Hunting Delilah

Anne Baines

Cover designed by Greg Jensen.
Formatting by Polgarus Studio.

ISBN-13: 978-0615955469
ISBN-10: 0615955460

Also By Anne Baines

Delilah Thrillers:

Chasing Delilah
Robbing Delilah
Breaking Delilah
Ice Cold Delilah

Sam Arbichaut Mysteries:

A Perfect Alibi
Butcher's Dozen
Cold Sweat

Standalone Work:

Bloodlines
Femme Fatale
Small Mercies
Out of Bullets
Not Quite Dead Enough

One

Alan's pointer scraped over the whiteboard, again, and Delilah sighed. She glanced around the hotel suite and noted that all three of the others were nodding, eyes focused hungrily on the plans being laid out before them. Amateurs. Sure, she needed the cash this job could bring just as much as anyone. Guaranteed to be a chunk of bills paid out, maybe twenty thousand a man in what looked to be an inspired hit on an illegal gambling operation.

Inspired by the movies. Delilah sighed again, mostly for effect this time, and rose to her feet.

"You can stop there, Alan. I'm out," she said.

The rangy, middle-aged man turned toward her, his pointer stick thwacking to a halt.

"There a problem?" he asked.

"Nah, no problem," she said. She had to be careful here, be nice but firm about it. She'd been referred to this job by

Cardiff, a mutual acquaintance. "I'm a driver. What you need for this," and she motioned to the parking garage plans and the ramp he wanted her to magically get a car over, "is a movie stunt team. Not worth the risk for me. Sorry guys."

One of the guys, a lock man, she guessed from his pinched look and small build, jumped up, too.

"This is what we get for lettin' a woman on a job. You just gonna let her walk?" His voice grated and made Delilah happier about her decision. She wanted out now, out of this room full of wishful thinkers, free from the miasma of stale coffee, staler sex, and old cigarettes that permeated the cramped suite.

"Yeah," Alan said after a moment. He nodded to the big man leaning against the door. "Yeah, she can walk. It's ok. She can't do it, she can't do it." And then to Delilah he said, "Tell Cardiff hi for me if you see him."

She nodded, keeping an eye on the jumpy little man as she moved toward the door. She'd hate to have to fake she had a gun in her purse or something. A man with a gun could scare people into doing what he wants. Delilah had learned the hard way that for a woman to scare people, especially bent types like these guys, she'd have to shoot someone.

Jumpy looked unhappy, but stayed put and only glared at her as she left.

The drive back to her own hotel was quick. Since it was only late afternoon, Delilah detoured the couple miles to the Florida beach, one of the ones that had a name like Seawind or maybe Seabreeze.

She'd driven down in a stolen car from her latest home base in Georgia and then liberated a nice new BMW from long-term parking at the Daytona International Airport. Car's owner had a hide-a-key tucked up behind the license plate. An automatic, not a stick shift, but she wasn't that choosy for just a drive-around car. Pity the job hadn't worked out, but at least the meet location was pretty, if touristy.

She stripped off her shoes, letting the soft pale sand slide between her toes. The waves hushed against the shore, the sound nearly drowning out the shouts of a few college-aged hardbodies playing volleyball somewhere behind her. Delilah shut her eyes, pushing away the other people, letting her mind wander out over that vast and shining sea. For a moment the salt air washed her clean, brushed away the staleness and disappointment from the hotel room she'd just left.

Then she opened her eyes and reality came flooding back in. Somewhere, on a different coast, with a different, colder sea, was a sick little girl Delilah tried not to think about much. But she refused to be like her own mother. She might lack the motherly instinct and disposition to actually take care of her daughter, but Delilah could help out with money. She was good at finding money, taking it from those who had far more than they needed. And Esther needed it. The weekly transfusions and visits to specialists were expensive, even if Jake, her daughter's father, refused to tell Delilah just how much.

Delilah did what she could, sent money. It was more than her own mother had ever done. A lot more.

She decided that in the morning she'd see about making up some of the cash she'd lost by refusing the job. Twenty grand was maybe out of reach for a day's work, despite the rich population, but a little breaking and entering was a lot less risky than stunt-driving cars off parking garages. She could head up to the Palm Coast area, pick out a couple nice big houses and work them over while their people were off earning the money to afford four-thousand square feet on the waterfront. Maybe this whole trip wouldn't be a bust.

Delilah rose just after 8am and drove out to a chain market. She bought a skim latte, a can of WD-40, some dog treats, and a leash. Outside the store she paused at the pay phone, fingertips lightly brushing the handset. It was only five thirty a.m. on the West Coast, but she knew Jake would be up already. Esther had a treatment this week, though Delilah couldn't remember the exact day. Jake hadn't been thrilled when she'd last called, telling her that if she'd wanted involvement in her daughter's life, she should have started before the kid got so sick.

Delilah took a deep breath and lifted the phone, digging into her pocket for change. She hesitated again and then let the phone drop with a muttered curse. She had no real reason to call. Maybe if her plans for the day went well, she'd call later. Jake might hate where the money came from, but he'd never turned extra down. Not when it was for Esther.

With a sigh she climbed into the car and headed back to the hotel.

Two

With her short, dark hair tucked under a blonde wig, and the right kind of make-up emphasizing her narrow nose and big eyes, Delilah could pass for white or maybe white mixed with a little Cuban and a lot of tanning hours clocked. Almost no one guessed at the Native half. That didn't bother Delilah. She liked being able to pass as white or Latina or even Asian, and carried the IDs to match. Made living on the sly a lot simpler when you looked like everybody.

A pair of khaki slacks with a narrow belt, and silky floral blouse with a nice oversize shoulder bag completed the bland suburban look. She just needed one more little touch and she'd be ready for work.

Delilah cruised a neighborhood outside Daytona proper until she saw what she wanted. The area was quiet, most people off at work and kids in school on a Tuesday. The palm trees were uncut here, their big shaggy fronds dancing in the slight breeze that shifted and promised more heat later. Taking the dog treats and leash with her, she approached the run-down ranch-style home. It had an open chain-link fence, about waist-high, over which a lonely, friendly golden retriever leaned his head, tongue lolling.

"Hey boy," she said softly, offering a bacon-scented snack. She smiled, a real one that actually touched her dark eyes, as he licked her fingers and looked at her, clearly hoping for more.

"Come on, Max," she said and opened the gate. She didn't really know what his name was, though she could have checked the tag hanging from his collar. But to her, all goldies were named Max. Just the way the world worked. She clipped the lead to the eager dog and took him back to her car.

Half an hour later saw her walking Max casually up and down the grid-like streets of the Palm Coast. Here the trees were trimmed, the lawns all green and manicured until they looked more like a TV representation of 'lawn' than grass and dirt.

She passed up the first house; it had too many windows near the road and an alarm system sign jammed into the lawn near the driveway. The next house was a sprawling Spanish-style home, but had a for-sale sign out front, so she skipped that one, too. While the lockbox in front might have made entry easier, and she certainly could just pass herself off as an interested buyer if she had to, homes staged for sale generally had fewer valuables left carelessly strewn about.

The next house looked perfect. It was set back on a nice circular drive, rising like a beige tower among its clean palm trees. Delilah and Max slipped around the back. A screened-in pool took up much of the backyard, with nice high vegetation to block out neighboring views. Delilah left Max tied loosely to an iron lounger in the shade and pulled on a pair of thin leather gloves.

Finding a way inside took only a moment. She checked the large glass French doors and saw an alarm panel on the inside. The alarm light was green and she could barely make out the digital text on the panel. "House Disarmed." Music to her ears. She took a deep breath, listening to the soft buzz of insects and the swish of the occasional car. After a few moments, sure that she was alone, she lifted a stone hedgehog lawn ornament and smashed through the glass door.

Another long pause. Max had flopped down after being startled by the crash and sat panting, staring at her. A car swooshed somewhere in the distance. She was in.

Delilah stepped through the door, unlocking it and swinging it wide. The floor was white marble tile with deep veins of pink and gold through it. Every detail of the house reeked of money, from the slab granite countertops in the adjacent kitchen to the design magazine furniture tastefully arrayed throughout the great room.

She stopped in the kitchen and opened the freezer. She doubted people with this much money would use the old tried and true method of hiding cash in the icebox, but it never hurt to look. No dice. Just a neat stack of low-calorie TV dinners and a couple athletic ice packs.

Delilah wandered through the main level, stopping in a small office and liberating about forty in small bills from a checkbook in the desk. She left the checks, wanting only cash or things easily turned into cash. She checked behind paintings and under the hand-knotted rug, but didn't find a safe in the office.

Upstairs were two guest bedrooms, their opulent luster marred by the dead flies in the window casings and the smell of air freshener. Delilah chuckled to herself since it was clear that the owners were paying too much for their maid service if they had one.

The master suite proved more lucrative. She found a set of gold and pear-cut diamond earrings lying on the night stand, as well as a few more small bills tucked in the nightstand drawer. There were no pictures; nothing to make this place lived-in. She wondered if Mr. and Mrs. Daniel Harkness, the name on the checks in the office, had only just moved here.

Delilah hesitated outside the walk-in closet. It was a large space, and well lit by the skylights cut into the ceiling. But there was only one door and no real windows. One exit. She took a deep breath and forced herself to walk inside, flipping on the light anyway.

Jackpot. The woman of the house was a purse collector. Delilah had never understood the point of designer handbags herself, but she appreciated the value others placed on them.

She stroked her gloved hand over a crocodile Chanel flip bag she estimated had cost about ten grand. Poppy, her fence back in Georgia, would pay at least seven-hundred for it. And there were more purses, seven more: Dior, Gucci, Hermes, Louis Vuitton. Delilah cursed herself for not bringing a better bag to carry this stuff. She'd have to use something here.

She made herself turn away from the nicely laid-out purses and explore the rest of the closet. On the back of a folding vanity mirror were earrings, none worth more than a few hundred, all tasteful solitaire diamonds or small gold loops and whirls. Delilah pulled them all down and slid them into her purse. She studied the expensive perfumes on top of the vanity, but left them. Their cloying and spicy scents were already giving her a headache.

Behind a large fur coat in a clear plastic bag, worth at least five grand, Delilah found the safe. It was a large combination safe, built into the wall. She studied it for a moment and then stepped out, relief pouring into her as she breathed the clear air of the bedroom.

Back downstairs in the office, Delilah sat down at the computer and jiggled the mouse until the screen woke up. No password needed. She shook her head. A quick search using the words "safe combination" yielded a document titled "passwords.doc". It was like these people were begging to be robbed. She memorized the combination and slipped back upstairs.

The safe opened easily, an inside light popping on. It illuminated papers in neat folders on the narrow top shelf, with perfect stacks of velvet boxes on lower shelves. There was a billfold with a couple hundred or so in it as well.

The lady of the house had very good taste indeed. Delilah slid a pair of white gold and diamond chandelier earrings into her own ears. She figured Poppy would give her a good one or two grand for those. She also slipped a three-strand diamond tennis necklace on under her blouse, clipping the matching bracelet onto her wrist under her sleeve.

The obligatory Rolex and a surprise Panerai watch went into her large shoulder bag, along with a set of huge vintage ruby and diamond earrings, and a black diamond ring.

She hesitated over a pair of large opal cufflinks. Colin, her father's partner, had always said that opals were unlucky for anyone not born in October. Having been born in June, Delilah didn't fit the bill. She bit her lip and smiled at herself. Superstitious bullshit. There was a lot of it in this business, a lot of talk of luck and chance.

She made her own chances. The cufflinks went into her bag.

The last piece in the safe was a set of yellow gold and diamond bracelets. The diamonds were tiny, cut to form flowers all around the bangles. She slid those onto her other wrist beneath her sleeve, thinking maybe she'd keep one for herself when this was over. It would depend on what Poppy offered her for the pair.

A large duffel bag tucked beneath the man's shoe-rack solved her purse issue. She loaded the designer bags and a couple pairs of new-looking designer shoes into the duffel and headed back downstairs.

Max gave a soft wuffling bark as she stepped out into the pool area.

"Hey buddy, ready to go?" She hefted the duffel. She should just walk away, get in her car, and go to the hotel, clear out of town. But she hesitated.

The purses and shoes would bring in maybe eight grand, since hot items never took in but a fraction of the street price. Jewelry, another six, perhaps, provided the stones were real.

Fourteen, maybe fifteen grand. A decent haul. But she'd come to Florida on the promise of at least twenty. She needed that twenty. That was the sort of amount that might really make a difference for her daughter, with the bonus of making Jake grateful for fucking once.

Twenty. She'd done close in one house. Just one.

"Maybe, two houses?" she muttered, fighting with her instincts to make good and go, and her desire to turn this stupid trip into a really big score, turn it into something worthwhile. She might not be so lucky at the next house, but this neighborhood clearly had stupid complacency mixed with money, and those were two of Delilah's favorite things.

With a sigh she set the duffle bag down just inside the screened in pool, making sure it was more or less out of sight. She'd pick it up on her way back to the car.

"Ok, Max, one more house. Let's go find the rest of my twenty grand."

The good one turned out to be about two blocks down. The yard was, like every other house, meticulous, but the sprawling home was tucked back behind lovely gardens and well hidden from the street and the neighbors. Perfect.

Delilah slipped into the back yard and was accosted at once by the heavy scent of blooming vegetation. The garden back here was meticulously laid out around a stone patio with a latticed lanai. She didn't know the name of even one of the tropical and exotic-looking plants blooming freely here, but she knew true care and passion for something when she saw it. She stood with Max for a long moment, gawking at the myriad colors and flavors available to her senses.

"In and out, Dee," she said, time ticking past.

She tied Max to an iron and marble birdbath and checked the back door. No alarm system that she could see and the lock was a simple tumbler, the deadbolt not thrown. She pulled out her lock kit and had the door open in less than a minute.

This house was homier than the last, a few more knickknacks cluttering shelves, some mail dropped negligently on the table.

"Mr. and Mrs. Theodore Whitechapel," Delilah read. "God, how pretentious. Poor saps."

She felt easy here, the garden scents following her into the home, lingering in the cooler air of the house. This was a nice place, something normal and calm about it, lived in. Even if they had countertops with granite the color of vomit.

She passed through the kitchen, noting photographs stuck with artful magnets to the fridge. The man, unfortunate Theodore, was tall, dark, and handsome, his smile white and perfect. The wife was smaller, a mousy blonde slip of a thing with nervous eyes. Delilah started to build a story for them in her head, with the man marrying the woman for money and then going around behind her back. A man that looked so confident, so perfect, had to be working some angle.

She stopped herself with a rueful smile and set her shoulder bag down on the vomit-granite countertop. She checked the kitchen drawers and found nothing of any value, though the silverware was real silver and tempted her, as did the authentic

Japanese chef knives in their bamboo block on the island. But she'd already pulled so much high-value stuff from the previous house that she felt okay with being picky here.

Out of habit, she opened the freezer and managed to stop her scream before it broke free of her lips.

Inside, between a pint of Haagen-Dazs cookie-dough ice-cream and a bag of stir-fry veggies, sat a woman's severed head. She was a young brunette, eyes wide and glassy and dead.

Behind Delilah, a man cleared his throat.

Three

She spun around and froze. A few feet away stood a man who was a dead ringer for the sly, handsome Theodore Whitechapel in the pictures.

"You shouldn't be here," the man said. He appeared as stunned as she felt.

"I was just leaving," Delilah said, an automatic response more than anything. She took a deep breath, adrenaline pouring into her body. The exit was behind him, she had no idea how he'd gotten inside and so close without her hearing anything.

"What—" the man began to say, but Delilah didn't give him a chance to finish.

She charged at him, aiming a straight kick at his groin. He caught and spun her, her kick missing entirely and throwing her off balance. With a jerk he slammed her into the kitchen island. She'd never seen anyone move so fast and, pressed against her, his body felt like it was iron instead of flesh.

She clawed at his face, but he tipped his chin away from her. The granite counter dug into her back and one of his hands caught her throat. She exhaled sharply, blinking away tears. She bucked, twisting to get free of him.

Then her body stopped responding, pain radiating out from her stomach. He stepped away from her and she stared down blankly at the paring knife protruding from her belly.

"Teddy?" A woman's voice cut through the heavy breathing and Delilah's whimper of shock. "The door was open, are you here?"

Teddy grabbed Delilah, lifting her like one would carry a child, though he bent her in a way that drove the knife deeper and she cried out. His mouth came down over hers as he rushed down a hallway, swallowing her cry.

"Shhh, stupid girl. It'll be over soon. I'll be right back for you, if you're still alive." His voice was soft, a horrible parody of caring.

Hot and then cold, Delilah twitched and a red haze clouded her vision. She wanted to fight him, to struggle, but nothing seemed connected to her brain anymore. Her body just lay in his arms.

He brought her into a large bathroom and dropped her into the huge soaking tub. She couldn't stop the scream as she landed and new agony speared through her.

Teddy grabbed a towel and rubbed the blood from his hands. With a warning look at Delilah, he ducked out of the bathroom, shutting the door behind him.

Four

Delilah wasn't sure if she'd passed out or not. Max barking outside, beyond the wall behind her, brought her back to a thinking state. She gritted her teeth and found a grip on the knife. It slid free quickly, a shorter blade than she'd thought. Blood rushed out after it, soaking more of her shirt and pants.

She took shallow, careful breaths, talking to herself through the pain. Max kept barking and she heard scrabbling and looked over to see a large frosted window with a dark shape dancing near the bottom. A way out.

Pulling her belt out of her pants meant having to lift her hips, the pain of which nearly knocked her out again. Delilah bit her fist to keep from screaming and then grabbed at a hand towel. She balled it up and jammed it over the wound, using her belt on its tightest setting to secure it in place. Then she crawled up over the lip of the tub and tumbled to the travertine tiles below.

She looked at the door. Scary, crazy Teddy would be back. She could grab the knife, try to surprise him. Stabbing the fucker had its appeal. But he'd been so strong, so fast. Bad idea. Thinking about facing him again brought on shivers.

Get out, Dee, she told herself. *Live.*

There was a vintage make-up table below the window. Only a narrow portion of the window opened, up at the top. She was sure she could fit through, if she could get up there. Without the wound it wouldn't have been an issue, she'd jammed her thin body through narrow openings before in her line of work.

With the wound, however.... Delilah shook her head. She'd cope. She had to get out.

Standing up straight sent her head whirling. Delilah clenched her jaw, focusing on the window. She dragged herself up using the table, knocking bottles and compacts to the floor. She turned her head and looked at the door, despairing when she saw a smooth handle, it had no lock. Who didn't put locks on their bathroom doors? She forced her gaze away. If he heard her and came back, there'd be nothing she could do.

Dragging herself up onto the table brought buzzing to her ears, her vision blinking in and out. She'd never known pain like this, it was worse than childbirth. She'd kill for an epidural now, she thought with a crazy half-smile around gritted teeth.

She got the window open after three tries, her bloody gloves slipping on the clasp. Her hands were too slippery to pull herself up and over. Frustrated, she bit down on the fingers of one glove, yanking it off. Survival was more important than prints, and she doubted this guy would be calling the police anyway.

She bit her lip and grabbed hold of the window edge. With a jerk she hauled her body upward, arms straining. *Don't think about it, just go.* Delilah jammed her leg through the narrow opening and twisted her body across the edge. Her belt buckle caught for a moment, then she tipped over the ledge and fell free.

Her belly exploded with pain as she hit a large leafy plant. This time, she couldn't prevent the scream. It felt good to get it out. Max bounded up and licked her face, whining. He'd slipped his collar.

She pulled herself up using the side of the house and checked her makeshift bandage. It had slipped so she jerked it back in place, using one hand to hold pressure on the wound. Leaning heavily on Max, Delilah stumbled away from the house and out onto the street. She moved as fast as she could, taking a direct route to the car.

Adrenaline and determination kept her going. The neighborhood stayed as quiet as it had been on her way through, none of the cars that passed stopping or even slowing.

Max leapt into the car as soon as she opened the driver's side door. Delilah fell into the seat and closed the door. The heat that had built up in the car hit her in a wave, sucking her down. Her vision blurred, turning from red to black and she gave in to the siren call of unconsciousness.

Five

"Teddy?" Cora called again.

Cursing under his breath, Ted pulled his bloody shirt over his head, popping a couple buttons in his haste. This little lunch-time dalliance wasn't starting out as planned at all. He had to get rid of Cora, beg off, get her out of the house so he could deal with the mystery blonde in his bathroom.

And where in God's name was that barking coming from?

With a growl, Ted stepped into the kitchen and found Cora bent down, touching her fingers to blood that had dripped on the floor.

"What is this? Are you okay?" She rose, her perfect salon red curls bouncing as she lifted her head. "Oh god, your hand, did you cut yourself?"

Abruptly Ted realized his tactical error. He should have wrapped his hand in a towel or something, anything to make an injury seem possible.

"It's nothing, it just seems like a lot of blood. I'll be fine."
He gave her his trademark beaming grin.

"Go wash that blood off," she said. "I'll get you some ice.
That's supposed to stop bleeding."

"No!" Too late Ted lunged for her as she opened the
freezer. He slammed it shut but the look of horror on her
overly made-up face told him all he needed to know.

"You stupid bitch," he said. "Fucking everything up. You
realize how many people are going to miss you? How many of
your girlfriends have you told about our affair? Five? Ten?
Everyone on your Facebook?"

"Teddy," she stumbled back from him, fetching up against
the island much as the tiny blonde dying in his bathtub had
done. "What are you saying, Teddy? What was that thing?"
The words came out faster and faster as he closed in and
gripped her arms. She didn't fight him like the mystery woman
had. Not a fighter, his pampered, sheltered Cora, not a bit.

"Please," she whimpered, "please. My dad can sort this out
for you if you're in trouble, but you gotta talk to me, Teddy,
please."

Her father was a lead prosecutor for the State's Attorney's
Office. It was why Ted had seduced Cora. She was a red-head,
not a brunette, and not nearly perky enough to be his "type",
but he loved flaunting his extra-curricular activities under the
nose of the daughter of a supposedly powerful law man.

Or he had, until today. Her disappearance would
eventually trace back to him. And he didn't relish the thought
of uncomfortable questions or anyone digging around in his
life. Or his garden.

Ted brought his hands up to Cora's throat and squeezed. She finally struggled, but his body pinned her arms and the counter did the rest of the work for him.

He loved the time strangulation took, the personal feel of flesh beneath his fingers. Her breath was sickly sweet as she exhaled out over his face. Her skin, so heavily made-up, hardly changed color, but her eyes bulged and blood vessels in them burst and hemorrhaged into the whites. So much tidier than a stabbing.

"Women," he said philosophically, as her eyes rolled back in her head. "Women ruin everything."

He'd known this fact since he was six and had been humiliated at a pool party when his mother insisted on breast-feeding him in front of the other mothers and children. He'd liked the warm feel of her breasts, the large dark nipples with their bumpy texture and sweet taste. But Ted had realized how stupid it was for a boy his age to breastfeed. Realized when the shocked looks and soft whispers started, had the point driven home by the ridicule and horrible names that only first graders could invent with special juvenile malicious imagination. His mother had begun it, destroying his chance at a happy school life with one beckoning gesture.

Ted bit his lip and leaned in; watching the panic fade to unconsciousness in Cora's terrified bloodshot eyes. When he killed her, he killed all women, if only for a moment.

When she was good and dead, a lifeless object in his arms, Ted dropped her and walked to the sink. He pulled a glass out of the cupboard and switched the faucet over to filtered water. He took a long drink, staring out the diamond-shaped window into his prize-winning garden. His pineapple guavas had a few late blooms left, the bright red stamens springing joyfully from between delicate pink petals. He smiled and set down the glass.

Ted walked back and bent over Cora's body, slowly undoing her shorts as his blood rushed in his ears and his groin tightened. Her skin was still warm. He stroked a finger down through her neatly trimmed light brown pubic hair, then sniffed and grimaced. Her bowels had vacated. That happened sometimes. If she'd been one of his special projects he might have bothered to bathe the body and enjoy a little more time with her.

She wasn't worth it. He kicked her body and stalked down the hallway to the bathroom. It was time to get some answers from the blonde intruder, if she still lived. He couldn't hear anything but his own breathing in the house now. Even that dog had stopped barking.

"Knock, knock," Ted said, tapping the door, his good humor returning. He opened it and stepped into the bathroom.

Blood was smeared across the tiles, the air thick with lingering perfume from a few of Emily's bottles that had come off the vanity and smashed on the floor. A bloody glove lay discarded on the table, the only trace left of the mystery girl.

Ted cursed, dashing up to the window and peering out the open top. She'd crushed one of his firebushes, leaving a smear of blood across the bright green leaves and a trampled patch of yellow-orange flowers in her wake.

He wished he'd grabbed a bigger knife.

He took a deep breath and walked to the master bedroom. He removed his Beretta PX4 sub-compact handgun and checked the clip. She'd been injured badly, she couldn't have gotten far. Of course, shooting a gun in the middle of the day was risky, but Ted didn't care. He was going to have to disappear anyway. He pulled on a clean shirt and tucked it over the gun in his waistband.

In the kitchen he nearly tripped over a large shoulder bag. It didn't look like something Cora would carry. He guessed it was the mystery woman's and had tumbled off the island when they'd struggled. A velvet box had slid out of it. Ted opened the box and found a pair of opal cuff-links. Men's, definitely.

A thief then. His smile widened. A new sort of prey for him, something rarer than his perky, preppy brunettes. Pity this woman was a blonde. He checked the bag and came up with a small wallet but no keys.

"Donna Utley," he said aloud, tasting the name. Probably a fake, if she was any good. There was a lot of expensive jewelry in this bag, and a few thousand in cash. She was probably good. But he'd find her, because he was better, he had to be better.

He started where she'd crushed his firebush and followed the dripping blood trail out to the sidewalk. Oh, he'd find her, and he'd make her suffer; make her pay dearly for ruining his life.

Six

Max's barking woke Delilah from her pain-induced stupor for the second time that day. The Golden Retriever was in the back seat of the BMW, clawing at the door. For a bleary moment Delilah stared at the steering wheel, wondering where the dark stains on it had come from and why she still had the dog with her. Her wig had shifted, the gum starting to degrade from time and sweat, blonde hairs sticking to her forehead and teasing her nose.

Then the pain hit.

And someone tapped on the window beside her head.

Agony blurring her vision, Delilah twisted her head and saw a smirking man leaning over beside the car. He had a nasty looking pistol, maybe a 9mm Beretta, and was lightly tapping it on the glass.

Theodore Whitechapel. Fear took over for a moment. She scrabbled sideways in the seat, trying to get away from him.

The tearing pain in her gut nearly put her out again and Delilah lay back, gasping and fighting to think.

Teddy held up a tan shoulder bag, her bag.

"Donna? Is that your name? Open the door Donna, or I'll shoot." His voice was muffled by the closed window, coming in as though through a tunnel.

Max fell silent at the sound of Teddy's voice, licking Delilah's arm from between the seats.

Donna? Donna Utley. Right. Damn. Her ID, the one she'd used for this trip anyway, was in that bag. Along with her stolen bounty.

But not the car key.

Delilah took a deep breath to steady herself, regretted it, and took a couple shallow ones to breathe through the pain. She reached up with her left hand to the sun visor in as quick a motion as she could manage, dropping it and letting the key fall into her lap. She caught it with her right hand and jammed the key into the ignition.

Outside Teddy let out a stream of curses and took a step away from the car. He raised the gun as the engine turned over and caught.

Delilah threw herself to the side as she slammed the car into drive and was grateful for an automatic transmission for the first time in her life. The car jerked forward as the gun cracked in the hot afternoon air.

The passenger window splintered as the bullet cut through it. Delilah straightened up, leaning over the steering wheel as she took a hard corner, praying she remembered the way out of this neighborhood.

She heard another gun shot and then they were away, zipping down the quiet lane. A sign for the I-95 loomed ahead. She'd chosen this neighborhood not just for its wealth, but also its proximity to the highway.

She took shallow breaths, fighting unconsciousness as Max whined softly in the seat behind her. The wig still itched, hair teasing her eyelashes and Delilah yanked it off with a hiss.

"Shh, boy, it's okay," she said as much to herself as to the dog. "Not a long drive now."

She merged up onto the I-95, checking her speed. She was covered in blood, wearing a thirty-thousand dollar pair of diamond earrings, had no ID, while driving a stolen car with a bullet hole in it. She wasn't sure whether to laugh or cry. Instead Delilah focused on the road, on the habit of driving.

She played games with herself, pass this Toyota Hybrid, stay two seconds behind that Ford Escort. Stay at two miles an hour over the speed limit, drop to the speed limit.

A horn blared and Delilah came to again, focusing back on the road. She swerved hard, just keeping control, to avoid the white SUV in the fast lane beside her. Her heart sped up and her vision cleared, the pain fading as a fresh jolt of adrenaline burst through her.

Then she was somehow almost there, off the exit ramp and into Daytona proper, turning right toward her hotel. She parked in front of her room, something she wouldn't have done if she hadn't been covered in blood in the middle of the afternoon.

Another moment of panic before she found her hotel key in her pant's pocket. She more stumbled than walked into the room, the bliss of the cool AC washing over her like fresh air. Delilah closed the door behind Max and half-crawled her way to the bathroom.

The towel was stuck to the wound with dried blood and Delilah lay on the linoleum as hot tears ran down her face. She didn't have the strength to deal with it. She needed help, real help.

Cardiff. He still owed her a favor from when she'd helped spring his nephew out of a situation with a loan shark in Detroit.

Crawling back to the phone, she tugged it down to the floor and dialed. When it stopped ringing she read the number off the hotel phone into the silence on the other end of the line.

Minutes crawled by. Max jumped up on the bed and settled down, his head only a foot from where Delilah leaned against the frame. She wished she'd gotten some water in the bathroom, her mouth tasted foul, blood and bile.

The phone rang, harsh and unreal in the quiet hotel room.

"It's Delilah," she said as she lifted the mouthpiece to her face.

"This a land line? Why aren't you using a payphone, Dee? And why not reverse the numbers?" Cardiff sounded upset.

"I forgot," she said. Her voice was weak and thick in her ears.

"Jesus, Dee. Are you all right? Alan called; he says some of the guys were pissed about you bailing on that job."

"It was amateur hour, Card." She swallowed. She needed help, but it was still tough to form the words. "I'm hurt. Real bad. I need a doctor, somebody who takes care of people like us."

"Jesus H Christ. You shot? Cops?"

"No, stabbed. Not cops. Look, I'm still in Daytona. There's got to be someone. You owe me, Card." She gasped out the last part as another unhealthy throb of pain went through her.

"All right. Where are you? I know a guy, I'll see if I can get someone out there." Cardiff didn't sound happy, but she didn't care. Happy didn't matter.

She wanted to live.

"Sunrise Lodge, room 159, on the end."

"I'll have the guy knock twice, and then twice again." She heard him sigh, then he added, "Hang in there, Dee."

"Thanks, Card." She let the phone drop from her shoulder and shoved it into the cradle.

He might not sound thrilled about it, but Cardiff wouldn't let her down. Even if he hadn't owed her, he'd still seen her raised up from a tiny girl. He knew her father, despite the disaster that had turned out to be. Card wouldn't let her down. She could count on him as much as she could count on anybody.

She hoped anyway. But the pain cut into her and Delilah felt crazy, beyond careful and caring.

She touched the phone again. Jake. She bit her lip and put her hands back at her middle, shifting slowly to try for a position that didn't hurt like hell. Jake was thousands of miles away, and even if he'd been willing to hear more than two words from her, he couldn't help. He'd probably tell her this was exactly what she deserved.

Delilah turned her face into the scratchy pastel comforter coverlet and let the tears squeeze out of her eyes. She just had to survive, wait for Cardiff's man.

"Think about living, Dee," she whispered, though hardly any sound escaped, "do only that."

Seven

Ted walked back into his quiet house and set the gun on the kitchen table. He stood for a moment, taking in the bloody floor and Cora's body. Regret stormed through him, sulfurous and annoying. None of this should have happened.

Emily was on a spa holiday he'd purchased for her, gone until tomorrow evening. Free of the wife for a few days, Ted had taken advantage to pursue his hobbies. His day was supposed to contain a leisurely lunch fuck with Cora, followed by the disposal of his latest toys, and rounded off with quality time in his garden.

Now he had three dead women to dispose of, one of which could be tied to him in a straight line.

It was that bitch's fault. All of it.

Hardly aware of what he was doing, Ted stormed into the kitchen. The smell of feces, death, and blood mingling with Cora's expensive Jean Patou perfume lit a fuse inside him. He slammed open cupboards, dragging the lightly patterned Pfaltzgraff dinnerware out and sending it crashing to the floor. The glasses went next, some flying off to the far walls.

He tore pictures off the fridge, an original Chagall off the wall, and flung each as far as he could throw them.

Ted's energy ran out after a few minutes and he stood gasping in the wreck of the kitchen, feeling mildly better. The rage was quenched for a moment and he needed a plan.

This life was over. Ted knew it; he'd always known that someday the careful façade he'd built here would have to end. But that had been abstract. The reality pissed him off.

He'd already taken the rest of the day off work, not that his boss would say anything if he hadn't. There were advantages to working for a company owned by his father. Emily was dealt with, though he was tempted to stay and finish her off when she returned. He put that thought away for later.

A tinny song interrupted his thoughts, Lady Gaga blaring through the house, singing about poker faces. Ted picked his way out of the kitchen and through the dining room into the great room. Cora's purse lay on a teak side-table, her cell phone vibrating its way half out of the top.

The screen identified the caller as her fiancée, a moderately successful young golf pro. A generally absent one as well. Ted cursed again as it went silent and then chimed that there was voicemail. Cora hadn't mentioned he was in town. More complications.

It was best to get things taken care of here and get out, then.

Ted grabbed Cora's body by the hair and dragged her down the hallway to the master bedroom. He pulled on cleaning gloves and removed her clothing before lifting her up to the bed. From the kitchen he grabbed the cleaver, the knife he wished he'd used on Donna the thief.

Rigor had started to set in, preventing Ted from crossing Cora's arms over her expensive saline implants. He wanted to create a nice image, something singular and memorable for his wife to find. A statement, final and true.

With a snarl, Ted stabbed first one breast, then the other, driving the knife in hard. He punctured each implant, pleased with himself. Then, almost as an afterthought, picturing the crime photos, picturing his pathetic little wife's face, he jammed the cleaver up between Cora's legs and left it there.

He collected the head he'd temporarily stashed in the freezer and went out to his garden cottage in the back yard. Ted's mind was full of regrets. He shouldn't have killed two women so close together. He'd always been so careful, waiting weeks or months between beauties. But with Emily gone it had been so easy. And the young women had both just fallen into his lap, one of them literally when she broke a heel coming out of the club he'd been hunting in.

It was that girl's head that had been in his freezer, her stupid dead eyes staring back at the intruder, accusing. If her head hadn't been in there, perhaps…. Ted shook that thought away in disgust.

But it wasn't his fault. It all came down to that stupid thief. She'd violated his space, ruining his perfect afternoon.

He dropped the head onto the floor of the cottage and took a deep breath. It hardly seemed worth processing the bodies into bone meal and mulch for his garden now. He'd have to leave it behind. All the neighborhood gardening awards lined up on the high mahogany shelf, the framed picture of him with the article from Better Homes and Gardens, these things taunted him. Ted's life was over. Ted had to disappear, become someone else.

He grabbed a shovel and walked back outside into the afternoon sun. A breeze danced through the silver-blue fronds of his Bismark palm tree. Bright purple Wishbone pansies spilled over Grecian urns placed around the stone patio. Birds darted in the foliage and the air droned with the healthy sounds of bees. He'd created something truly beautiful, with the help of all the stupid women who'd always thought they were better than he, and he was its master. Their master.

A glint caught Ted's eye. A dog collar with tags lay on the patio, still attached to a leash.

Donna's golden retriever. He bent and picked up the collar. The tags had an address, south of here, near Daytona Beach. Was this really her dog? Ted shrugged. It was a lead, a start.

And he realized what his new life would be, the act that would begin it. Donna Utley had given him a new purpose, a new game. She should have died, her body going to nourish his domain. He grinned, then laughed. He'd never felt so alive, so much emotion. He hated her, truly hated, and not in an abstract way, for thinking she was superior. This thief was different from those perky bitches. Escaping him meant she'd won, for now. No one had ever escaped him before. She was worthy of hunting, her rejection of his power was tangible, a thing he could almost touch, could taste.

He pictured her face, thin and shocked, the blonde hair at odds with her dark cinnamon skin and wide brown eyes. She'd smelled of very little, not covered in perfume. Shampoo maybe? Something cheap and generic, like you'd find in a hotel. Her clothes had been basic, tasteful. The earrings, he was sure she'd worn earrings. Diamonds or maybe just cut glass. Big though, he remembered them pressing into his chest as he carried her.

And her mouth, tasting of blood and panic and berry lip gloss. He'd swallowed her whimper and it had been so weak, so beautiful. He wanted to taste her again, press his mouth to hers as she screamed and screamed. As she died.

Ted walked into his house, renewed energy bringing a fresh spring to his step. He went to the library and booted up his computer. While it was starting, he opened the floor safe and removed an envelope. It contained a safe-deposit key. Emily didn't know about this. He'd gotten a good set of fake IDs made up and stashed it, along with fifty thousand in cash, in a local bank. Enough to hunt down Donna on. Then he could use the passport and take off for Belize or somewhere nice. The money hidden in overseas accounts under his other name would keep him until he found something else to do.

But first, he had a thief to hunt.

Ted carefully put on gloves again and made a shallow cut with a knife on the back of his left arm. He wandered through the house, dripping blood around the kitchen and then through the great-room to the front door. He bandaged his arm in the bathroom.

As an afterthought, he wrapped the bloody glove that Donna had left behind into the towel he'd used to wipe her blood off his hands and shoved the bundle into a plastic garbage bag from under the sink. Ted wanted the whole scene to be as baffling for the police as possible. He was a lawyer, though a corporate one, and knew that law enforcement could waste days if not weeks trying to sort through this kind of mess.

That thought also made him happy, those busy stupid men and women in their little blue suits, digging through the mess he'd created for them. They'd never figure it all out. They just weren't good enough.

He used the computer to get directions to the address on the dog tags and left. He took the jewelry, the bag with the bloody towel and glove, Donna's ID, and his gun with him. Ted felt good. Today had not gone as planned, but it would work out. He deserved to win.

He tucked his Bluetooth device into his ear and called up information. Time to start seeing if Donna Utley had checked into any Daytona Beach hotels. With a grin, Ted merged onto the I-95, going to see a person about a dog, and a tiny blonde thief.

Eight

A firm knock woke Delilah out of a half-conscious state she was starting to get accustomed to falling into. Max started barking and she shushed him, trying to stand upright.

Pain doubled her back over and she half-crawled, half-staggered to the door. She forced herself to straighten long enough to stare out the peephole. A man stood there with a bag and a large hard suitcase.

Had he knocked twice?

He knocked again, tap tap. Then waited, and again, tap tap.

The doctor. Delilah wanted to shout with relief but instead pulled the chain off the door and threw back the bolt.

Max tried to overwhelm the man in greeting.

"I'm sorry," Delilah said through clenched teeth, shuffling out of the way, her hands supporting her against the wall.

"No problem. Though I can't work with him jumping around." The man's voice was soft, with a slight Cuban accent.

"Put him out the back, there's a construction site there, and he probably needs to go out." Delilah leaned against the wall, one hand pressing the towel in place at her belly. She studied the doctor as he closed the door behind him and crossed to the back sliding door, calling the dog to come with him.

He looked late thirties and a lot more like a biker than a doctor. The man had broad shoulders, his dark brown hair pulled up into a pony-tail, and tattoos visible winding down his arms where his sleeves had been rolled back. He wore a leather vest and leather pants. But he moved with confidence, and his dark eyes were gentle as he returned and looked Delilah over.

"I'm Morales," he said. "I guess you're the one hurt."

She wanted to laugh but choked the hysterical sound back. She was half-covered in blood, with a bloody hand-towel crusted to her abdomen. This guy had a gift for the obvious.

"Stab wound, in my belly. You really a doctor?"

He tsked and put his bags up on the table underneath the main window. Delilah leaned into the wall, wondering what she should do. Standing hurt like hell and she wasn't sure she'd remain conscious long. She took a tentative step toward the bed.

"Come on then," he said and reached for her.

She jerked away, slamming back into the wall, then looked at him, chagrined.

"I'm sorry," she said. "It's been a bad day."

She let him half-carry her to the bed. He didn't smell very sterile; his vest was warm leather, with an undertone of pipe tobacco and peppermint.

"Okay, Delilah," he said in his soothing voice. "I'm going to move the towel, see what I'm dealing with."

She lay back on the bed and nodded. Vague annoyance with Cardiff for giving this guy her name swirled up but was quickly shoved away. If this man could stop the pain, she'd do anything. Tears burned her eyes as he pulled on gloves and then gently tugged at the towel. Delilah turned her face to the side and bit her fist. She felt like a child, helpless, stupid.

Morales shook his head, muttered something under his breath in Spanish. She turned her face back and looked up at him.

"No chance I can get you to go to a hospital?" he said. She couldn't read his eyes, or even focus well on his features, but guessed that question meant it was bad.

"No chance," she said. "No hospitals."

"You need exploratory surgery. I don't know exactly how deep this wound is, but it doesn't look great. Without surgery there's no way to know if the peritoneum is punctured. If it isn't, great. If it is, you'll probably die in a few days." He was definitely glaring at her. "Do you understand?"

"It was a paring knife," she said wearily. "And no hospitals. Just fix me like you're supposed to."

He stared down at her for a moment, a long moment. Delilah started to worry he'd call an ambulance anyway, wondered if she had the strength to stop him. Doubted it.

Morales sighed. "Sure. I guess we go with the 'stitch and pray' option."

He moved away, setting out things from his bags. He put a double hook over the headboard and hung an IV bag. Then he disappeared for a little while and she heard running water in the bathroom.

She faded in and out, barely registering the pinch of the IV needle as the doctor stuck her hand. Morales let the drip go for a couple minutes as he busied himself setting up.

"I'm going to give you morphine," he said. "Then local for the actual stitches. You've lost a lot of blood."

"Tell me," she started to say, then licked her lips, "something I don't know."

"The Riverside Cathedral in Manhattan is the tallest cathedral in North America."

Delilah half-choked on a surprise bubble of laughter, her diaphragm tensing and sending a new wave of pain over her.

"Sorry," Morales said. "I shouldn't make you laugh." He depressed the plunger on the syringe.

"No," she said. "Thanks."

The pain faded abruptly away, pulling Delilah with it into blissful unconsciousness.

It was fully dark outside when she came to, but the pain stayed at bay. Morales sat in a chair pulled up near the bed, reading a tattered paperback romance novel.

"Hi," Delilah said. Her mouth tasted terrible, sleep and blood mingling into sticky paste on her tongue. "Can I have water?"

"Sure, how are you feeling?" The doctor rose and filled a plastic cup from the sink.

She reached for it, sitting up gingerly, and felt the tug of the IV line. Switching hands, Delilah took the cup and sipped. Tiny swallows didn't seem to hurt too much and she leaned against the headboard, relieved when the pain stayed only a dull ache.

"Better. Am I good to go?" She sipped more water. It was time to get out of this place. She'd checked in under the name Donna Utley, which that psycho killer now had, and she'd rather not stick around. No reason to stay in Florida anyway. She'd recover better at her home in Atlanta.

"Go?" Morales chuckled. "You are a firecracker, aren't you? You shouldn't go anywhere for a while." At her upset look he waved his hands, shaking his head in defeat. "All right, at least until that IV bag runs down. I added some broad-spectrum antibiotics to it, as well as more morphine. You need the fluids, too."

"So when?" she asked.

"Two, three hours."

"I can live with that." She sank back down.

"Perhaps." Morales stood up. He picked up two pill bottles from the table and set them down next to her on the nightstand. "The white ones are painkillers. Take them as you need to for the pain. The pinkish ones are antibiotics. Take one four times a day until they're gone. I don't know if it'll save you, but it can't hurt."

"I thought you saved me?" Delilah tried to focus on him. Her body wanted more sleep, exhaustion catching up to her after a day of adrenaline and pain.

"I stitched you up, stopped the bleeding. But if your abdominal cavity was punctured, you'll likely get peritonitus, go septic in a few days, and die. Horribly."

She looked at his grim face, knowing what he wasn't saying. "I'm not going to a hospital."

"Not yet," he muttered. "Look, if you get dizzy, lots of nausea, so much pain you can't stand or even move, or a high fever, then you've got to get to a hospital. I realize they might call the police, but is risking death worth whatever you're avoiding?"

Delilah closed her eyes and thought about the one time she'd visited Benny, her father, in prison. The walls all closing in, the people staring at you all the time. The tight spaces and tiny rooms. The locked doors, so many locked doors. Rooms with only one exit and barred windows or no windows at all. Even the air had tasted like something a hundred others had breathed before her. She'd gone to see Benny because she felt a vague familial tie. He'd helped her find her calling in life, teaching her some of the best short cons, showing her how to hotwire her first car.

But she hadn't been back to visit. Thinking about it gave her chills and sometimes she woke from sleep shivering with the after-images of concrete walls and windows that wouldn't open. If there was a hell for her, Delilah was sure it would look like prison.

"Yeah," she said softly, opening her eyes. "I'll take my chances."

Morales shrugged and packed up. Delilah pulled the yellow gold and diamond bracelets off her wrists and offered them to him. She wasn't sure if Cardiff had worked out payment with the doctor, but Morales hadn't mentioned it.

"Thank you," he said, "But I feel cruel taking payment from a dead woman."

"Take them anyway. For all you know, they're fake." She tossed the bracelets at him.

Morales caught them easily. "God's truth," he said with a ghost of a smile.

She stopped herself from asking him how he knew Cardiff, why a guy like him was even willing to patch up crooks. No questions, nothing personal. Those were the rules if you wanted to be a pro. But she couldn't help wondering, turning over possibilities in her morphine-clouded mind.

Delilah managed to stand long enough to relock the door after closing it behind the strange doctor, holding her IV bag up with one hand. She stumbled to the back door and flipped on the rear light, looking for Max. There was no sign of the dog. Fog clouded her head, her body begging her to lie down again.

"Stupid mutt," she whispered. She knew she was probably better off without him, but part of her felt guilty for dumping him outside in a strange place. Delilah hoped he'd come back.

She promised herself she'd look for the dog before she left and staggered back to the bed.

She slid back onto the mattress, replaced the IV on its hook, and dragged the coverlet over her legs. Her tired body and the morphine did the rest and she dropped into a dreamless sleep.

Nine

Poor yard hygiene, Ted thought, was definitely one of the markers of the lower class. The palms in this neighborhood were overgrown; the lawns more weed than grass. He cruised past the house that belonged to the dog collar, watching the neighborhood. It was quiet enough, through his open car window he could hear the occasional child's laugh or shout, but nobody was out in the street or their dilapidated front yards.

The house was a run-down ranch, lacking pride of ownership. The chain-link fence looked like it belonged more in a junkyard than a suburb. Ted doubted that there was a man in that house. No real man would let his domain look so slovenly.

Ted parked his Mercedes down the street and walked to the front door, casually holding the dog collar. He had tucked the Beretta into the back of his pants, letting his shirt billow over it. Ted knocked, then pressed the doorbell. He heard the sound of tinny chimes ringing inside.

An older, overweight Hispanic woman opened the door, peering up at him with suspicious dark eyes. She took in his pressed shirt, shiny leather shoes, and the opal cufflinks and her expression shifted to confusion.

He put on his best and brightest smile for her, swallowing his disgust.

"Excuse me, Ma'am, but did you lose a dog?" Ted held up the collar.

Before the woman could answer, a bouncy teenaged girl ducked into view and peered over the fat lady's shoulder.

"Bobo? Did you find him?"

Heat suffused Ted's face, spreading down into his chest and then his groin. The girl had large dark eyes and beautiful chestnut hair. Her nose was straight, her skin cinnamon and clear. She wore a tiny pink tank-top with a built-in shelf bra that did little to disguise the tips of her plump young breasts.

She was glorious, just like those perky girls who'd taunted him for so many years. She was perfect. The universe had handed him another gift, as good as an angel coming down and saying he was on the right path.

"May I come in?" Ted asked. "I'd like to talk to you about your dog."

The woman glared at him for a second, evaluating his looks, and then sighed. "Yes, sir, of course."

"Is Bobo okay? Where is he? We got home and he was just gone." The perky girl crowded in on Ted, reaching for the dog collar.

Ted let her have it. So Donna had stolen the dog. Dead end here.

He smiled at the teenager. Or perhaps not. She smelled of strawberries and baby powder. He cursed himself for not having made up a new kit. He had no ropes, no knives.

Oh well. He'd just have to make do.

"Where did you get this collar?" the fat woman asked.

Ted nearly snarled at the distraction. He didn't want to deal with this overgrown hag, he wanted to focus and enjoy the bouncy young creature enchanting him with her lovely eyes and smooth skin. With a quick gesture he drew the gun from behind his back, flicking the safety off.

Both women shrieked, eyes going wide. They crowded together, the hag putting the girl behind her.

"Don't," she wimpered. "We don't have anything. You can have it. Don't hurt her, don't hurt my Estrellita."

Estrellita. Little star. She'd be his little star soon enough.

"It's okay, ladies. No one has to get hurt." Ted kept his voice calm, soothing. No need to sound mean, he'd learned it just made things worse. People liked to have a little hope; they liked to cling to the lies. Ted could let them do that, he wasn't cruel. Let them keep their delusions until the end. It made them more cooperative.

He moved them into the crowded little dining area, made the mother sit down. Estrellita pointed to a drawer in the kitchen that held duct tape and he had her bind her mother up. The girl's hands shook and Ted smiled, his blood singing at her fear.

She was a good girl though. No heroics in this one, no real fight. She still believed that everything would turn out just fine.

"Sit down on the floor, Estrellita," Ted told her once the mother was bound and gagged to his satisfaction.

"Please," she begged, "Please, we won't do anything. We won't tell. Just go. We don't have anything."

"You do," Ted said soothingly as he moved around the galley kitchen, picking out the knife he wanted. "It's okay. Now, Estrellita, where's your father?"

Ted glanced at the old woman as he said this, noting the lack of a wedding ring on her clenched left hand.

"He's going to be home any minute now, so you'd better go," Estrellita said, showing a small amount of pluck.

"Don't lie to me." Ted let a little edge tinge his voice, pointing the knife at her while he tapped the gun against his thigh.

"He lives in Miami," she said, tears sliding down her plump young cheeks.

"Siblings?" Ted wanted to make sure they weren't disturbed, though his heart sped up at the thought of sisters, pretty girls like his little star.

She nodded toward the far living room wall, curling her legs up to her chest and wrapping her arms around them. "They don't live here anymore."

Ted glanced at the fake fireplace. Pictures in cheap frames lined the fake mantel. The girls in the pictures looked like their mother more than the sister on the floor at his feet. One stuffed wedding cake into her fat mouth, the moment of disgusting gluttony frozen forever in its frame.

Cows. And not yet past their twenties if Ted guessed right. Estrellita should be thanking him for sparing her their obese fate. She would forever be young and fresh and smiling in those picture frames, caught in youth and preserved. A lily among weeds.

Ted set the safety on his gun and laid it down on the fake wood dining table. He touched the knife blade as Estrellita stared up at him with bloodshot eyes, her face wet from crying. Her slender body, just growing into itself, shook. She was so brave, so beautiful. She didn't scream or beg.

Not like her slovenly worn out mother. Even with the layers of tape, the cow's protests and cries bled through, marring the peace and quiet of Ted's perfect afternoon.

His little star didn't struggle until he cut her mother's throat. After that she fought him for a moment. But not long.

Ted cut away the dying girl's clothing, enjoying the heavy rasp of her breath as she struggled for air around the wound in her ribs. Her breasts were as lovely as he'd expected, better than Moira Stafford's in tenth grade when he'd been caught in the girl's locker room peeking.

His little star. Strawberries and baby powder. Ted swallowed her weak cries into his mouth and thanked the universe for giving him such a lovely present.

Ten

Ted washed the blood from his hands, the pink water swirling around the stainless metal of the kitchen sink before draining away. Outside the ranch house, the sky darkened with clouds as the afternoon sun dipped toward an orange and grey horizon.

This had been a nice interlude, a little gift of the universe to affirm he was on track in his new life, but Ted felt the hunt awaken in his blood. The dead teenager was an appetizer to the real prey.

Donna was still out there, taunting him by living on while he was forced to abandon his carefully constructed existence.

After wiping his hands clean and rolling his sleeves back down, Ted pulled the opal cufflinks out of his pocket and replaced them. He rubbed a thumb over the brilliant red, purple, and greenish gems. Donna had stolen these. Where was she?

Ted left the ranch house, walking back to his car. He opened the trunk and took out the plastic bag with the bloody glove and towel. Time for more fun with the police, though he imagined that Donna would be long gone and dead before all the evidence was sorted out. The cops were so slow about things like DNA and fingerprints, reality being nothing like the TV shows, for which Ted was always grateful.

The neighborhood had more cars in it than earlier, more lights shone from the surrounding houses, but no one gave Ted a second glance as he walked casually back to the house and entered. He removed the towel and glove from the bag. The blood had dried to a thick brown and black paste on both. He dropped the glove on Estrellita's still body, admiring the curve of her breast and the dizzying scent of her skin one last time as he bent down and rolled her over onto her face, careful to keep his hands out of the sticky mess.

Ted smeared the towel around in the pool of blood under the dead mother and then hung it in the hall bathroom. He turned up the air-conditioning on the window unit in the living room and left the house.

He drove toward Daytona Beach and pulled off the highway, circling until he found a pawn shop. He parked, watching as a man in a loud floral-print shirt emerged from the shop and got slowly into Mustang and drove away, head down, shoulders slumped.

Ted opened Donna's shoulder bag and looked more closely at the contents, tucking his face near the bag and inhaling, hoping somehow this might reveal the fatal clue to her whereabouts.

The purse smelled like a purse, the absence of perfumes or noticeable female items bothering Ted. This woman didn't behave like a woman should. She'd worn such nice jewelry, yet no perfume? Her bag held no make-up, no keys, no personal items at all. Cool and professional.

Ted took a deep breath and forced his mind to calm. She was just another girl, though a different type than he usually hunted. He had to relax, to think more like her.

The jewelry in the boxes was expensive, the handful of earrings dumped carelessly in the bottom of the purse less so. She had to have broken into a safe. So, a good thief. The address on the driver's license listed her as living in Nashville, but Ted guessed that with what he knew about her, that address was fake.

She stole the dog as a decoy, a disguise to blend in. No one would question a nicely dressed woman out walking a friendly dog. Ted could appreciate that, he'd used puppies bought with cash at pet stores to lure in victims before. Women did stupid things for pets and children, put themselves in danger in ways they'd never consider if faced with just a man by himself.

Donna was a professional, and from out of town. Ted thought about the trips he'd made, the hunting he'd done in other cities. His neighborhood, the one Donna had chosen to rob, was wealthy, and right off a main freeway. Easy access, easy escape.

Mulling that over, working out how to narrow his search of hotels, Ted left the car and went into the pawn shop. He blinked in the dimmer interior, grimacing at the sudden assault of musty foreign scents. This place was full of the discards of others, curios and bright jewelry, guns and even a crossbow, relics of lives that couldn't hang on to what they had.

An older man, with crooked teeth and bright green eyes that were lively and incongruous with his age-spotted tan skin and straggling salt and pepper hair, sat behind the counter. There was plate-glass around him, but the half-door was open, slid aside for the business day.

"Evening," Ted said and put the purse down on the counter.

"Let's see what you've got," the man said. He looked at the women's shoulder bag and his bright green eyes narrowed.

Ted didn't care how suspicious it looked. Theodore Whitechapel was still a good ID and Ted would get the mileage out of it before he disappeared. Knowing how much these things might be worth could help him define his prey, sort out how good of a thief she was.

He upended the purse onto the counter, stacking the velvet boxes to one side. He'd removed the cash already, leaving only the jewelry and watches.

The man got out a magnifying glass and turned on a brighter light. He spent a long time looking over each piece, enough that Ted had to fight not to shift around or glance too often at the door. It would do no good to look suspicious.

"High quality stuff," the man said at last. "But you know that, being the owner and all, right?"

Ted chuckled, though there wasn't much mirth in it. He thought about the stupid little thief and her escape from him, her wide brown eyes and the blood smeared all over his house. A house he couldn't go back to, because of her.

"Bitch thinks she's leaving me, wants a divorce," he said, staring right into the emerald gaze of the clerk. Ire tinged his voice, his eyes, just as he wanted it to.

The man blinked and then a slow smile bared his uneven teeth. "Guess she won't need these anymore then. I'll just need some ID from you."

Ted relaxed a hair, the tension draining from his shoulders. "No problem," he said.

The amount was less than Ted thought it should be, but he was a few grand richer now and didn't care. Besides, it wouldn't have fit the persona he'd taken on to argue about the price. Angry, hurt husbands wouldn't quibble over sold gifts.

He punched on the phone in his car and hid the money in the glove box. Hotels near easy egresses. That's where he'd stay. Places small enough to take cash, maybe rent by the week, places without cameras or requiring too much ID.

He started calling hotels again, asking for Donna Utley, focusing on ones in the vicinity of the Daytona Beach airport. If she'd left town already, he was going to have to let her go. It twisted his gut to think about losing her, about her out there, surviving while Theodore Whitechapel had to disappear and re-invent. Donna going on living, his one failure.

If, of course, she survived the gut wound he'd given her. But the thought of her dying alone and unmarked made him even angrier. She wouldn't know why she was dying, who he was, how she'd ruined everything. She wouldn't be able to appreciate his power in her final moments.

"Let her be in Daytona Beach still," he murmured, and called information.

Ted got a hit on the eighth one, a place called the Sunrise Lodge. Donna Utley, staying in room 159 and had she not answered when he'd called before? Would he like to leave a message?

Ted swallowed a laugh, beating one fist against the steering wheel. Someone had called for her before? That was interesting. It meant she was likely still in town. He asked to be put through, let the phone ring once, and then hung up. His heart raced, blood pumping into his arms, rushing in his ears. So close, only twenty minutes away with the evening traffic.

Her tan skin, her short blonde hair, the soft moist lips that had cried out so beautifully as she lay like a child in his arms. She should have been his, there in his bathroom, bleeding out into his soaking tub. She'd denied him his pleasure; she'd violated his domain, trespassing into his perfect garden. Donna Utley had soiled and snubbed him.

But not for long. Not long now at all. He'd have her back, and she would give him what was due.

Grinning hard enough to hurt his cheeks, Ted turned on a Johnny Hartman CD, and pulled out onto the road. It was time to tie up the final end, to finish Theodore Whitechapel's final victim before setting out on a new adventure. Rain started to fall, streaming like tears down the Mercedes' windshield.

Eleven

Delilah awoke with the disorientation of a diver ripped from the depths. She lay on her back, listening to the rain, and wondering what had woken her in such a panic.

Then something scraped against the door again. Someone was picking the lock.

Delilah sat up, biting back a cry of pain. The morphine was wearing off, the IV bag nearly empty. The clock glowed sinister and red in the dim light of the table lamp. She'd slept barely two hours.

Scrape. A tinny jingling sound of metal on metal pinged through the quiet hotel room. The lock was giving this guy trouble, probably because Delilah had disabled the light outside the door.

Now she wished she hadn't. Not that she needed to see who was there. She knew.

It would be him. He'd hunted her down. Pain and nausea ripped through her abdomen along with a dark wave of fear.

She ripped off the tape and pulled the IV needle from her hand. Gritting her teeth against the pulling pain, she slid off the bed, staying low so as not to cast movement shadows on the front window. She grabbed her coat off the chair and dumped the pills from the side table into her pocket. There was no time to find a clean shirt.

The door handle wiggled and she heard a muffled curse. With her own suppressed curse, she glared at the vent grate. There was no time to unscrew the grate and retrieve her cash and ID.

Teddy was outside, a thin wooden panel away, and staying here wasn't an option. Fear tingled through her, cramping her hands, clogging her brain with the sound of her pounding heart.

She couldn't face him again, that horrible soft voice, that bright tan smile. He was an enervating presence in her mind, large and powerful. Terrible. Evil.

And clearly he wasn't going to give up before he'd finished killing her. She knew she'd have to hope he didn't find the ID and money in the grate. Would he follow her to Atlanta?

He's just a man, she told herself. He'll give up. She hadn't even done anything to him, except bled helplessly. He'd have to give up. If she could get away again.

Delilah half crawled across the floor, dragging on her hooded sweatshirt and sandals as she moved. She pulled the sliding glass door open and took off at a run across the construction site, feet squelching in the mud.

The rain slammed down in sheets, the street lights barely visible in the downpour. Car headlights zoomed past as she gained the sidewalk behind the hotel. Delilah spared a glance behind her. The construction site was empty looking, no movement coming from the lighted hotel beyond.

Parked cars lined the street. Delilah walked alongside them, trying door handles and checking for open windows. An older Honda sedan's passenger door popped open. She nearly cried out with relief, the dark expanse of the empty lot behind her making her neck itch. She wanted to be gone, far far away from the nightmare that Daytona had become. She reached around and unlocked the other doors, glancing back again and again.

Sitting hurt. Thinking hurt. She took shallow breaths and dug the painkillers out of her pocket, popping a large white pill into her mouth. Then she pawed through the glove box, looking for a screwdriver or anything hard with which she could pry the steering column open. She wished for her tools but shoved that desire aside. Wishing and whining wouldn't get her away and safe.

She found a flathead screwdriver, a short little thing, and tears of relief choked her throat.

The plastic shell peeled away. She blinked hard and tried to remember how to do this by touch since the overhead light was too dim to help and bending over for too long made her want to scream, destroying her focus.

She gave in after a moment and leaned to the side with a careful breath. Red wires, there. She scraped at them with the head of the screwdriver, stripping them down. More shallow breaths, then she twisted them together. Now she just had to find the ignition wire. Brown, usually. She leaned to the side again, trying to keep her torso as straight as possible.

Movement in the corner of her eye brought her head up.

Delilah jerked her head around, staring out into the rain. Had that been a person, there, down the street, outlined for a moment in the streetlights? A shudder went through her.

She sucked in a breath and leaned forward, fear winning over pain. White wire, red wires. No brown wire. *Wait, there.*

She gripped it, stripping the stubborn rubbery plastic away.

Car in neutral, parking break engaged, foot on accelerator. She touched the ignition wire to the twisted red power wires. Click, click. Again she touched it, praying for the engine to catch, to turn over. Click, spark, click.

Ignition. She pushed down on the gas, giving the engine juice, feeding it. With one hand she jammed the plastic casing back into place over the steering column and dropped the parking break with the other.

Lights on, time to go. The drive back to Atlanta, back to her home, would take at least six hours. She'd grab her emergency cash and ID from the house, then get out. Someone would eventually find the driver's license and cash tucked into the wall of her motel room here. Just hopefully not evil Teddy, and not tonight. Atlanta wouldn't be safe forever. But it was as close to a home as she had, and Delilah needed to rest.

The painkillers kicked in as she found the US-1 and headed toward the I-95. Delilah squinted through the sheets of rain painting her windshield opaque or glittering depending on the amount of tail lights and street lights. The world was fuzzier on the pain killers, but she could lean back, relax a little. She turned on the radio and winced at the loud country twang that poured from the front speakers. A quick scan with the dial found classic rock and she eased back in the seat, making a few adjustments to the mirrors.

Delilah loved driving. A car was perfect. She had complete control of it, all the power in the world. No car had only one exit, either. Windows and doors were everywhere. She knew many ways to escape a car, on the chance that she couldn't control it. Inside a car, Delilah was safe, free. She could go anywhere, get away from everything, and just drive. It was hard to find someone in a car, hard to reach them, harder to kill them. Moving target, free and perfect.

Bennie, her father, had taught her to drive in a 1951 Willys truck when she was eleven. Delilah had never wanted to do anything else after. She'd make up excuses to drive to the store, to school, to the beach, any errand, any time, as long as she could have a car underneath her.

She wondered, driving away from Daytona in a haze of rain and drugs, if Jake still had her '67 Mustang, the powder blue one she'd bought and had restored with money from her first big take. Maybe someday he'd teach Esther to drive in it and then it could be her car.

"Can't say I never gave my daughter anything," she muttered into the darkness. She missed Jake like hell sometimes, but the baby, a little girl now, was just an abstract in her mind, a smiling dark face in photographs sent to the P.O. Box she used as a drop site. That was all she'd ever be.

Especially if this gut wound kills me.

Delilah sighed. Maybe she'd take that strange doctor up on his advice. Go to a hospital when she got back to Atlanta, if all was quiet there. She had cash, she could con her way into an emergency room and fake that she didn't understand enough English to be worth talking to. They'd treat her and then she could run. She hated hospitals on principle. Never enough space, enough exits. Plenty of cars, though. She'd manage okay.

Delilah blinked back exhaustion and turned up the volume on the radio. She had a plan. She had the necklace and earrings still on her, which she knew Poppy would pay good cash for. She would live, thrive even, and leave Daytona and its nightmare behind her for good.

She merged up onto the I-95, twisting her head to watch for cars. She turned her head back and glanced down at the display. The needle of the gas gauge sat solidly in the middle between Empty and Full. With a little luck the car would make it far enough away, though not all the way to Atlanta. She'd figure out what to do then. But she had a couple hours.

High, in pain, and hopeful, Delilah drove off into the storm.

Twelve

Jimmy Black cursed softly and then looked around the quiet Sunrise Lodge parking lot. No one out and about, everyone sane was hiding inside from the downpour. He was good with locks, though safe-cracking had become his specialty, but it was damned dark out. He wished he'd just brought a bump key instead.

Jimmy crouched back down and turned his attention to the lock. He closed his eyes and took a deep breath, gripping his tools between boney fingertips. Another jiggle, a twist of the smaller pin, and he heard the click. Finally.

He dropped his tools into his trouser pocket and eased the door open. The place looked empty, as he'd thought it would be. Jimmy had been watching the room for the last hour, crouched down in his rented sedan in the parking lot. Though a light was on, he'd seen no movement.

He figured Delilah was out, doing whatever she'd come into town to really do. Jimmy fingered the .38 special tucked into his belt and checked around the room. Found a bit of blood on towels in the bathroom and the place smelled a bit like a hospital, all iodine, soap, and something sharp like rubbing alcohol. An empty IV bag hung on a hook over the headboard. Someone had been hurt here. Her boyfriend? A mark?

Maybe they'd tortured someone here, getting information about something. You had to do that sometimes, with the really big scores, the ones that took a large crew and a lot of planning. Delilah could be on to a big take, a real deal. And didn't he deserve some of that after how badly his luck had been? Sure he did.

He checked the closet and found a few women's clothes hanging up, pants folded neatly over hangers, a couple nice blouses. Good, she was still in town. Jimmy knew she'd be back and he'd just settle down and wait for her, ask her a few questions.

Like why her car was in the parking lot when she wasn't here. Meant she had to be with somebody.

It had been blind crazy luck that he even knew where she was staying. After she'd quit the job, there'd been a big argument about what to do. The whole plan wasn't possible without a driver and they needed a pro. The illegal casino could be closed up or moved at just about any time, so the job had an uncertain clock on it as well.

Jimmy had left in disgust as the arguing and ideas came to nothing. It looked like the job might be called off entirely.

He'd wasted a trip. Just his fucking luck lately. He needed that twenty grand, bad. Dolmetti wasn't going to stay off his ass for long and a goodwill payment would set Jimmy back up just fine, buy him some breathing room, time to plan a way to repay, or get out of paying, the last hundred grand he owed.

This job was supposed to buy him time. *Until that stupid broad ruined things.*

He'd headed down to the beach, thinking an umbrella drink and hard tanned bodies to ogle would cheer him up.

And there she'd been, standing in the sand in her bare feet. Delilah was too thin for his taste, could use a boob job at the least, but pretty in an exotic kind of way. Asian maybe. She'd stood with her eyes shut for a while, her short dark hair floating around her face in the wind.

Jimmy had decided then and there to follow her. He wanted to know what her angle was. He'd bugged Al about her credentials, not liking the idea of a woman on a job, especially not a job with wetwork, and not doing something as important as the driving. She was a con artist, too, a small timer but a pro. Apparently her family was in the business, though Al didn't know much more about it.

Jimmy had carefully trailed her back to her hotel, smug that she hadn't noticed him. Guess she wasn't so good after all. She was too young to be seasoned, to be paranoid yet. Which is why he figured she had an angle, maybe wasn't working alone.

He knew guys who weren't above putting a pretty face out to get info on a job going down so they could steal it or cut themselves in. She was the kind of broad who'd do that,

Jimmy was sure. Some guy had to have a handle in her back; women in this life always had a handle on them.

He'd thought about confronting her right there at the hotel, but he didn't have his gun. Not that he wanted to hurt her, not really. But a gun scared girls and scared was good. Scared talked. He figured if she was what she said, she'd leave town that day. No reason to stay if she wasn't working anyway. If she stayed, then she was definitely double dealing somehow and Jimmy Black would be the man to set her straight.

And she was still here a day later. Proof enough for Jimmy. Her car was in the parking lot, but she was gone. Probably her man picking her up. Handle, just like he'd thought.

Jimmy turned the beige office chair so that it faced the front door, relocked the door, and then settled in to wait. He hoped she came back alone. He wasn't a big guy, so it'd be hard to deal with two people. But he had his gun, he'd work it out. She owed him answers.

Yeah. Maybe she had a new job here, or maybe a different crew doing the old job. She could cut him in, keep things nice and professional. Friendly. It would only be fair.

With a smile, Jimmy rested the .38 on his thigh and leaned back. He sniffed at the air again and sighed, then pulled a cigarette from his jacket pocket and lit up. He'd get what was his and the lady thief was going to give it to him, one way or another.

Thirteen

Ted stopped off at a hardware store, dashing through the pouring rain. In the past he'd been far more careful about putting together his hunting kits. He'd go to five or ten different stores all around the state, sometimes driving for hours, and of course he always paid cash.

This time he only went to one store. He paid for the cotton rope, duct tape, utility knife, crow bar, plastic zip ties, lighter fluid, motor oil, and latex gloves with his Visa card. Let the cops track it. By the time they even thought to, even knew about the first killing of ditzy spoiled Cora Swarsky, it would be too late. Theodore Whitechapel would be gone, one for the history books.

After tonight.

He grinned at the cashier, making the awkward, overweight woman blush through her orange tan. Ted felt alive, turned on, ready. This wasn't just any hunt, this was the ultimate hunt. The one who got away.

Away, but not too far.

He pulled up to the Sunrise Lodge and watched it for a moment, hovering at the curb in a fire lane. There was a light on in room 159, soft gold shining through the curtains. She was there, then. Maybe dead, maybe not. Well, not yet.

Time to go get her. Not through the front. That would be a mistake. Ted pulled around the side, parking on the street. The backs of the units on the first floor had sliding glass doors which opened onto a construction site. Ted approved. He'd always been fond of places that had extra exits.

Well, for him, extra entrances. Besides, sliding glass doors, provided there wasn't a stick blocking them, often were simpler to open than a lock and certainly a deadbolt. A knife and a credit card would usually do the trick.

Ted pulled on a black slicker, of which he always kept two or three hidden in his trunk, and a pair of latex gloves. Grabbing his hunting kit, he made sure his Beretta was in easy reach and climbed out of the car. The rain fell, thick and warm, and dripped off his hood.

He edged along the backside of the motel. It was more likely he'd be noticed walking along here, but he despised the thought of miring his shoes in the muddy tough of the construction site. Besides, anyone noticing him would probably think he was headed to his room and just staying under the eaves, out of the rain and muck.

The curtains of each room were pulled as he went along, counting the doors until he got to the eleventh one. Room 159.

The curtain was partially drawn, but Ted ducked past it and peeked around the side through the opening. The light from the one lamp shining inside outlined a figure sitting, facing the front door. Ted's heartbeat picked up, his face flushing.

Then he squinted, looking more carefully. It was a man. The blonde hair was balding in a tonsure pattern at the crown.

A man. Ted shook himself and turned away. Donna might have fled town already then. Or this room was a decoy. Or this man could be her man, a boyfriend perhaps. Some protector he'd turned out to be. A pretty little girl like her should have a real man, someone who provided well enough that she didn't have to break into other people's homes.

Ted took a deep breath. He wanted Donna, not some man. He turned and looked back into the room, eyes searching about for some sign that the woman was there, or had been there, or might return.

Was that an IV bag hanging from the bed? Ted thought so. So Donna was alive then, had gotten some medical care. Good, good. She wasn't allowed to die, not without Ted's help. So who was this guy?

Curiosity spurred Ted into action. He looked down at the door latch and was pleased to find it unlocked. He set his kit down on the concrete patio, careful to make no sound, and drew the Beretta, flicking the safety off. *Time to get some answers.*

Ted knew he could slide the door open without much sound, but once it was open the air would change and the rain would get louder, alerting the man inside. So Ted yanked the door open and stepped through, slamming it shut behind him in one clean motion.

Baldy jumped up out of the chair, holding a .38 Special in his hand, his pale blue eyes wide and his mouth hanging open. Ted bit back a laugh at the smaller man's comical expression, holding his own gun casually in front of him.

"Drop the gun," he said. "I want to talk."

"You with Delilah?" Baldy said.

"The lady thief?"

Baldy nodded, licking his lips, eyes flicking between Ted's face and the Beretta.

Delilah. So, this guy knew his thief after all. *Not Donna. Delilah.* A fitting name for her. Temptress, liar, destroyer of strong men. His Delilah. Ted was giddy with this discovery. He wanted more, to know everything about this woman.

"Delilah," he whispered, savoring her name the way he'd run a good aged scotch over his tongue. Then he said, louder, "Drop the gun."

The guy tossed the .38 onto the bed and backed away, toward the front door.

"Look, man, I don't want any trouble. I was just going to ask her some questions. But I don't have to do that." Baldy kept backing up as he babbled.

"Shut up and sit down," Ted said, kicking the chair toward him. He guessed he made a wonderfully imposing figure, all in black plastic with the black gun and latex gloves. Maybe the guy thought he was a pro hit man or something. Dangerous. Powerful.

Ted had never felt any real need to dominate men or scare them. They didn't matter, not really. He was an alpha male and that sort of thing didn't need proving. Men understood. They only had to look at Ted's car, his beautiful home, his clear and perfectly tanned skin, his six-pack abs and nicely cut, but not too large, muscles. Other men just knew they weren't as handsome or successful. Men bought into the façade easily.

It was the women who needed reminding. Women tried to control him, to change him. Women talked with their eyes, needing to be shown their place, to be taught what to care about. Men understood, could read the signs of an alpha staking his claim on life. It was always the women who tried to ruin things.

Baldy glanced at the door behind him, then sighed. He stepped forward and sat in the chair, taking quick breaths.

Ted held still for a long moment, letting the tension build. Then he strode forward quickly. He slapped away the man's hands as they came up to protect his face at the last moment and smashed the pistol's butt down into the scared little man's temple.

The guy passed out, sagging down in the chair. Ted grabbed his hunting kit from the back patio and went to work securing the man. He used a couple zip ties to bind his hands behind his back. Then he yanked him down onto the floor as Baldy started to wake up. A length of rope bound the man's legs.

Ted pulled a knife from the kit and sat down in the chair, letting his foot rest on the bound man's stomach. Slowly the pale blue eyes opened and fixed on him, confusion and fear swirling through Baldy's expression.

"Now," said Ted. "Tell me all about Delilah."

Fourteen

Turned out Baldy's name was Jimmy and he broke easily. Which worked well for Ted, since he wasn't sure about cutting up a man. No joy in it, no true lesson, nothing beautiful about a man's pain.

"She's a thief, that's all I know," Jimmy said, his voice an irritating whine. "Does she owe you money or something?" The little man kept trying to pull information out of Ted, though he wasn't as sly about it as he might have thought. Fear overrode manipulative ability, apparently.

Ted sat in the chair and ran his fingers over the small packet of lock-picking tools he'd taken off Jimmy. Lock-picking tools. Something didn't add up.

There was an IV bag, but no pills or medications. Bloody towels were balled up in the bathtub, soaked in cold water. Traces of iodine in the sink. The bed was rumpled, clothes still hung in the closet. Clothes that smelled like his Delilah, clean soap and that indescribable scent of woman, pure and untainted. A pair of silver, strappy fuck-me heels, as Ted thought of them, and Nike running sneakers were the only shoes. Size five and a half.

Small feet, he liked that. It fit her slender form, his image of her lithe body writhing against him.

It looked as though she were just out; leaving this stuff here, ready to return. Ted left Jimmy curled on the floor and walked back over to the closet. He picked up one of the running shoes.

Clean tread, almost no wear. New shoes or else she wasn't much of a runner.

Ted bet they were new. A woman didn't survive what she'd survived without being in excellent shape. And he'd touched her body, if only all too briefly. Delilah worked out.

Lock picks. For a sliding glass door? Ted had assumed that Jimmy was the one who opened the back door and left it unlocked behind him. Delilah wouldn't have left the door unlocked, she didn't seem the type to be that stupid, not injured as she'd been.

"The door, you picked the lock?" Ted turned back to Jimmy and kicked the man in the ribs to get his attention.

Jimmy groaned. "Yes. I told you. I just wanted to ask her what she was doing here. She's yours, I don't care. Just let me go, man. I'm gone."

"Which door?"

"What?" Jimmy squinted up at him. "The front door. Jesus."

Ted froze and looked around the room again, turning in place to get a full three-sixty view.

"Fuck," he said. He'd missed her. This bumbling, stupid, useless beta male had fucked it all up. Delilah would be miles away by now, headed who knew where. She'd escaped him.

Rage burned white inside him, rising like acid into his throat. He picked up the knife and bent over Jimmy.

Jimmy struggled, seeing the anger in Ted's face, accurately reading his intent.

"Help," he screamed, too late. "Somebody help—"

Ted cut him off with the knife, slicing deep into the pathetic man's vocal chords. Then he stood back and watched Jimmy's body twitch for a long moment. Thick red blood gurgled sluggishly out of the wound after the initial rush from the blade coming out.

Ted watched and waited to see what he would feel. He'd never killed a man before. Disappointment, perhaps? Had he killed the idiot too soon, missed some bit of knowledge about Delilah that he needed, missed the key to finding her? He doubted it.

Other than the mild worry he'd missed asking a few questions, Ted felt nothing. No rush of elation, no arousal. He could have been staring down at the dishwasher after he'd finished loading it for all he felt.

That, too, disappointed him.

Delilah. Ted shoved off his annoyance at the dead body and stepped in close to the wall that neighbored the next unit over. The rain made it difficult to hear but he made out the sound of a TV going. Good. The dead man's scream, which had sounded loud in the small room, likely hadn't traveled much beyond these walls.

Delilah had left in a hurry it looked like. Probably as soon as she heard the idiot at the door with his lock picks. She was a professional, Jimmy had confirmed that, though Ted had already assumed as much from the jewelry and other evidence. And she'd gotten medical care, the IV bag was evidence of that.

Ted sat on the bed, fingering the plastic tubing. The bag was almost empty. He ran his hand over the dented pillows and then bent down low, rubbing his nose into them. Something tickled his skin and he carefully lifted a hair from the pillows. It was short, about the length of his middle finger, and black.

Delilah was a blonde, wasn't she? He rose and went back to the closet. Extra blankets were stacked on a shelf above the clothes hangers. Ted yanked them down and grinned at the small bag behind them.

He pulled it down and unzipped it. Wigs, two of them, in plastic and carefully packaged. One was short, cut in a page-boy style, and auburn, the other long and brown. Both were good quality and made of real human hair. There wasn't a blonde one, but Ted guessed she'd shed it either in the car or while running away from his home.

Dark Delilah. Her frightened, exotic features better fit a dark-haired image. Ted's heartbeat picked up, his fingers tingled. She'd left in such a hurry, so what else had she left behind?

He tore the room apart; searching underneath the mattress and slicing open the box-spring beneath. He emptied the trash, pulled up the corners of the carpet, and came up empty.

Jimmy's bowels had given way when he died and the room reeked of drying blood and shit. But Ted couldn't leave yet. Not without some hint.

He picked up the phone and hit redial. It picked up after one ring, beeping twice and then silence. A pager or an automated message machine. Curious, Ted punched in the numbers on the hotel phone and hit the pound key.

He sat on the edge of the bed and waited. The clock's minutes turned over once. Twice. Then the phone rang.

Ted picked it up but didn't say anything.

"Delilah?" A man's voice yelled through the line, "Goddamnit, what the fuck are you doing?"

"I'm wondering the very same thing," Ted said, amused. "Who's this?"

Silence then, and Ted wondered if the man would hang up on him.

"Who the fuck are you, pal?" the man said after a moment.

"I'm going to kill Delilah," Ted said. "And anyone who gets in my way."

"Jesus fucking Christ," the man said, and the line went dead.

That had been amusing, but ultimately fruitless. However, Ted guessed his little warning might create a few questions for his Delilah. She'd called this guy at a time when she had to have needed a lot of help, injured like that. She might get in touch with the angry fellow again.

Ted took a deep breath and regretted it. *Damn dead body.* He needed a new plan, a next step.

Jimmy had spilled the information about the job that wasn't going to happen, though Ted hadn't cared about the particulars. Ted doubted that anyone was still using the meeting hotel anymore, or that this Al man would know more than Jimmy had. It would be his next stop, however. He couldn't give up on Delilah yet, she wasn't allowed to win.

She was out there. Living, breathing. Knowing she'd beaten him, escaped him. Laughing at him.

Ted's eyes settled on the square vent. This hotel had central air. He hadn't taken apart the walls yet.

Heart starting to race again, Ted picked up the bloody knife and cut into the drywall around the vent, prying the covering loose.

It came away with a few hard tugs. The screws were loose; the vent had already been tampered with.

Tucked inside was a little cloth wallet, like a traveler might carry against his body in a foreign country. Delilah hadn't had time to pry open the vent and retrieve it. Ted grinned. She'd left him a present, a clue. Clearly the universe was still on his side.

The pouch contained two hundred dollars in cash, two keys on a ring, and a Georgia driver's license with the name "Lily Chung" on it. The tiny picture was his Delilah, however, staring dark-eyed and quiet. It was basically the same picture that was on Donna Utley's driver's license, only with dark hair instead of blonde. A woman of many names, it seemed. Deceitful Delilah.

And there was an address. Atlanta, Georgia. Ted had never been there. But he knew that when humans were injured and scared and on the run, they all wanted somewhere safe, somewhere familiar. It was human nature, plain and simple. She might be special, but she was just a girl in the end, and she'd run home.

Run right to him.

He called the airport from the hotel phone. There was one flight left tonight from Daytona to Atlanta, leaving in less than two hours. Ted booked a seat. She'd either be on the same flight, he guessed, or driving home. Either way, he'd arrive before she did or catch her on the plane. He'd have to ditch the gun and his car, but that was all right.

He had no plans to use a gun on his little Delilah anyway.

Ted tucked her picture into his pocket. One last thing to do before he caught his flight. He didn't want Delilah to think she'd gotten away. It was time to put a little pressure on his prey.

Before slipping out the back door, he dialed nine-one-one and left the phone off the hook.

Fifteen

The orange glow of the low-fuel light caught Delilah's attention. She slammed her fist down onto the steering wheel, cursing her luck. Pain stabbed through the painkilling fog and she winced.

The rain fell hard enough to bounce off the road, leaving a bright mist in front of her headlights and turning the tail-lights of the cars ahead into dim patches of bloody water. There was an exit coming up. She'd made it out of Daytona, almost to Jacksonville.

Not close enough, however. She'd hoped for another sixty, seventy miles, to at least get away from the rain.

The drugs swathed her mind in a thick cloud, but the pain waited along the edges, testing the boundaries every time she shifted or took a deep breath. It was hard to think, to process anything. She just wanted to be home already. Then she'd sleep for a year. Heal and figure out what had gone so wrong.

She'd made mistakes here in Daytona, she knew that. Delilah was young, but she'd grown up around professionals. She'd figure out what she'd done wrong and make damned sure she never repeated the stupid things.

Delilah knew bad men. Men who killed without a thought if they had to. She'd even met a pro hit-man, a guy working for an outfit. He'd cut a deal with her father, weeks before the crime that got Benny incarcerated. She remembered that man's eyes. Cold, empty.

Not at all like the eyes of the man who'd stabbed her. His had been warm, intense. Bile rose in her throat as she merged into the exit lane and remembered the feel of his lips on hers as he swallowed her scream.

He'd been so fast, so strong. Miles away and safe, she still shivered.

The men she knew killed when they had to, when they needed to protect themselves, either from physical danger or from jail. A good thief should never have to hurt anyone. Benny and Colin had taught her that. A good con man stayed ahead of everyone and a good thief was gone long before the crime got reported.

Delilah blinked hard and the dead staring eyes of the woman's severed head flashed across her closed lids.

Teddy wasn't a professional. He was a predator. Probably a serial killer, though she'd only seen one head. But he'd stabbed her without thinking and his words to her, those whispered promises: those were the words of a man with plans for more.

"Shh, stupid girl. I'll be right back for you," Delilah said the words from her memory. He hadn't killed her because he hadn't finished with her yet. It would have been easy for him to pull out the knife and finish the job. He was strong enough that he could have just broken her neck.

But he hadn't wanted her dead. Not yet.

Alone in the car as it floated through the rain like a submarine, Delilah let the hot tears slide down her cheeks. She'd made so many mistakes and that man had almost killed her. With the space to think, finally, it hit her how close she'd been to really dying. Dying horribly. A man who kept a woman's head in his freezer probably wasn't the type to kill her quick.

The car's engine stuttered as she reached a stop light and Delilah forced her attention back to the road. She ran the back of her arm across her face, rubbing the tears out with one sleeve.

She had no money, so a gas station was out of the question. If she hadn't been injured, she would have just done a gas and run, but she didn't want to take the chance that an attendant was paying attention. So that left the options of either finding some money, or stealing a new car.

The neon light of a sign caught her attention. A bar. Delilah nursed the dying car into the parking lot and twisted the ignition switch to kill the engine. She noted that the fuel needle rested at the midpoint. Stupid broken things. The owner clearly didn't take care of his or her things.

Him. The name on the registration in the glove box confirmed that. She searched the car for anything useful, coming up with a few pennies and a dime. She took the change and the screwdriver.

Delilah thought about popping another pain pill but pushed it away. She wanted her head clear, or at least as clear as it was going to get. She dashed across to the awning of the bar, hood up against the rain. There were a few cars in the parking lot and traffic was steady on the road. All the cars she could see were more modern models, nothing cheap and easy to break into or hotwire.

Movement and light caught her eye. Across the parking lot from the bar was a garage, one of the bay doors open. Dim gold light spilled out into the rain, refracting off the water. Two men stood under the protection of the raised door, smoking cigarettes and talking. One man rested his foot up on an older model Buell motorcycle. The harsh bark of laughter sent a shiver down her spine. The guy resting his foot on the bike turned and seemed to look across the parking lot at her.

Too many people, too much traffic. Stealing a car here was going to be a problem.

No, she told herself, not a problem. Just a challenge. Stop making mistakes. Stop rushing.

With a sigh, Delilah walked into the bar. She was cold, exhausted, and hurting. She needed a minute to think. Just for a minute. Get warm, reason out her next plan, then she'd go. She was nearly an hour outside Daytona now. There was no way killer Teddy could find her here.

So why did she still feel like a rat on the run?

The heat inside the bar blasted into her and she started to shiver. Smoke and beer and peanuts assaulted her nose and her sandals crunched on the floor as she moved further into the bar. She slid along one wall, taking in the place, the patrons.

Looking for the rear exit. She needed an exit if she wanted to stop hyperventilating.

Delilah had been in a lot of bars and this one had a pretty typical layout. Booths lined one wall, with a couple small tables scattered around the room. There was a pool table off to one side and two young men leaned on it, chatting with a blonde waitress whose skin had seen too much sunlight and many better days. The bar ran in a half moon through the back of the room, with one bartender washing glasses. He glanced her way.

Delilah pushed her hood off her head and ran a hand through her hair. Through a side hallway were the restrooms and at the back of that hall was the fire exit. She walked past the ladies' room and checked the door for an alarm. None, just the bright friendly glow of the exit sign. Her heartbeat slowed.

She turned and stepped into the ladies' room. Delilah pushed into the handicap stall and sat on the toilet. She dragged up her shirt and checked the bandage.

It was dry and clean. No blood. She wished the wound would stop throbbing.

Time to figure out a plan. The bar wasn't crowded by any means, but there were enough people, mostly men. Delilah liked men, especially men alone in bars. Her plan shifted, forming in her mind. She needed a ride, and she needed some cash. Any car she stole would have to be gassed up before she arrived in Atlanta and she didn't feel healthy enough to go through with the routine of steal, ditch, steal.

Not tonight. She just wanted to get back to her stash, clear out, head some place far away. Maybe she'd go to New York, see about finding someone who needed something run across to Canada.

After sleeping for a week. And maybe seeing another doctor. Just in case.

Plus she still wanted to send money to Jake and her daughter. For a brief instant Delilah entertained the thought of heading across the country, going home to Oregon. Seeing her daughter, seeing Jake. His crooked smile, the way his cornflower blue eyes filled with life and joy when he laughed.

But Esther wasn't really hers, any more than Jake was. She'd given her up to Jake and Nancy. Nancy wanted a kid and Delilah had no idea what she'd do with one. How she'd make a living. A baby might be good for some kinds of con jobs, nothing like single-mother sympathy after all, but for a get-away driver children just seemed like a liability.

And if the law ever got Delilah, well, the kid already had a grandfather locked away for life. Esther was better off with her dad and the woman he'd chosen over Delilah.

She was no kind of mother for a kid. Delilah suppressed the bubble of laughter that danced in her throat and threatened to rise with tears. She couldn't even take care of herself. Here she was, maybe dying and totally broke in a bar somewhere in the boonies of Florida.

Fuck this. She was alive. She'd escaped that crazy killer, twice.

Delilah twisted the tennis bracelet still on her wrist. Then she removed the necklace and tucked it into her pocket. The earrings followed. They looked too rich for this place.

She had about ten grand stashed in her home in Atlanta and she could get more as soon as she saw Poppy at the pawn shop. Between the necklace, earrings, and bracelet, she guessed she was walking around with a good seven or eight grand on her. It was almost funny. Almost.

If she hadn't been in so much pain, or so cold, or so damn scared of a man who couldn't possibly know where she was.

Delilah stood up and pulled the pain killers out of her pocket. The choice to take one or not was a devil's bargain. Either fight the pain and be fuzzy from the drugs, or suck it up and let the pain stab at her with tiny blades. She wanted a clear mind, but it wasn't going to happen.

She took a pill. It was chalky in her mouth and she stepped out of the stall. A couple handfuls of water from the faucet cleared the worst of the taste out.

The bathroom door opened and the overly-tanned blonde waitress came in. She leaned against the little shelf beneath the mirror and pulled a small makeup bag out of one of her apron pockets.

Delilah smiled. This would work, this would be okay. She was in a bar, one of her natural hunting grounds. Suckers were born each minute and half of them regularly haunted bars.

"Hey," she said to the waitress.

"Yeah?" The woman looked over at her. Took her measure.

"I've had a kinda rough night," Delilah said. The woman's eyes narrowed suspiciously and Delilah hurried on, "Could I maybe borrow a little lipstick, fix myself up? I just wanna have a good time, you know?"

The woman smiled, suspicion fading from her eyes. Asking for help usually got people over their initial fear of someone. Everybody liked to be a hero, and to feel superior to those around them.

"One of those days, huh?" The waitress passed her lipstick to Delilah.

Delilah shrugged and dipped her head, going for bedraggled and pathetic. She knew with her wet hoodie and the hollows under her eyes, it wouldn't take much acting. A little hot water on her face and some lipstick went a long way toward making herself presentable.

Evie, as the waitress introduced herself, offered up some eye shadow and blush as well. Delilah suffered through five minutes of Evie's whining about men, nodding occasionally and murmuring sympathetic nonsense sounds. It was good to let people talk. Let them think she cared. Trust was important, useful.

The drugs were kicking in, flooding her system with relief from the pain. Delilah felt floaty and insulated, as though there were a thin layer of plastic between herself and the real world. Bubble plastic, like the kind used to ship packages and keep them from breaking. She imagined that if she reached out and squeezed the air there'd be a pop.

"Thanks, Evie," she said when the woman's rant wound down.

"Sure thing, honey. I got to get back to work. Good luck finding a little comfort. Pretty thing like you shouldn't have no trouble."

No trouble. That sounded nice to Delilah. She'd had nothing but trouble since she'd walked off that job and tried to make a little money on her own. Two days. Jesus, but it felt like forever. She wanted to turn around, swim backward in time and undo it all.

Delilah shook herself and the shocks of pain helped wake her out of her fugue. She'd almost gone maudlin there. Damnit. She didn't have time for this. Money, then a car. Those were the priorities now.

She looked at herself in the mirror and unzipped her hoodie enough that most of the lacy bra beneath showed. Her short dark hair was tousled in a way that looked almost intentional, Evie's lipstick was too pink for Delilah's taste, but it looked good on her full mouth. With the green shadow and a light dusting of blush, she looked good, exotic instead of thin and sick.

It was time to go hunting.

Sixteen

Delilah hadn't even noticed the old jukebox or the music playing on her first pass through the bar. Now the strains of a woman's voice wafted from the jukebox, muting the conversations. There were two TVs flanking the bar, one tuned to a golfing tournament, the other to a local news channel.

The peanut smell mingled with something fresher, fried. Her belly gurgled, hunger nudging her through the painkillers. Delilah guessed this bar had a small kitchen, probably just a counter with a line of deep fryers. Fried and salty worked well to soak up booze and get people thirsty for more.

Sweet smoke from a clove cigarette drifted to her as she surveyed the room looking for a mark. She followed it out into the middle, pinpointing its source.

A middle-aged man with thinning brown hair sat alone at one end of the bar, smoking a clove. Djarums, she guessed. He wasn't good-looking enough to be arrogant, but not so ugly he'd be suspicious of a woman coming on to him. Perfect.

She ran a hand through her hair one last time and walked over, taking the empty seat next to him.

"Want to be my hero?" she asked him. She noticed his keys were on the bar by his elbow, along with a twenty dollar bill. He had a couple of beer bottles and an empty shot glass in front of him.

"Hi," he said, shifting to face her.

"Can I beg a clove off you? I've had one of those days." Delilah smiled at him, putting just enough flirt into it to light up her eyes but keeping the down-on-her-luck persona she'd pitched to Evie the waitress.

Consistent characters were important. Tell the least number of lies to get what you want, that's what Bennie had always said.

"Sure, I like being a hero," the man said and he reached into his jacket pocket for a clove.

While he lit it and she sucked in on the hot smoke, Evie stepped up to them.

"Come on, Sam, buy the pretty girl a drink." Evie winked at Delilah in what she probably thought was a subtle way.

Excellent. Delilah smiled at the waitress and took another drag. The smoke heated her up inside, tingling against her throat. She didn't smoke usually, preferring to keep her body whole and healthy, but this certainly seemed like a smoke 'em if you got 'em situation.

And she liked cloves. She and Jake used to park her Mustang at a lookout over the ocean off highway 101 and sit, talking and smoking cloves, watching the waves as the sun settled down into the sea. They'd kiss the sweet aftertaste from each other's lips and laugh. Sometimes they'd sneak down onto the beach in the dark and make love on the old army blanket.

Those were the best times, bright glowing memories nestled in the happier parts of Delilah's mind. The times before she got pregnant. Before Jake went straight and she realized he'd finally made a choice she couldn't make with him.

"What're you drinking?" The man in the bar brought her back from the fog of memories.

"Shirley Temple, with a shot of vodka on the side. Thanks."

"I'll have another beer, Evie," the guy said.

Evie laughed and moved away from them, waving at the bartender.

"That's cute," he said. "I'm Sam."

"Lia," Delilah said, offering him her hand.

They awkwardly shook and she took in his lack of a wedding ring. His hand was warm and dry, dwarfing her thin fingers.

She asked him the basic questions as she waited for their drinks to arrive. The flicker of the TV above his head kept drawing her eye and she forced herself to focus on his eyes. *Connect with the mark, make them believe.*

His eyes were hazel and a bit small for his face, close together but saved from seeming beady by thick, almost feminine lashes.

Shit, but she needed to focus. The drug haze clouded her brain and she just wanted to sleep now that she was warm again. Delilah took another deep drag of the cigarette.

The bartender came over, set down a beer and a tall glass full of fizzy pink liquid. He then poured a shot of vodka, bottom shelf stuff Delilah was sure, and nodded to Sam.

So, Sam had a tab. That was good. She'd already guessed he was a regular since Evie knew his name. A tab meant he could pay up, which meant he had money on him. But she'd focus on that twenty first. Then maybe she'd set her sights on whatever was in his wallet, and finally, on the Camry he drove.

The keys beckoned to her but she forced herself to stick to script. Money first. Then car. Then she could flee, get back out onto the open road and say see-ya to Florida. Maybe forever. Screw this State anyway.

"Want to play a game, Sam?" Delilah leaned in, giving him a nice view of her perky breasts inside the thin blue lace of her bra. She bit into the cherry she'd pulled out of her Shirley Temple and twisted it off at the stem.

He swallowed. "What kind of game?"

"Stupid bar game. Here, give me that twenty and your empty bottle there." She laughed, keeping it light, friendly.

Sam raised his eyebrows at her but did as she asked. Delilah took a deep breath, hiding it by letting the air slip slowly out of her lungs as she exhaled. She didn't want to push this too much, too fast. That would ruin the con, break the rapport she was trying to build.

But she hurt and the bar was fuzzy from the drugs, her mind hazy and slow. She leaned into the cool metal rail edging the bar and prayed for the dexterity to pull off this simple trick.

"Okay, Sam," she said with an exaggerated wink she hoped looked silly and fun instead of just stupid. "The way it works is this." She put the twenty flat on the bar and balanced the beer bottle upside down on it. "We each try to pull the bill out without tipping over or touching the bottle. Winner keeps the bill and buys the next round." She made sure to make a yanking motion with her hand as she explained. It was always good to give unspoken cues that might induce the mark to do the wrong thing.

"You've done this before," he said, shaking his head.

"Yeah, okay, you got me." She put her hand on his arm and leaned in again. "I'll give you three tries. Come on, can't you beat a girl?"

Sam shook his head. His face was flushed, a good sign. He shifted and examined the bottle. Then, carefully, he used two fingers to try to slide the twenty out. The bottle wobbled and then fell over.

"Any tips?" Sam looked sideways at her.

"Nope. That would be cheating." Delilah picked up her shot of vodka and held it up in salute. "Try again." She took the shot but held the alcohol in her mouth.

Sam set the bottle up again and stared down at it. With his attention elsewhere, Delilah slowly spit the vodka into her Shirley Temple as she faked chasing the shot with a drink from the sickly sweet cherry soda.

The bottle clattered to the floor as Sam failed again.

"Third time is the charm," Delilah said.

"Sure." Sam set it back up and this time almost got the bill out. He slid it carefully, letting the bottle stabilize after wobbling, but the bottle finally tipped over again.

"Let me show you how it's done." Delilah leaned in over Sam and set the game back up.

"Go on, Lia." Sam took a long drink of his beer. "But you only get one try."

Delilah flexed her fingers. Her hands were shaking a little, which was bad. Don't fuck this up, she told herself. Losing here might be a good strategy, get the mark all confident that this was just a silly game, but she didn't have time for a lot of games tonight.

She carefully rolled the edge of the twenty up and then kept rolling it until it hit the bottle. Keeping her fingers away from the bottle, she continued slowly rolling the bill, sliding the bottle along a bit at a time until finally the rolled twenty slid out from under the bottle.

"Just got to think outside the box," she said, holding up her rolled twenty with a grin.

"Damn. You got me." Sam smiled at her and pulled out another clove.

"I'll show you some more tricks, they're good for parties. After we get another round, right? My treat now." Delilah took the clove from his fingers and took a drag before slipping it back between Sam's lips.

His body was turned toward her now, his posture forward, his pupils dilated. All good signs. She had him hooked, now to reel the man in. The painkillers had kicked in fully now and

Delilah felt all right. Fuzzy, but better. She was in her element now, safe and sound.

The TV above Sam's head at the end of the bar, the one with a news channel playing, caught her attention for a second as a picture flashed onto the screen.

It was a driver's license photo, blown up. And underneath it, the captions flowing past said things like "wanted" and "murder".

It was Donna Utley's license, blonde-haired Donna. Blonde Delilah. She stared up over Sam's head at her own face and felt the world closing in again, tighter and tighter.

Seventeen

Delilah's hands started to shake again. She glanced wildly about, imaging that every pair of eyes in the cozy bar had turned and focused on her. No one was looking at her except Sam.

He leaned toward her. "You okay?"

"Yeah." She smiled at him, wondering how he couldn't hear the crazy pounding of her heart. Her eyes went back to the screen above his head. Her picture was still there.

"Something on TV?" Sam started to turn his head but Delilah quickly grabbed his arm and brought his attention back onto her.

"Nah, I just think the vodka has run right through me," she said. She slipped the twenty into her pocket and got off the bar stool. "I'll be right back, order the next round."

"You okay?" Sam's eyes narrowed. Damn, she was losing him.

Stop panicking, Dee. "Totally." She leaned into him, letting her breasts brush his arm, and gave him a soft kiss on the cheek. "You have already made my night better." With a hand behind his back, she gripped his keys and brought them off the bar in a quick motion, hoping her grasp was tight enough that they wouldn't jingle.

"Back in a sec, hero," she said and quickly stepped away from the bar, heading to the bathrooms.

Walking fast hurt, the muscles in her abdomen pulling on the stitches, but she couldn't slow down. She had to get out. Peanut shells crunched beneath her sandals and she thought she heard someone call out.

Delilah didn't look back. She walked right by the bathrooms and out the rear exit, glancing for an alarm again before pressing down on the bar to open the fire door. No alarm light, and no sound when she opened it.

Then she was out in the rain and open air. Free.

The rain was down to a misting sprinkle now. She pulled up her hood and picked out the ignition key for the Camry. There was a remote door opener as well, and she pressed it twice, watching for lights in the parking lot. There, not far from the door. Good.

The two men were still smoking and messing around with the motorcycle across the lot, but Delilah ignored them. She'd be away in just a moment.

She got into the driver's seat of the silver Camry. Sam's car was messier than she'd expected. Empty wrappers and coffee cups were scattered on the passenger side floor. The tree-shaped air freshener labeled "Applewoods" laid a thick fruit and Pinesol layer over the stale cigarette, coffee, and potato chip scent that greeted her as she adjusted the seat for a shorter driver. She'd adjust the mirrors once she was on the highway.

Key into ignition, lights and windshield wipers on. The gas gauge said it was three-quarters full and Delilah hoped that was true. That and the twenty might be enough to get her to Atlanta. Camry's got good mileage generally. Another automatic transmission. Delilah sighed. Nobody drove a stick shift anymore. Lazy people.

She started up the car. The two men across the lot were moving toward her, waving their arms. What was this? She hadn't checked the tires. If one were flat she was going to cry. Just break down and sob. *Damnit.*

Then she heard the shout and glanced to the side to see Sam coming at the car, fast. He had something in his hand. Something small and shiny. He slammed the thing against the passenger window.

A badge.

"Oh fuck me," Delilah said aloud and hit the door locks just in time to prevent Sam from opening the door.

She hit the gas and sped out of the parking lot toward the freeway, almost hitting an oncoming truck. In the rearview she saw Sam sprinting down the road, his hand pressed to his ear. A cell phone, she guessed. Reporting her. This night just got better and better.

Delilah took the onramp going south, knowing that Sam would report her actions and wanting to misdirect. Normally a stolen car wouldn't get a huge amount of attention. Sure, the license plate would be put out and cops would look out for it, but no real pursuit would be mustered. This wasn't normal. She'd stolen a cop's car. Every stupid pig in the vicinity would be out looking for her within ten to twenty minutes.

Sam hadn't looked like a cop. Cops all had an air, a miasma of power-tripping and authority about them. Damnit, but she could tell. She thought she could anyway. He'd seemed so normal, without the edge or awareness that cops usually carried. The drugs. It had to be the stupid wound and the pain. She was so damned tired. Her instincts were frazzled. Not good.

She replayed the events in the bar from her memory. That had definitely been a badge pressed to the window. He'd nearly made it into the car, and she'd seen the shield clearly. Shield. Detective. Crap. Worse and worse. Cops with ranks.

Delilah stayed southbound until the next exit. Then she swung off the freeway and back around, heading toward the Jacksonville airport. She was in a car, she could out run them. Not in this car though. It was a cop's car. No way in hell she was going to bet it didn't have Lojack or some sort of tracking system. The GPS was switched off, but that didn't mean shit.

Not the way her luck had been going. She'd head to the airport, ditch the car and pick up a new one in long-term parking. The cops wouldn't know if she'd caught a flight or what. She'd be away by then. She just had to stay ahead.

Just get home, she told herself. Get home, sleep this stupidity off, and everything will be fine. Everything will go back to normal.

Except it wouldn't. Home couldn't be home anymore.

Donna Utley's name was burned, but she'd already known that. Murder though? What murder? The news probably got her name and that picture from the hotel desk. The clerk had photocopied her license.

She had a bigger problem though. Who got killed at the hotel? Teddy had found her there, he'd almost gotten inside. Had he been so angry when she was gone that he'd killed someone else? What did the asshole want with her, anyway? She hadn't even stolen anything from him.

She thought of his cold, psychotic eyes and shivered. Yeah, she could see him killing someone randomly. Easy. *Crazy bastard.* She hoped the weird doctor hadn't come back to check on her. She forced away the image of Teddy laughing over Morales's bleeding corpse.

If that crazy bastard had murdered someone in her hotel room, that would create more issues. Make it more likely that someone would see the tampering with the vent and find her stash. The money and her Atlanta address.

At the thought that she shouldn't go to her safe house, Delilah's tears finally broke through. She had nowhere else to go. She needed money; she needed to get her other IDs. Even if the law found her stuff in the vent, she had time. The cops were slow, especially across state lines. And her prints weren't in the system.

Hell, finding prints and such and identifying them in a cheap hotel room had to be about as hit and miss as printing a public restroom or a New York subway station. She had at least a week. The cop would get his car back, probably tonight, and that would be that. She stared down at her bare hands, pale and thin, gripping the wheel. They'd print the car. But those prints might not catch up to the Daytona Beach prints. Not for a long while.

Still, she was leaving a hell of a trail behind her. Like a snot-faced square straight out of Juvie.

"Damn you, Sam. You seemed so stupid and nice." She sighed. Hopefully, Sam was at least kind of stupid. There were so many risks, no matter what she did.

She took a deep breath and winced. The pain was returning, the drugged gauzy haze wearing thin with the adrenaline and emotion pouring through her. Tears dripped off her chin and she found it hard to breathe with her nosed clogged with snot. All she wanted to do was sleep. Sleep without fear. This whole day had been so fucked up.

I'll go. But I won't stay. In and out. Get the money, get a new car, drive somewhere else and book a room. Start over.

There would be other houses. Other jobs. She'd never screwed up so badly that she'd had to lay low before, but she could do that, too, if she had to. There was money enough, especially with the jewelry in her pocket. She'd stay ahead. Running. Delilah was good at running.

Wiping the back of her hand angrily over her cheeks, Delilah sped off toward the lights of Jacksonville.

Eighteen

Ted sipped the atrocious, over-priced red wine from a plastic cup and stared out the airplane window into the darkness. Far beneath the plane, the skies rained down, drowning the world in cleansing dark water.

He was above it all. Those tiny, pointless lives scurrying around like maggots somewhere thousands of miles below. Ted loved flying. He just wished the drinks they served in first class were higher quality. The stewardess was high quality, however, and Ted gave her a friendly grin as she walked by.

Nice ass, legs in clean, light brown pantyhose. Her breasts were small, but looked perky inside the airline uniform. She had on too much makeup, but her face wasn't haggard yet from the job and her eyes still had some life in them. Old enough to be a good fuck, young enough to still enjoy it.

Ted knew he could have her. Even without his hunting kit, he could easily find a way to either convince her to join the "mile high" club with him, or force her into it. She wouldn't protest too much. They never did.

But it might create complications. Even delay him. He sighed. This wasn't the time for play. His blood still raced. He felt so good, so alive. So free.

But first, Delilah.

He'd find her. Sit in wait for her, a hunter waiting in the blind for the prey to bed down. It would be too late at night to rebuild his kit, the hardware stores would all be closed. That was okay with him. Delilah wasn't on this flight and the next one out wasn't until the morning. Unless she drove, but even then he'd still arrive hours before her. Plenty of time to find a knife and some duct tape or rope.

From there, he'd improvise. It occurred to Ted that she might not live alone and that thought brought on another rush of anger. She was his. The idea of another man touching her, putting his cock in her, running his hands through that soft hair and breathing in her clean, soapy smell, burned in Ted's mind. *Mine.*

The empty plastic cup crumpled and cracked in Ted's hand, bringing him back to himself. He shook his head, reaching for his iron control. If there was another man, well, he'd fix that. He could kill a man, hadn't he proven that with the whining idiot in the hotel? There would only be one man in Delilah's life from now on.

Her very, very short life.

Ted set the damaged cup down and gave himself a mental shake. He needed to get control of his feelings, his urges. His head must stay clear, ready. Ted pushed the button for the stewardess and asked her for a blanket.

When she returned he briefly entertained the idea of propositioning her, as first class was almost empty, but discarded that. No complications. Not tonight.

Ted hit the overhead light and flicked it off. He slid one hand under the blanket draped over his lap and unzipped his pants. The pretty stewardess' and Delilah's faces blended together, their bodies merging in his mind as he stroked himself. She was there, somewhere in the darkness below him, struggling in the mud with the other lesser creatures. She had gotten away, but she was coming to him now.

Ted looked out into the black void, and smiled.

Nineteen

Detective Sam Arbichaut stood under the awning of the Bold Bass tavern and pulled out his cell phone to make a series of calls he really, truly didn't want to make. He'd already waved off the two men who'd been in the garage across the way. Nothing they could do, they'd seen what he'd seen.

Him getting left in the drizzle while a woman stole his car. He sighed and started making calls.

The first was to his dispatch to report his car stolen so it could be entered into the database and the VIN checked against his LoJack number. It would take Emerelda about five to ten minutes to beat the system into submission and get his LoJack activated so he could track his car.

"Sure thing, boss," Emerelda said when he gave her the news and asked her to start the trace. He could hear the amusement in her voice, but she was nice enough to keep her trap shut.

"It's Rocco and Petty on tonight, isn't it?" Sam asked with a sigh. He already knew the answer, he'd made the schedule.

"Yeah. They're out and about. You want me to call them?" He heard the click of her keyboard in the background.

"Nah, I have the number. They'll have to come pick me up anyway. Thanks, Em." Sam hung up and then popped up a new number from his contacts list.

This call, this was the one he was really dreading. As senior detective and a shift supervisor in Robbery for Jacksonville, having to call the two clowns of the Auto Theft division, his underlings, and ask for a ride was just insulting. But the worst would be when they found out he'd had his car stolen. By a girl.

"Fuck," Sam said and hit send.

"Rocco here. Hit me, boss, we're bored as hell." Rocco's voice buzzed through the phone and Sam heard the deep bass throb of the noise those two guys called music in the background.

"I need you to come pick me up, out off I-95, at the Bold Bass."

"What? Why? Get a little too drunk?"

Sam wished he were more drunk, but his buzz had worn off the moment he'd realized that the face up on the TV screen was the woman who had just left with his keys.

"Just come get me. I'll explain later." He hung up. They'd do what he said. Both of them were still in the dog house since an incident involving a bait car and a pacemaker a couple weeks ago. He'd stuck them on graveyard patrol in an unmarked just to get them out of everyone's hair until the inquiry finished.

Sam leaned back against the building and watched the drizzle. He had more calls to make, but those could keep until he was back at his desk. He didn't believe for a second they'd find his car with the woman still in it.

Donna Utley, that's what the news had said. Breaking Story. Someone murdered in a hotel room in Daytona Beach. News was speculating a drug-related thing or domestic disturbance. Not that the reporters ever knew anything real. But damn.

He'd liked her. She'd been so tiny, so vulnerable looking. Evie had vouched for her, more or less. Ever since his divorce a few years ago, Sam had been wary of women. But he was still a sucker for a damsel in distress. Had a bad day, she'd said. He guessed that hadn't been a lie.

His brain was clearing out and Sam went back over the last half hour in his head. She'd looked tired. She hadn't had a purse. That should have clued him in, but it was his weekend, he hadn't been in cop-mode. Okay, and he'd had a few beers already. Sam shoved away the reproaches. Not useful now.

Scared. She'd looked scared. Even before her face popped up on the screen. Tense, too. Well, if she'd killed somebody, he guessed she would be tense. But he didn't want to think about her being a killer. Maybe she just knew something, saw something. Needed help.

Sure and pigs were growing wings all over. She'd worked him over like a pro. The little smiles, the arm touches, the way she'd used a "bar game" to hoodwink him out of a twenty.

She'd slid his keys off the bar easy and clean, too. If his instincts hadn't given him that little shove, he might never have turned to see what was on the TV as she went to what he'd assumed was the bathroom.

But she'd tensed up, gotten a hollow, scared look for a moment. Warning enough for Sam. He sighed again. He should have known that a pretty woman flirting with him was too good to be true. She was a looker though. A bit on the skinny side for him, but she'd had nice cleavage, and very smooth cinnamon-brown skin. Wide eyes, straight nose, thick lips. Maybe Cambodian or Chinese? With a bit of Caucasian mixed in, that he was sure of. A typical American mutt. Would make her harder to describe later.

Sam slapped his palms flat on the wall and then went inside to talk to Evie. She'd seemed to know the girl, so maybe she could shed some light.

"I met her in the bathroom, Sam, honest." Evie bit her lip and wrung her hands in her apron. "She said she'd had a bad day and asked to borrow a little lipstick. She seemed nice, a bit lost. I figured a fight with a boyfriend or something."

"It's all right, Evie. She sold us both a story. My car has a tracking system. We'll find her." Sam patted the waitress on the shoulder and went back out into the cool night air to wait for Rocco and Petty.

He knew what the first thing they'd say would be. Sam had a bit of a weakness for damsels in distress. Even in his divorce he'd still let his ex-wife take whatever she'd wanted. Including his dog. Some days he regretted that. He missed Nitro, the Collie-Rottweiler mutt he'd raised from a puppy. But hell, he could always get another dog and Denise had made big eyes at him, sniffling about how lonely it would be without the dog.

Denise. She'd had big brown eyes, too, just like that waif who'd stolen his car. Donna Utley. *What is it with me and D-names?* Sam sighed again and leaned into the wall of the bar. The rain looked to be letting up. He wondered where this latest damsel in distress had headed and felt a pang of embarrassment about the state of his car.

That's how much of a sucker you are, Sammy, he thought. *Woman steals my car and I'm embarrassed about the mess.*

Lighting up another cigarette, he shook his head and stared out into the night.

Twenty

Delilah drove up to the ticket machine and pulled the long-term ticket. This was going to bite into her twenty bucks, but twenty was worth nothing if the cops caught up to her. At least the rain had stopped.

She parked Sam's car in between two huge SUVs where it would be a little tougher to spot. Then she dug around, looking for spare change or anything useful. She found a better screwdriver and then hit pay-dirt with a car break-in kit like the professional lock guys used. That left her wondering what kind of detective Sam really was. The kit would be handy.

"Guess you turned out to be useful after all, Sam." Delilah smiled, then hissed as she straightened up too fast and pulled on the stitches. She pressed her fingers into her abdomen around the bandaging and found the skin warm and swollen. The bandage was damp and her fingers came away faintly pink when she checked on the gauze. Probably a bad sign, but she had no time to worry about it.

She hesitated and leaned against the car for a long moment. There was no way she could tell the cops what she knew, they'd never let her out even though she'd done nothing wrong that they could pin on her. They'd lock her in a room without exits and she'd be in hell.

But maybe she could toss a bone Sam's way, and put a roadblock in the path of the psycho who had tried to take her out.

She reached into the car and grabbed a pen from the glove box. Rummaging around, she found a receipt with a blank back. It hurt to bend down so she sat in the passenger seat of the car and penned Sam a note.

As a final afterthought, she signed it "sorry". He had seemed like a nice guy, and probably one of those people with a weak spot for pretty girls in distress. It couldn't hurt to play that angle. Right now, she definitely counted as a damsel in distress. She left the note on the front seat and closed up the car.

Minutes ticked past in her head as Delilah combed the parking lot for a good candidate. She checked for hide-a-keys behind license plates and under wheel wells, lips pressed together against the pain of bending down. But she hated hot-wiring cars and really didn't want to deal with any alarms right now. Finally she came up with a key on a dark green Subaru. She tossed the lock kit into the car with her anyway, knowing she might need to change vehicles before the long drive to Atlanta was over.

The Subaru Legacy had nearly a full tank of gas and Delilah prayed that the gauge was telling the truth this time. She hardly had to adjust the seat for her five-foot-six-inch height and the mirrors were almost perfect. The car smelled a bit like Cheerios, but was pretty clean. There was a pink kiddie car-seat in the back with a colorful Giraffe toy sitting in it. A little pang gripped Delilah's heart for a moment and she sighed.

Esther wouldn't be in a car-seat anymore, probably. The last picture that Jake had sent showed a smiling little girl with black pigtails on her way to her first day in Kindergarten. Delilah shoved away thoughts of Jake and her daughter and started the car.

The man in the parking booth didn't even raise an eyebrow at the tiny amount of time on her ticket. He just took her money, made change, and waved her through. *Must be a good book.*

She headed away from the airport, toward the US-1 north. She was finally going home. She could get money, get new IDs, and get the hell out. Maybe she'd call Jake, just to check in, let him know she might be laying low for a while. The money she could get from the stolen jewelry would help pay for some of Esther's testing. Jake would deal with it.

Meanwhile she'd get a hotel room, sleep off the injury, and then maybe head to Canada, do a few driving runs for Mikey up there. He always had something going with either booze or cigarettes and dodging the taxes and tariffs. Everything was going to work out just fine. Florida had been a hiccup. She'd survived. She could run away, move on. Like always.

Delilah flipped on the radio, scanning for a moment and finally settling on a bluesy station. She glanced in the rearview, adjusted it, and sighed. It was time to leave Florida—the violence, the pain, the bad luck, all of it—far, far behind. She drove off into the darkness, free and safe.

Twenty-one

Sam crammed himself into the back of the Mustang GT, silently cursing the department for getting these smaller, new cars. The Mustang was fast, sure, and looked nice, and got a hell of a lot better gas mileage than the old Crown Victorias or even the newer Impalas. He wished that they'd signed out one of the new Impalas anyway; at least those had leg room in the back.

Petty was driving, which didn't surprise Sam at all. Rocco liked to ride shotgun, handling the radio and dispensing jokes and wisdom in a seemingly endless stream of bullshit. Petty had only just made Detective, but he was a good guy, always had a smile and a willing attitude. Petty might have gone a little further, a little faster, but he was too easy going and too into the practical jokes to play the political games necessary.

Rocco was a few years older than Sam, but hadn't given him any shit over being a transfer or getting the promotion.

Rocco seemed to like his position just the way it was. Plainclothes, without too much responsibility but enough seniority to get the probies and rookies looking up to him. He was on the job and decent at it when it counted, however, and that's all Sam really cared about.

"What's the story, boss?" Rocco twisted his head around, giving Sam a good view of his straggling attempt at a beard.

"Waiting on Dispatch to call me back," Sam said. He sighed. Might as well get this out of the way. "My car was stolen, Em's got the trace started on it. Head south for now."

"Your car got stolen? How?" Petty looked back at Sam through the rearview mirror.

Sam clicked his seatbelt on and leaned back into the shadows. "A girl stole my keys off the bar. Just drive, Petty."

"Damn." Petty laughed and Rocco beat his fist against his thigh, hooting. "That's sad."

"Should have guessed it would involve a woman." Rocco twisted back around and the whites of his eyes gleamed in the passing headlights as they pulled out onto the freeway.

Sam's phone buzzed, saving him from finding an appropriate comeback.

"Give me good news, Em."

"Lojack has the car stationary, at the airport," Emerelda's voice rasped through the phone. "I've got a patrol car near there, they'll meet you."

"Thanks, Em." Sam hit end and shook his head. "Flip around, Petty. We're going to Jackson International."

"What about airport security?" Rocco asked.

"No point. If the car is stationary, she's gone." Sam didn't think she'd take a flight, either. Not with her face plastered on every late-night TV news program in the state. No use involving the Homeland Security guys, he'd just be teased even worse, and possibly get flack later from the Lieutenant. Better to keep this whole mess as quiet as possible.

Rocco looked like he wanted to say more, but the expression on Sam's face warned him off. The drive to the airport was carried out in relative peace and quiet, only the low-volume bass of the music interrupting Sam's thoughts.

He checked his watch as they arrived at long-term parking, heading toward the flashing lights of the patrol car. Petty grabbed a ticket, though their badges would get them out for free anyway.

The patrol car had found his Camry sandwiched between two large SUVs. Petty pulled up and Sam climbed out of the Mustang, flashing his badge at the two officers.

He recognized Aldo Vasquez—that belly would identify the quiet, soft-spoken officer anywhere—but couldn't remember his partner's name.

"Car's empty, keys were on the front seat, along with this." Vasquez handed Sam a receipt with some writing on it.

"She left you a love note, boss." Rocco hooted and leaned on the hood of the Mustang.

"Stuff a sock in it," Sam said. "And grab an evidence bag, will you?" He looked down at the shaky writing in the flashing lights. It made his head ache to read this way.

Sam, the note started, *I'm sorry. I didn't hurt anyone. It's Theodore Whitechapel, has house in Palm Coast. He stabbed me, he's the killer. He's after me. Help me.*

Sorry.

She was sorry? Sam sighed. There was a smudge on the note, as though a tear had fallen and been wiped away. Jesus. Was he that much of a sucker? And yet, if he let this go without at least a little checking, wouldn't he be a bad cop?

Sure, and an asshole. He slid the note into the plastic bag Rocco handed him and walked around his car. At first glance nothing seemed to be missing, but the interior was such a dump he wasn't sure even he'd recognize something out of place. At least his service weapon was locked up at home, though he had his ankle spare on him.

"Shit." Sam kicked a rear tire as he checked the trunk.

"What's up?" Petty had waved off the uniformed cops and now walked up beside Sam.

"My lock-out kit is missing." Sam shook his head. He'd been on the verge of letting all this go, willing himself to believe that she'd run for the airport, climbed on a plane, and disappeared.

But she wasn't getting on a plane with a lock-out kit. The slim jims alone would put the TSA's panties in a wad. Unless it was a distraction? Was she trying to make him think she wasn't getting on a plane? He rubbed his temples.

"Better file a report then, yeah?" Petty clapped him on the shoulder and then flushed and backed off.

Sam smiled at him and shook his head. "Yeah. I'll head back into headquarters. You two can go."

"You don't want CSU to dust for prints?" Rocco came forward from where he'd been leaning on the Mustang.

"Look at my car, it isn't exactly CSU-friendly," Sam said.

Rocco peered into the car and swallowed a low whistle. If he'd been less tired and annoyed, Sam would have felt even more embarrassed. Denise would never have let him drive a mobile dumpster around. But she was in Daytona Beach and hadn't been in his life for a while now. Long enough.

"All right, boss. See you later." Rocco grabbed Petty's arm and gave him a look. The two of them slipped back into the Mustang and headed out after a quick friendly lights-flash at Sam.

Sam stood in the cool night, alone between two SUVs in the dark parking lot. He held his keys in one hand and the evidence bag with the note in the other and stared into the mess that was his life. This Donna or Lia or whatever her name was, she hadn't even pegged him for a cop. He'd been a mark. She'd wanted his car, and even stolen his money.

Well, not stolen. He'd handed it right over.

He could pick a career cop out from a crowd a hundred yards off. Most criminals he'd encountered, at least the repeat offenders who were smart or lucky enough to stay out of jail for any amount of time, they could do the same. This woman should have known.

But he'd seen her face when he slammed his badge into the window. She'd had a perfect "oh shit" look in those wide brown eyes.

Sam sat down in the filthy Camry and sank low into the seat. He'd lost it. That edge. That indefinable something. He slammed the car door shut and took a deep breath full of stale coffee, staler cigarettes, and decaying food. He felt as though he'd been sleepwalking, going through the motions. He hadn't even noticed the smell in his own damn car.

He reached into his coat pocket for the cloves and stopped himself. When had he started smoking so much, anyway? It used to be a weekend thing, a smoke and a drink. *Used to be a lot of things*, Sam thought.

The dome light clicked off, leaving him in relative darkness. He shoved a couple of mostly empty chip bags and some other debris off the passenger seat and set the note down.

Sam, I'm sorry. Help me.

"Damsel in distress," Sam murmured. "Fuck me." He jammed his key into the ignition and backed his car out. Maybe it was time to wake up, start caring a little more. Sam headed toward the parking exit, dragging out his badge. It looked like he had a few more phone calls to make tonight.

Twenty-two

Sam set the note down on his desk and picked up the receiver. It was almost midnight, but he guessed that his former supervisor would be up and taking calls. If the news had even half the information right, tonight had been a busy one for Homicide in Daytona Beach.

She picked up on the third ring. "Lieutenant Brown."

"It's Sam Arbichaut, Ronnie." He couldn't help but smile at the sound of her clipped, serious voice. God, it had been too long. He hadn't really talked to anyone down in Daytona since the divorce.

"Arby?" She used his old nickname, one of the things he was glad hadn't transferred up here with him. "You know what time it is? What's up?"

"Sorry it's late, but I figured you'd be up." Sam decided to get right to the point. "That woman on the news? Donna Utley? I think she stole my car."

A moment of silence, then the sound of something being shuffled. Sam was willing to bet money Ronnie had scrambled for a pen and her notepad.

"Stole your car? Damn. In Jacksonville?"

"Yeah, but it gets better." He took a deep breath. Donna/Lia wanted his help? Well, he could at least ask, check out her story. Be a good cop. "Does the name Theodore Whitechapel mean anything to you?"

He heard the hiss of a sharp intake of breath and then another long moment of silence. Sam was just about to ask if she was still on the line when she spoke.

"How do you have that name, Detective?" Ronnie's voice was deadpan.

Sam sat up and made sure he had his own pen handy. So, something was up. Something serious. Maybe the pretty thief hadn't lied about everything.

"I'm looking at it on a note your fugitive left in my car for me. I know I'm not one of your detectives anymore, Ronnie, or hell, even in Homicide, but come on. I'll show you mine if you show me yours."

Another deep breath from Ronnie and then he could almost hear her cracking that lopsided smile of hers. "Shit, Arby. But this is serious. You can't hold out on me."

"I'm not. I won't. Spill it."

"You first. How the hell did your car get stolen?"

Sam took a deep breath and then told her the whole humiliating story. He didn't leave anything too important out, but emphasized how tired Donna had looked, how scared. He read the note aloud.

"Always with the women in need, Arby." Ronnie sighed. "So you think she could have been injured?"

"Sure. Though she was walking all right, so I don't know how badly," Sam said, thinking about how Donna had moved. A little unsteady, her eyes glassy. Pills? How hadn't he noticed all this at the time? Because he hadn't wanted to, he could admit that. A pretty girl had hit on him and he'd seen only what he wanted to see.

"So who is this Whitechapel guy?" Sam asked.

"This doesn't get out, Sam. Big shit is hitting the fan here and we're trying to keep press out until we can sort the asses from the elbows."

"I don't exactly have Fox News on speed-dial, Ronnie."

"Ok, so Theodore Whitechapel is a lawyer, he's listed as missing at this time. His wife got home early from a spa thing, came in this evening and found," Ronnie hesitated and he thought he heard her swallow hard. "She found D.A. Swarski's daughter's mutilated corpse displayed on her bed."

"The Governor's cousin, Nicholas Swarski?"

"Yeah. So she calls the cops, they show up and find some women's body parts in the freezer, and more out in the garden shed. There was also blood all over the bathroom, including a trail out the bathroom window and into the garden, though the rain kind of fucked us there. Was another blood trail through the house, too. We don't know whose blood it is yet, but Whitechapel's missing, his car is gone, as well as some money and a gun registered to him. We're getting his credit card and phone records. So far I got fuck all and the damn DA and the whole head cheese breathing down my neck wanting immediate answers and an arrest."

"Jesus Christ, Ronnie." This was the kind of case that made or broke a career. Solve it and get a strong collar, set for life. Screw it up and push paperwork in the basement until you either eat a bullet or pension out.

"Yeah. Making things more fun, we got this guy in your girl's hotel room stabbed to death, maybe even tortured. There's medical equipment there and some women's clothing, but it's a low-brow hotel room. Going to take CSU a couple months to sort through the DNA and prints in that place. Room was registered to Donna Utley, they took a photocopy of her DL." Ronnie's voice shifted and changed and Sam could picture her shaking her head and taking a sip of what was probably her tenth cup of coffee. "And now you go and tell me this shit is related? Thanks, Arby."

"What if it is?" He might not be in Homicide anymore, but Sam was still a detective. Gears dusted themselves off and started grinding in his brain. "You said there was blood going out a window, right?"

"At the Whitechapel scene?" She said it like a question, giving him some room. She was listening, that was good.

Sam just hoped he wasn't talking out his ass.

"My note says she was stabbed by this guy. Nobody knows about the DA's kid yet, right? So she didn't pull this name at random, Ronnie. What if Donna was there? She might have bled while escaping. Theodore comes after her, finds her somehow. Maybe the guy dead in the hotel is a boyfriend or something. Tried to protect her. She runs, has to take my car when something happens to her's." Damn. He should have checked the parking lot at the bar. He'd get uniforms out on it as soon as he was done with Ronnie. It was going to be a long night.

"Theodore is a corporate lawyer. He doesn't have so much as a speeding ticket. But the Captain and Chief both think this is a serial, which means we're supposed to call the FBI in."

"You got what? Two, three dead women and an 'upstanding' citizen missing? Sounds serial to me."

"And your car thief might be the only one who knows what happened. If these scenes are related."

"You got blood and fingerprints at both, right? Run them." Sam tapped his pen against the pad of paper. Donna really was in trouble. No wonder she'd seemed so scared. This guy had killed at least four people and probably was after the woman who had run away from him. Sam's fantasy scenario made sense. He wanted, no, needed to find Donna first. Whoever this girl was, whatever she had done, she needed help.

Sam, I'm sorry. Help me. He pictured her saying it in that low, soft voice. Big brown eyes brimming with tears. *Help me, Sam.*

Ronnie's voice dragged him back to his office. "Sam? You paying attention?"

"Yeah, sorry."

"Look, I'll follow up on your theory, but it's going to take at least a week or two to get this stuff pushed through. Even with the DA pressure, I'm not sure how fast our lab can handle this. I guess if we bring the Feebs in, maybe." She sighed again. "I hate to see this lead go cold. I wish you'd caught her."

"Me too." She had no idea how much he meant it. "Maybe you should fax her face around up north, hit the major cities. I think she's driving, so the Staties can keep an eye out for her."

"I'll do it. Thanks for the call, Sam."

She was winding the call down, pushing him out. But Sam wasn't done.

Now the delicate part. "Ronnie, you said you got lots of blood out of the scenes, right?"

"Yeah?" He felt her impatience like a hot breath through the phone.

"I've got a friend who owes me a favor or two down in Miami. I know you hate the idea of the FBI snagging your case, but they'll be coming in anyway, we both know that. It's a serial."

"If. If it's a serial. What are you getting at, Arby?"

"Can you overnight blood samples from the house and the hotel crime scenes to Mike Davidson at the Miami lab? I'll fax over the address and details."

"The Miami FBI lab?"

"He owes me; he can get the matching done fast. Hours maybe." Sam chewed on his lip and forced himself to set the pen down. He was going to find Donna, help her, and maybe stop a killer, too. Excitement shivered through him. He was a cop. He could do this.

"Okay. Okay." Ronnie repeated it as though she were trying to convince herself she meant it. "I'll get my CSU guys to put together some blood samples and some DNA from the victim and Mr. Whitechapel. You think this Donna's DNA is in the system?"

"Yeah, 'cause we could be that lucky. But we'll see. Thanks for trusting me on this, Ronnie."

"You had good instincts when you worked for me, Sam." She didn't say the "except when it came to women" part, but Sam heard it in her tone.

"I'll fax stuff over. And a copy of the note. Night, Ronnie."

"Night, Arby."

He stared down at the note, one hand resting on his phone. It was too late to call Mike, so he shoved the note aside and logged onto the computer. Mike always got in early; he'd get an email in time. Hopefully.

A couple of calls later, Sam had done all he could think to for now. It was nearly one in the morning but he didn't feel tired yet. He was more awake than he could recall being in a while. A quick Google search gave him the location of the nearest self-service car wash.

It was time to clean up his life.

Twenty-three

Ted's first stop in Atlanta was a twenty-four hour Walmart. He needed to rebuild his hunting kit. It wouldn't do to be unprepared for his grand meeting with his little Delilah.

Ted was amused that for the second time in twenty-four hours he found himself buying rope, duct tape, a couple of nice chef's knives, and other sundry items all at once. The old Ted, the careful, mask-wearing Ted, squirmed deep within, screaming warnings.

But he didn't listen. He paid with cash and went back out to the rental car, tossing the duffle bag into the front seat. He plugged Delilah's address into his phone, asking for directions. Ted smoothed his thumb over the tiny picture. Delilah. Soon.

The directions guided him across Atlanta, to a homey, quiet suburb off of I-85. Ted turned his phone off as he pulled up along the semi-dark street. He didn't think anyone would be after him yet, but it wouldn't hurt to be a little careful and keep them from tracing his phone to Georgia just in case. The phone was part of his old life, part of secret Ted. It would go, as soon as he was done here.

Ted cruised along the street, passing Delilah's address. The house was set back a little from the road and a porch light illuminated a grey and red wrap-around-style ranch. Two overgrown trees flanked the front steps. There was no car in the driveway.

After flipping around, Ted parked across the street. It was after midnight and he saw no one else moving around. Both of the neighbor's lights were mostly out, nothing shifting behind curtains. He pulled his duffle bag from the front seat and slid out, locking the car manually to prevent the lights flashing.

Delilah's front yard was mostly bark dust and those hideous, bulbous bushes that were the main staple of what Ted had always called "lazyscaping". Normally, this would have bothered Ted. But not tonight. This yard and the house's appearance in general were promising. No man in her life, at least no man taking care of this place. His heart rate elevated in anticipation as he fingered the keys he'd taken from the hotel room. Maybe she was already here, asleep inside, waiting for him to come kiss her awake.

He forced himself to think rationally, taking a deep, calming breath. There was no way she could have beat him here. He was sure she was injured, and he knew she'd likely left that hotel room not long before he'd arrived. The last flight of the night had already left, and besides, with the little present he'd given to the cops, Delilah probably wouldn't be flying anywhere out of Florida anytime soon. She'd have to drive here, and that would put her a couple hours behind him.

Ted tried a key in the lock. It almost fit, but not quite. He tried a second one and the key slid home. He wasn't worried about an alarm system. The pathetic little dead man had said Delilah was a criminal, and Ted knew all about being a criminal. It meant secrets, and staying away from the law.

He opened the door and stale, warm air blew out over him. She hadn't left her air conditioning on. Thrifty, forward thinking. He approved.

The front door opened into a small foyer which led into the living room. Ted flicked on the light near the door, stepped inside, and locked the door. A painting, a garish bit of art nouveau, greeted his eye on the far wall above a gas fireplace. A curl of hot excitement unfurled in his belly. He was here, inside Delilah's home, at last. Her things, things she touched, things she'd wanted. Laid out for him, his to touch, his to explore. Ted dropped the duffle bag and pulled the heavy crowbar from it. First he had to check and make sure he was alone.

Then, well, then he could get to know his Delilah so much better.

Ted checked each room. There were two bedrooms and one small full bath as well as a galley kitchen and a little utility room that had a door out to a listing back porch. He was alone in the house, which was good. But as he slid like a hunting shadow through the hallway and into each room, flicking on and off lights as he went, Ted felt a growing sense of disappointment.

This house could have been a cheap model showroom for all the personalization it had. A blue hard plastic cup overturned in the dish rack was the only sign anyone had really lived at all in this place. The house told him as clear as if a catalogue had been left out that Atlanta boasted at least one Ikea in the vicinity. The living room had two black chairs positioned facing the wall where a TV might have been if there'd been one at all. A modern cubic coffee table sat in front of the chairs and a large white paper lamp jutted up between them, plugged into the wall where the switch would turn it on.

Books lined a white shelf set back against a white wall. Paperbacks, Ted saw, romances mostly, the kind that you'd find in bulk at a library sale. A few outdated magazines lay on the coffee table, lending to the home's façade. Everything in the living room was white or black, except a huge rug that covered the laminated click-together flooring. The rug stuck out, bright blue geometric shapes against the faux maple.

Ted glanced into the bathroom and found more generic things. A bottle of combination shampoo and conditioner. It didn't smell like Delilah, not the woman of his memory at any rate. He moved on, back to the bedroom. Surely something personal, something of *her* would be there.

A grey rug with floral designs in it covered the floor in front of a queen bed. There were no personal pictures, no little knickknacks or small items. No jewelry left out or perfume, nothing to show a woman might live here. The bed was unmade, the blue and white floral comforter bunched to one side as though its owner had merely risen in the dark for a glass of water.

When Ted touched the sheets, he half-expected them to be warm. They weren't. There was nothing warm about this house, nothing special or secretive. Nothing personal.

It wasn't fair. He was free now, divorced from his old life, away from the careful patterns that had kept his own secrets all these years. He was hunting in the lair of his prey for the first time. Ted hardly counted the girl and her mother from earlier. They had been a snack, like eating a piece of bread while waiting for the real meal, the rare and tender steak, to arrive. A light repast to quell the hunger and sharpen his edges for the real deal.

He wanted Delilah but now he could feel her slipping away again. This place wasn't the home he'd hoped it would be. It was even more of a fake place than his own. A parody of a home, set up as a stop along the way. Nothing permanent, nothing personal, nothing of any real value. Ted couldn't hold onto her this way. Doubts gnawed at him, twisting his stomach into writhing serpents and bringing on a mild heartburn attack.

The clothing in the closet was clean and smelled of fabric sheets and a clove bouquet that rested on the shelf above the hangers. Even her underwear was boring, plain black or grey cotton panties and bras. She wore a 32B, but he'd already guessed at her cup size from his too brief contact with her. Nothing racy, nothing lacy. It was all clean, boring and sterile. He yanked a sundress that she could have bought at Nordstrom's, or any mall store, off a hanger and growled as the disappointment grew into a cancer on his heart, clutching and insistent.

He walked back into the kitchen and opened the fridge. A jar of mustard, a two-liter of diet Coke, and a jar of green olives were the only contents. Again, nothing of home. No real perishable food. Ted started opening the cupboards, slamming them shut again as he found only generic crockery, a few cans of tuna, and ready-made soup. The freezer had a bag of peas, a half gallon box of vanilla ice-cream that was icing over from disuse, and two plain ice trays.

There was nothing here. He wanted something tangible, a window into her dark little soul, a connection to her. Not this boring, generic place that could belong to anyone. Ted took deep, calming breaths and forced himself to stop slamming the cupboards shut. He winced at the acidic taste of bile in his throat and pulled out a blue cup and the Coke.

The cold, sweet bubbles eased his throat. He walked out of the narrow kitchen and stood in the living room, looking about. He needed to think, not rage.

The bright rug with its geometric designs drew his eye back to the floor. Delilah was a criminal, a thief. Her ID and keys were hidden in the hotel room. Ted smiled slowly. Of course. He had to stop thinking of her as a normal woman. She wasn't normal, not his Delilah. She was special, a predator like him. She wouldn't put her dirty little secrets just anywhere, not like most women. Delilah wouldn't leave them lying about. She was like a little mouse, hiding in the corners and behind the walls.

Subtle, secret Delilah. But Ted was better than that. He'd found her little hideaway, hadn't he? He could find her out again.

"You won't escape like this, girl," he said aloud. He finished his drink and walked back to the kitchen, leaving the cup on the counter.

It occurred to him that she might not return to this place at all. She might have other places, other little holes to bolt into and hide away in. Ted refused the panic that rose in him. He would find her out, wherever she ran. His little mouse would get caught in a trap eventually.

And the secret to that was somewhere within these walls, Ted felt it in his bones. The disappointment eased its grip on him. He could not fail, not here, not with something so simple as hunting down a woman and showing her exactly what her place in this world was meant to be.

Devious Delilah. But she was his, and she'd left the key to herself for him to find. It was here.

Ted dragged the coffee table off the rug, spilling the magazines onto the blue expanse. He caught one woolen corner and, like a layer of skin, peeled the rug away.

Twenty-four

The laminate flooring below looked normal at first glance, but Ted got down on his knees and felt along the edges where the pieces snapped together. There, his fingers touched where one of the boards had a larger groove. He dug around the edge and lifted. The board came up easily, its edges smoothed so that it lay next to its neighbors without snapping into place.

The subfloor beneath had been cut away, leaving a narrow chamber in the insulation beneath. Nestled there were two plastic bags wrapped with duct tape, and a manila envelope. Ted pulled the bundles out and sat back on his heels.

The plastic bags contained cash, Ted guessed around ten thousand dollars worth though the bills were mostly twenties and hard to estimate in the bundles. He set those aside and opened the envelope, dumping its contents out onto the floor.

A few creased pieces of paper, another, smaller envelope, and a handful of pictures fluttered out and scattered across the floorboards. He focused on the pictures first, gathering them up.

A smiling brunette woman, pretty in a cheerleader gone-to-seed sort of way, held a black baby wrapped in a pink blanket with little green frogs printed on it. On the back of the photo "Esther, 9 months" was written in neat black lettering. In another picture a little black girl stood smiling shyly at the camera, clutching a white kitten against her blue dress. This one was labeled "Esther and Snowman." The same little girl, but older, stood with a backpack in the next picture, looking nervous. The label said "Esther, kindergarten." The next picture was a typical family portrait, this time with the brunette, a slender black man, and the little girl all smiling fake plastic smiles. Ted could almost hear them saying "Cheese!" for the camera. The back was labeled simply "Jake, Nancy, Esther" in the same handwriting as the others.

The last picture had Delilah in it. She was pale and unsmiling, staring up from a hospital bed with a tiny swaddled baby on her lap. She was barely holding the child, one hand lightly touching the pink-capped head, the other more draped over than clutched at the blanketed baby. Delilah's eyes were huge and dark. She looked terrified and young.

Vulnerable. Helpless. Perfect.

Ted held that picture, rubbing his fingers along the edges, bringing it up close to his face. Delilah. His Delilah, and she had a child, a daughter. Anger burned into Ted, turning his stomach to ropes as he thought about a man touching her, that skinny black guy putting his hands on exotic, lovely Delilah. Breeding on her. He wanted to rip the guy apart, even if it was clear that this "Jake" wasn't in her life, at least her life here in Atlanta.

But that baby would tie them together. He knew all about children, the way they wormed their way into their parent's hearts and could take over every part of a person's life. Children made people weak and stupid. And nobody deserved the responsibility of raising other people anyway. His own parents hadn't done so great.

But maybe he could use this discovery to trap Delilah. As the thoughts began to build in his mind, ideas percolating, Ted turned to the other envelope, reluctantly setting down the pictures.

Inside were more pieces of, Ted assumed, stolen or fake ID. There was a passport under the name he already had, Lily Chung. Lily Chung had a birth certificate, neatly folded. There was a Texas driver's license as well, Delilah's picture auburn-haired with modish reading glasses propped on her thin nose. Another ID was a New York driver's license under the name Donna Rowe. That name had a couple of credit cards and a library card.

The New York address might be worth checking on, if she didn't show up here. Ted shook his head at the extent of her deceptions. His Delilah was certainly a woman of many guises. But he could strip all the bullshit away; lay her bare and naked before him.

He would destroy her, layer by layer, in his final act as Theodore Whitechapel. Destroy her as she'd destroyed his façade, his carefully constructed double life.

Not that he particularly minded. He had that morning, but Ted was changing, growing. She'd freed him from shackles he hadn't realized were there, binding him to a definition of normal he'd clearly outlived. He was overdue for an update, and Delilah had been the catalyst. He was sure he'd remember to thank her, before she finally died struggling beneath his hands.

Ted set down the IDsand took a deep breath. So many choices. His mind whirled with possibilities. Would she come here? How long would it take her to return? He could wait, he guessed that he could live in this house for days without anyone thinking too much of it. Delilah was likely a reclusive sort anyway, given her proclivities.

Hungry for all he could learn about her, Ted picked up the pieces of folded paper.

The first he smoothed flat was a medical sheet of some sort. Test results. He skimmed it as he realized it dealt with Esther Leventon, the little girl. Negli's something or other, some sort of blood thing. So, she was a sick little girl. With that sheet was a quick scrawl in shaky cursive informing Delilah that Esther was sick and he thought she might want to know. Signed, Jake. That black guy in the picture. Ted took a deep breath, shoving away the acid rage. He needed to stay calm.

The other piece of paper was a note from Jake, telling Delilah that he'd sent a picture of Esther, but that she should stop calling the house because it upset Nancy. The note told her to call the bar and gave a number if Delilah needed to reach him for some reason. It also thanked her for some money, but made it clear he was only accepting it because he wanted the best care for his daughter.

Ted noticed that Jake worded it "my daughter" and not "our daughter". Interesting family tensions there. So, his Delilah wasn't quite an optimal candidate for worst mother ever. At least it seemed she cared enough to send money. He wondered how strong her attachments were. If the child were threatened, for example, would Delilah care? Would she race to help her child?

Ted rose and pulled out his phone. He turned it back on and went into the kitchen, searching for a pen. He found one in a drawer with rubber bands and a couple coupons for soda pop. Then he dialed the number that Jake had given for this bar.

A woman picked up on the third ring. "No Man's Land," she chirped. Ted heard music and the hum of conversation in the background.

"Yes, hi," he said, "I have a friend coming to town and wanted to recommend your bar, but I can't find the address, can you give it to me?"

"Sure," she said, "ready?"

Ted was and he wrote down the address. Portland, Oregon. That was a long way from Atlanta, Georgia. He hung up and tapped the pen against the counter, running his tongue over his lips. Stay, or go? He could track down this Jake, this little girl Esther. But it came down to Delilah. He wanted her, wanted her to hurt, to suffer, to see her life crumbling around her and to know it was because of him, all his doing. Her world would fall apart and he would be its destroyer.

Ted turned his phone back off and decided to tear through the house, see if she had any other secret stashes.

An hour or so later and he'd found two, one in the crawlspace above a hallway, and one beneath the bedroom rug. The crawlspace held more cash, another five thousand or so. The bedroom stash was more pictures. They were all of a younger Jake, with a few of him and a hardly recognizable teenaged Delilah. Jake, his shirt off displaying his gleaming dark skin and muscles, smiling from the top of a cliff with the grey expanse of ocean beyond. Jake leaning on a beat-up Mustang, holding a wrench in one hand and laughing at the camera. Jake, with stripes shaved into his short curly hair, sticking his tongue out as he held a clearly squirming Delilah, her hair long and black and shining.

Ted couldn't contain his acid rage by carefully breathing this time. It ran through Ted's body like an angry swarm of wasps, murderous intent burning in his blood. The rage spoke, the rage wanted, the rage decided.

Delilah, his Delilah, still cared about this man. Why else would she keep so many pictures of him near to her bed? She'd had his child and clearly stayed in touch. The pictures in his hands told a story of young love. Each picture she appeared in showed a girl smitten, her eyes focused on this slender, stupid boy, her body language all but screaming that she was in love and wanted him.

Ted tore every single picture to shreds except the one with Delilah and the baby. That one he kept after tearing the child out of the picture.

He turned on his phone for the last time and booked himself a seat on the morning flight to Portland. If Delilah hadn't shown up by the time he needed to go to the airport, well, he'd leave her a present and a warning. She'd follow him, or she'd run. But either way she would know his power, know that he could take everything away from her.

His heart rate slowly returning to normal, Ted stood in the trashed living room and stretched. He was tired, but he could sleep on the plane in the morning. Right now he had work to do. It was time to make his first mark on Delilah's life.

Twenty-five

Delilah drove in a haze of pain and exhaustion, singing under her breath to keep herself alert. She played her little games with the few other cars on the freeway, but it felt as though she were driving in another world. The green and blue lights from the stereos in the cars that passed her made it look as though they were all driving underwater, each person drowning slowly, locked away and pulled along by the invisible tide.

She stopped finally at a gas station. It was closed, the sign on the door saying it would open at six a.m.. An hour or so away. Delilah decided to wait. She took another pain pill and one of the little antibiotic pills. They stuck in her dry throat, tasting of bitter chalk.

She locked the car doors and sank down into the driver's seat, letting the drugs go to work. An hour of rest wouldn't kill her. She was probably safe enough out here, far enough away from Daytona and all the issues she'd had there.

The painkillers kicked in, taking her down into the comforting blackness.

Tapping on the car window woke her. For a panicked moment she was trapped and dying in a vat of blood as a laughing man who morphed between her father's jowly face and Teddy's handsome one pinned her beneath the thick red mire.

Then Delilah surfaced, forcing herself to breathe through the panic and the pain. She hurt only when she moved. Somehow this was funny, amusement bubbling up, as irrational as her sleepy panic the moment before.

A middle-aged, skinny man wearing a brown jacket with the gas station's logo on it tapped on the window again. Outside the world had turned from gray predawn to full light.

Delilah forced herself upright, gritting her teeth against the agony that radiated from her stomach like shards of broken glass, and rolled down the window.

"Hey," she said, giving him a tired smile, "can I get twenty bucks of regular?"

On the road with a mostly full tank of gas and headed home in the daylight, Delilah felt a hell of a lot better. Not great yet, but she could see a future now instead of just running for her life in a crazy daze of pain and reaction.

She winced at the tightness in her stomach, poking gingerly at her bandages with one hand as she drove. They felt dry enough, none of the wet pink leaking like it had the night before, and she hoped that was a good sign. No way could she go to a hospital at this point, not with the police heat down in Florida. Maybe once she got to Canada. They had free care there anyway from what she'd heard. She hoped they'd ask fewer questions.

Her bottle of painkillers looked emptier than it had and she wondered how many were left and how many she'd taken. It was hard to count, but she knew she should ration them, at least until she could figure out how to get more.

It took Delilah just over an hour to reach Atlanta. She pulled off the highway and onto familiar roads, her mood improving the closer she got to home. She'd never realized how attached she'd become to this place, but the idea of curling into her blue sheets and sleeping for a week safe and bundled away from the world lifted her flagging spirits.

She turned onto her street and looked about. No police presence, that was good. The street was quiet, just about everyone would be off to school or work or wherever normal people went during the day. She drove past her home as a habit, scouting around just in case. She was tired, but not so exhausted that she could afford to let caution go completely.

Something was off. The quiet street looked fine at first glance, the trees dancing in the morning breeze, lawns turned yellow with summer. Nothing looked out of place and no one was around. But yet, the scene nagged at Delilah and she circled again with the car, trying to pin down her growing feeling of dread.

Then it hit her, that thing, the missing piece of the picture.

Mr. Palmer, the retiree and Nam vet who lived next door, wasn't out on his front porch. Delilah drove by slowly and noticed his paper sat on his white front steps, still in the little thin plastic baggie. The heavy rocking chair was unoccupied, no large green cup of coffee cooled on the railing.

In the nearly eight months that Delilah had been living at this address, at least part time, she'd never seen a morning without Mr. Palmer's gap-toothed, crooked smile as he read his paper. Even when it rained he'd sat on his covered front porch and watched the water stream down the copper chains that hung from his gutters.

He wasn't there. Delilah swung around and parked across the street from her house. She took a slow breath and thought about this new development. He could be sick, she supposed, or on vacation. Or he'd slept in for once. After all, she hadn't been here in a few days and any number of things could have happened. He'd always joked about the shrapnel inside his chest killing him someday. Perhaps that day had come.

She shook her head slowly. She didn't like any of these possibilities. It felt off to her, wrong. What if the police were waiting inside her home? Wouldn't they tell the neighbors to stay inside? She couldn't be sure. She wished she'd risked taking a few moments to get her ID out of the hotel room.

Of course, a few moments might have killed her.

"Damnit. Damnitdamnitdamnit." Cursing didn't actually help. Her throat was dry as though she'd swallowed sand.

It could be nothing. Or this anomaly could be the only warning of her impending death or capture. Death. She wouldn't go with the police, not to jail. Walls closing in, doors locking, chains binding her.

"Stop it, Dee," she muttered as her heart rate spiked and the wound in her stomach started to throb in time to its pounding.

She should drive away, go with her instincts and let this go. It was the smart thing to do, the professional thing.

But she needed the ID and money in that house. Her other stash was in Kansas City, way too far off to be of use at the moment. Delilah couldn't keep going as she was, there was just no way. Whatever might be lurking in there for her, she'd have to just face it.

Her heart beating a rhythm in her throat, Delilah climbed gingerly out of her car and slipped across the street.

Twenty-six

Delilah avoided the front and moved as quietly as she could around the side of the house. With a wince, she reached over the wooden fence and opened the back gate. The back yard looked the same way it had when she'd left. The grass was dying and in need of a mow and the pecan tree had started to shed leaves. She glanced at the house, but the shades were drawn as they always were and nothing looked disturbed or out of place.

She hesitated for a long moment, listening to the distant hum of the freeway and the closer intermittent rustle or chirp of insect and bird life. Delilah pulled her hoodie straight over her bandaging and took a couple careful breaths. The sunlight felt good and the yellow plastic chair on the back porch looked inviting. Her bed was close, just inside her home. She fought the urge to charge inside.

Besides, if all was well, the house should be locked and she'd left her keys in Daytona Beach.

Tiny hairs on the back of her neck rose as she forced herself to turn away and walked to the pecan tree. A small blue birdhouse was tucked into the first branching limbs. Delilah had added it and made a few modifications to suit her needs when she'd moved into the home.

She undid the little hasp on the side and swung the birdhouse open. A clear sheet of plastic covered the entry hole, making it impossible for a bird or any other creature to nest within. Inside was a .32 revolver wrapped in a sealed plastic baggie and a spare key to the house.

Delilah checked the gun. The ammunition looked all right, no rusting or weirdness. She spun the cylinder before snapping it back into place. The gun seemed to be fine, though she guessed it needed a good cleaning after being in this tree for a few months. She'd cleaned it sometime last spring, but couldn't recall exactly when. Sloppy of her. She sighed.

With the key in one hand and the gun held against her thigh by the other, Delilah approached the house.

She unlocked the back door as carefully as she could. The utility room was dark, lit only by the slim beams of light filtering through the venetian blinds over the window. The house was warm, warmer and closer feeling than the bright and airy back yard.

It wasn't until she stepped into the kitchen that the smell hit her. Death, cloying and pungent. Blood and bile and a scent underneath of burnt plastic and ash.

She slid along the counter, noting a cup sitting in the sink that she hadn't left there. Then she jerked around the side of the kitchen, gun out and ready as her eyes swept the living room.

What was left of Mr. Palmer lay in a grotesque heap displayed across her coffee table. He'd been gutted and drained in a horrific parody of a hunting kill. Delilah crept closer, her ears searching for any sound of movement from the back hallway and bedrooms. Mr. Palmer's blue eyes were clouded and stared at nothing. She gritted her teeth and bent to touch his foot. Rigor had set in, so he'd been dead at least a little while but not so long that the body had gone pliant again.

The blue carpet had been pulled up and Delilah could see that her stash in here had been raided and emptied.

Delilah forced herself away and walked, pressed against the wall, down the hall, checking each room. Someone had tossed the entire house and her clothing lay strewn about as though a temper tantrum had been thrown.

She found the note sitting on her pillow.

Delilah, it read, *Yes, I know who you are. I know all about you. I know about Esther and Jake and Portland. Do you like your gift? I'm going to Portland to get you another one just like it. I'll be seeing Jake and your daughter real soon. Love, Ted.*

She read the note twice and then crumpled it. That wasn't enough. She tore it to pieces, her entire body shaking until she couldn't stand upright and she collapsed onto the bed.

"No, no no no no no," she sobbed into the bed sheets, curling around herself. He'd found her, found this place. All those pictures she'd kept, the recent letters.

She had to warn Jake, had to get him to take Esther and get away. If Jake would even listen. Once in the past a man had threatened her family, thinking to use them against her after she ran a little real estate con on him. It had amounted to nothing in the end, the man not knowing as much as he'd threatened he did. But Jake hadn't forgiven her for her panic at the time, especially since she hadn't even talked to him in the two years prior to that crazy phone call.

But this wasn't an empty threat. Ted was real and she trusted that he'd do exactly what he said he would. He'd tracked her to the hotel, traced her here. Found her IDs and money and all her pictures of Jake and her daughter.

The money. Her IDs. *Fuck.*

Delilah forced herself to uncurl. She needed to know if he'd found everything.

He had. The bedroom stash was empty, as was the crawl space. He'd burnt something in the fireplace, pictures it looked like. The grate was still warm and Delilah started shivering all over again as she realized she'd missed him by an hour at most.

She had nothing. No ID, no money. Just a gun and the scariest man she'd ever known going after the only people she gave a shit about. All because she'd gotten greedy and robbed the wrong damn house.

She stood carefully. The freezer. Had he found that? She went back into the kitchen, avoiding looking at the poor dead Mr. Palmer. She yanked the ice trays out of the freezer and reached her hand up behind the ice compartment. Her fingers touched tape and Delilah's heart lifted. She had an ID.

She unpeeled the tape and plastic and retrieved the Kansas driver's license. Lily Fairchild. The ID was barely professional-looking and had nothing else attached to it. It was the sort of thing an underage college student could use to get served in a bar and little more. It would get her into a storage unit in Kansas City where she had a better ID and some money and other things stashed.

It, and the lump of diamonds and gold in her pocket, was a start.

She had to warn Jake. The nearest phone was at a convenience store four blocks away. Delilah doubted that Jake would take a collect call from her and she lacked even so much as a dollar to her name at the moment.

Another wave of nausea washed over her and she knew that whatever she did, she had to get out of this house with its stench of death. Nothing was going to help Mr. Palmer now.

Mr. Palmer. Of course. He had a phone. It was a risk, but Delilah didn't care. It would probably be days before anyone noticed anything wrong with either house. And if Ted got to Jake and Esther before she could warn them, well, this mess wasn't going to matter anyway. Psycho Ted already had the IDs tied to this house anyway. It wouldn't matter if the police traced things at this point. Her whole life was so fucked, all because of that bastard.

She unlocked the front door and walked over to Mr. Palmer's. His front door was unlocked. She brought his paper in; hoping that it would buy her some more time before anyone came investigating either place.

Feeling a little bad about it but unable to help herself, Delilah catalogued the things in his house as she walked through the living room to the kitchen, searching for a phone. Nothing of easy value presented itself immediately. His furniture was old but comfortable looking, the house smelled of the cheroots he smoked and the bourbon he favored as well as that somewhat metallic undertone that Delilah associated as "old people" smell. He'd had a cat until this last winter. Tufts of cat hair still clung to the edges of the couch and claw damage marred one of the overstuffed chairs.

Delilah picked up the phone, took a steadying breath, and dialed Jake's home number from memory. With the time difference, he'd be just getting up, maybe getting Esther ready for school. She prayed that he would pick up instead of Nancy. She didn't blame Jake's wife for hating her, but this call was too important to wait on bullshit and cattiness.

And Delilah was just too damned tired and hurt to care about what Nancy might think anyway.

Jake picked up after four rings.

"Jake? It's Delilah," she said, her throat tight and dry. God she didn't want to say what had to be said. Not over the phone.

"Fuck, Delilah. I told you not to call here." He sounded as though he might hang up. He used her whole name, not her nickname. Not a good sign.

"No, wait, don't hang up. A man is gonna come kill you and Esther." Shit. She hadn't meant to say it like that, but it was out now.

"What?" Jake's tone spiked. "What did you do?"

"I didn't do anything. This guy's crazy. You gotta get out of town."

"Some guy is coming here to kill Esther and me, because you didn't do anything? Sure, I totally believe that. Either you come clean with whatever is going on right now or I'm hanging up."

Fuck. Fuck. Fuck. She never could seem to reason with him, it was why she rarely called. The last six years had been conversations like this, round after round.

"Don't hang up," she said and took a deep breath, gasping as a spear of pain ran from her stomach into her chest. The painkillers were wearing off, again. "This guy, his name is Ted. He's crazy, okay. I didn't do anything. But he knows about you and Esther, he broke into my house. He's coming after you. I know it doesn't make much sense, but you have to believe me." She spit it out in a desperate rush, leaving aside most of it. Jake didn't need to know about Florida or the mess here in Atlanta. That part would just piss him off. He only needed to know enough to convince him to grab Esther and run away from Ted.

"Jesus, Lil. Are you drunk? On drugs? You sound horrible."

"Painkillers," she admitted. "This guy stabbed me, Jake. He's serious. This isn't like before." Even as she said the words she wished she hadn't brought that up.

"It isn't? You don't fucking ask after your own daughter for months and now you call saying I should just pack up everything and run? That's what *you* do, Delilah. I've got a life here. Esther has a treatment tomorrow. We can't just go away and miss appointments. You know what happens if she doesn't get her regular transfusion? She dies. Do you give a shit about that?"

"Yes," she said softly. She must have sounded more broken and vulnerable than usual because she heard Jake sigh heavily.

Then he said in a quieter, almost gentle voice, "Tell me what I need to know about this guy. I'll go to the police and see if they can help. But you have to be honest with me."

The police? She shook her head, even though she knew Jake couldn't see the motion. "The cops aren't the answer, damnit. What'll they do? They can't just put a twenty-four-hour guard on you guys. They're stupid and reactive. Trust me, I know cops. They'll be no help at all against this guy, not until it's too late."

"Yeah, well, some of us don't live on the shady side anymore. Cops are paid to do their jobs and I'm going to let them. So tell me what I need to know and then let me decide how to protect *my* family."

She didn't miss his emphasis. Despair bloomed inside her, a deep dark well, cold and empty. Jake wasn't going to run. He'd stay put, thinking the law and a little extra vigilance would protect him against a man who cared nothing for law and was far deadlier than anything Jake had ever had to deal with. Ted was outside the understanding of someone like Jake. Hell, Delilah barely understood. She knew what she knew in her heart because she'd stared into his cold eyes with a knife sticking from her belly and then seen his gruesome work firsthand in her own living room.

Anyone who could do *that* to an old man was on a whole other level from the rest of humanity.

"He's in his thirties, white, handsome in a tanned playboy way, with dark hair." She hesitated. If she gave Jake a name and he went to the police, things would eventually tie back to Florida. She didn't want that mess crossing over. The police already had her DNA and fingerprints, the fewer names they could tie to those, the better.

"You have a full name, besides just Ted?" She could hear Jake rummaging for a pen.

"No," she lied. Behind the despair floated a terrible certainty. This wasn't something she could flee from. Jake couldn't help her, wouldn't be able to protect himself or their daughter.

"Delilah?" His voice sounded far away as she pulled the phone away from her ear.

She hung up and leaned heavily into the counter. There was only one thing to do. She would have to go to Portland and protect her family herself. The shakes started again at the thought of confronting Ted, but she gripped the counter until they faded.

Delilah turned away from the phone and started searching through Mr. Palmer's house for cash. It was time to stop running and show this crazy Ted that he'd fucked with the wrong woman. She had to stop him. Somehow.

Twenty-seven

Delilah's newfound anger and resolve dissipated as she rummaged through her neighbor's home. She found Mr. Palmer's wallet and learned his name was Walter. There was eighteen dollars in the wallet and a wad of coupons clipped from Sunday's paper. She pocketed the money.

She found an old revolver in the bedroom and a shotgun half-buried in dust under the couch. A Porky Pig cookie jar yielded another forty dollars and change in small bills and coins. As she half-heartedly searched, feeling time pressing in on her with a tangible pressure like water on her skin, Delilah realized that she'd have to fly.

She tried to think of a way to avoid the deathtrap tin can option. But the drive across country would take thirty some hours in the most ideal circumstances. Injured, exhausted, and with a murderer gunning for her family was not her ideal.

Forty hours, at least. How much damage could crazy Ted do in that time? She looked around poor Walter Palmer's house.

Enough. Too much.

She'd have to fly. Which meant she needed more money. And she couldn't take the guns with her. Delilah could live with that. She wasn't fond of guns and part of her hoped she could grab Jake and Esther and get the hell out. Confronting a man who could do what Ted had done, well, thinking about it brought the tremors back to her hands and ran chills down her spine.

With heavy steps she walked back to her own house. She needed to stay sharp, stay smart. *Smarter, cause I've fucked this whole thing up.* She stepped into the moist heat and tried to breathe through her mouth. Palmer's body was growing riper as the day warmed up.

She knew she had to pack a bag, look normal for the airport people. Just a woman going on a flight. Normal, safe, boring.

Her tongue stuck to the roof of her mouth and she breathed in little gasps as she grabbed a duffle bag and started stuffing clothes into it. A plane. Thousands of feet in the air. No exit. *Fuck.*

She sat down heavily on the bed and unzipped her hoodie. The bandage was stuck to the skin, but though a shower sounded like heaven, Delilah forced away those thoughts. She didn't have the time. No time. Even now a killer could be watching her daughter or grabbing the only man in the world who had ever given a damn for Delilah.

If she turned away now, if she let the fear make her run again, she'd be responsible for what happened to them. She guessed she wasn't quite the hardened bitch that Jake had accused her of being, after all.

Thinking about Jake, sending money and secret prayers for the baby they'd made together, it kept her more grounded than she'd realized. But if he, if they, died, if she lost her last human connection to the girl she'd been, then she wasn't sure what she'd become.

She left the hoodie on the bed and pulled on a tee-shirt. Getting a clean pair of pants on was more work and she felt something tear, almost heard it in a teeth-grinding, internal-sound way. Pain sent icicle spikes through her lower back and she slammed her fist against the bed frame, chewing her lip.

Her stomach was in ropes and her throat unbearably dry. Nausea radiated through her. Delilah went into the kitchen, avoiding looking at the corpse in the living room, and pulled out the bottle of diet Coke. Her hands shook so hard as she poured that she sloshed it onto the counter and floor. She started to replace the bottle, then snorted in horrible amusement. It didn't matter if the Coke got warm. Wasn't like she was ever coming back here.

The bubbles settled her stomach a little and she swished the final mouthful of cold sweetness around before swallowing. She set the empty glass down. No putting it off now. She had to go.

Her first stop was Poppy's pawn shop. It was just after eight in the morning when she reached the barren parking lot. Poppy's truck was parked by the dumpster behind.

Delilah pounded on the thick steel back door. After a minute she heard movement and a slit opened in the door. Poppy's yellowed eyes squinted out at her.

"You alone?" he asked.

"Yes, of course. Come on, Pops." She didn't have time for his normal paranoid bullshit. She needed money and to get to the airport. There was no way to know when flights left, not without a computer to check times or other tech she didn't have at the moment. No way to know if Ted had jumped a flight already or if Delilah could catch him beforehand.

Not that she'd have a clue what to do in that case. *Come up with something. Stop him. Somehow.* She shivered as Poppy unlocked the million locks on the other side of his door.

He motioned her into the dim interior. The air conditioning was going strong, recycling the cigarette smoke and thin, acidic scent of instant coffee.

"You shouldn't be here, Dee." Poppy led the way to his office and flopped down in the bright orange leather chair.

"What are you talking about?"

"Cardiff called. Says you got trouble. Your face all over the news or something. You kill somebody?"

"Fuck." Delilah sighed. "No, I didn't kill anyone." *Yet.* She reached into her coat pocket and pulled out the necklace, earrings, and bracelet and dumped them on the desk in front of Poppy. The diamonds glittered in the fluorescent light.

Poppy whistled through his dentures and scratched a weekend's growth of salt and pepper stubble on his thick chin.

"You can't be here, Dee. Card—"

"Fine, I was never here." She cut him off with a sharp gesture. "I need cash, Pops. Now."

That had been a mistake she realized as his eyes locked on her face and narrowed to predatory slits. She had a playbook, rules, customs and personalities she adopted to deal with the people she had to deal with to do what she loved doing.

But this whole thing with Ted, with Florida. God, she couldn't stop fucking up. It was like the whole book had been thrown out the window. On fire.

Poppy poked at the diamonds, sorting the pile out into individual pieces.

"Because I'm a nice man," he said, "I'll give you two hundred."

She wasn't sure she'd heard him right. "What? Fuck that, Pops. This shit is real, you can see that at a glance. It's worth at least fifty grand. I want my usual ten percent."

"Usual? You're in trouble, kid. I wonder if they got one of those information bounty things on you yet. Would that be worth fifty grand, you think?"

She swallowed and shook her head. She was alone, inside a locked shop. She hadn't even thought about it. She liked Poppy, more or less. He'd always dealt fair with her. Until now, apparently. *Blood's in the water and the sharks are circling*, she thought.

She ran a hand through her hair. The last couple days had seemed like a nightmare from which she just wanted to wake up, but now, slowly, she was starting to realize that maybe the rest of the time had been the dream. She'd been so busy running around, pretending to be whomever she wanted that she'd lost sight of the consequences.

You're never truly free, Colin had always told her. Shit has a way of falling out of the sky.

Shit was sure falling now.

She forced herself to breathe normally and took a different tact with Poppy.

"Hey, Pops, come on." She lifted her shirt a little, showing the blood-stained bandage. "There's a guy, he stabbed me and now he's gonna kill my little girl. I need at least enough for a ticket to get there first." When in doubt, the truth couldn't be the worst way. She hoped. It was all too easy to let the emotions roiling through her build up and large, heavy tears burst from her eyes, making cold streaks down her face.

"Jesus," he said, unconsciously mirroring her as he ran his own hand through his graying curls. "A thousand. Take it or leave it."

A thousand. He was screwing her over, but it would be enough. Probably. She had no idea how much a plane ticket cost.

"Okay, fine. I'll take it." She barely waited for him to count out the bills before bolting from the shop.

She slid into the car and rubbed the back of her hand against her wet eyes. "Suck it up, Dee. Move on, keep going." There wasn't time to sit around feeling sorry for herself. She wasn't the one who'd be sliced into a million bits of viscera and—she shoved away the image of Walter. It wouldn't happen. Not to Jake. Not to the sick little girl who probably didn't even know Delilah's name.

She twisted the key in the ignition and pulled away from the pawn shop, tears still streaking down her cheeks in glistening lines.

Twenty-eight

Angry thoughts swarmed through Delilah's mind like wasps, bright and dangerous. Cardiff. That damn paranoid bastard. This whole thing was his fault, in many ways. He'd set her up with Alan and the dumb job in Florida in the first place. Why hadn't he vetted those people better? He knew Delilah well enough to know she'd never sit in on amateur hour like that.

And now, now that the whole thing was a giant mess and it was her face, if not her name, yet, plastered across screens all over the South. Cardiff had called Poppy. She wondered who else he'd think to call, probably anyone who he'd recommended her to over the last few years.

Her stomach twisted, sharp pains digging into her lower back and down into her legs like cheap fingernails rending her skin from the inside out. Sweat beaded on her forehead and ran down her spine. She jammed on the brakes and pulled over to the side of the road, flipping off an asshole in a Chevy Suburban who leaned on his horn before charging around her.

Even if she stopped crazy Ted, got Jake and Esther out, what kind of life would be waiting for her? There was no way but time and prayers to clear up the shit in Florida. Her prints and DNA would always be tied to imaginary Donna Utley and whatever Ted had done in her hotel room. They might even tie her to that cop and the carjacking.

And now Cardiff had essentially told her to fuck off, withdrawn his help. Favor repaid.

She leaned forward, resting her forehead on the steering wheel. She ran her tongue over dry lips, forcing herself to breathe in shallow, slow breaths.

My choices. My world. Jake had offered to leave Nancy, to try again with Delilah after she'd found out she was pregnant. Was all magnanimous and shit about it, like he hadn't been the one cheating on Nancy in the first place, like he hadn't walked out on Delilah after their high school graduation over a year before that. But he'd told her that for that to happen, she'd have to give up the crooked business. Offered her a waitress position at his dad's bar. *Seriously.*

The bitch of it was, even with the year of no contact, even with him coming back to Portland with another woman, all of it, Delilah would have forgiven it.

But not that last request. She did what she did because she loved it. The thrill of a good con, the ease with which thousands of dollars could come and go in moments, based on skill and intelligence and power. So much power.

And she hadn't wanted the baby. Just Jake. Jake and the life of the heister. The way it was when they were skipping school and boosting cars and small electronics. The perfect team.

And now. Nothing. None of that mattered. She was worse off than ever.

Delilah bit down hard on her lower lip, forcing away the tears. She was fucking maudlin when this exhausted, apparently. Exhausted, alone, injured.

"One thing at a time, Dee," she muttered.

She had two options, the way she saw it. Go, or run. Protect Jake and their daughter, or leave them to fend for themselves and get the hell out. She'd make it. The nice thing about crime was that she could pretty much work anywhere. That thought made her chuckle, which hurt. Hurt because of what crazy Ted had done.

He was so fast, so strong, and apparently so fucking persistent. Mr. Palmer had been a soldier and while old, wasn't exactly a weak slouch either. Ted clearly hadn't had any issues subduing him.

"Damn it." She sat up slowly. She'd chosen this life over Jake and the baby before. And it had gotten her here. To this moment.

She glanced out the window and then pulled the car out onto the road again. She had to get on the plane and protect them. She was the only one who had any idea what Ted was. Maybe Jake could take him, but probably he wouldn't. Ted wasn't the kind of guy who set off alarms and Delilah had never met someone with empty eyes who didn't get that way through lots and lots of practice. Killing practice.

She'd save them. Even if it meant getting into a tin can and hurtling thousands of miles into the air.

Delilah turned off the freeway, toward the airport, with a tiny smile. She'd finally found something that scared her more than small, closed spaces.

Ted.

A white car came up on her quickly, and the blue flash of lights warned her just before the sirens started up.

Delilah looked down at her dash and realized she'd been driving twenty miles an hour *under* the speed limit. Without her seatbelt on. With a muttered curse, she floored the gas.

Twenty-nine

The airport was so damn close that she could see the long-term parking lots and beyond that the shiny bodies of planes taking off in the morning light. But running toward the airport would just mean more security and quicker backup for the cops behind her.

The exit ramp was a long one, up ahead Delilah saw where it merged with another road. She stayed on the gas until the last moment, slamming the brakes and hauling on the emergency brake as she jerked the wheel hard and took the car into a mostly controlled spin. Her car flipped around, the cop car sailing by. She jammed the gas again and hit her horn, heading down the one-way street away from the airport.

In the rearview mirror she saw the cruiser scrambling to turn and come after her. She shot down the tree-lined road and they fell out of sight.

She was in the sweet spot now, the small space of time anyone running from the police had once they'd lost immediate sight. Backup would be called in and the cruiser would come down this road behind her. She had only moments to get away.

The road dead-ended at a busy four-lane highway. Right turn only. Delilah slowed for the briefest of seconds and then gunned through a gap in the traffic, turning the car to the left hard as she shot through the traffic. She merged into the right lane and slowed down, watching her mirrors for a sign of the police.

She heard sirens but didn't see the car. She was still in that window, perhaps away safely, perhaps not. And she couldn't risk coming back around and getting to the airport this way. She needed a new plan.

The adrenaline faded, leaving shakes behind it. Nausea burned in her stomach and Delilah pressed a fist to her abdomen. Too many close calls.

A blue information sign with a bunch of hotel decals on it caught her eye. *Of course.* The airport would have many hotels around it. While the cops had a description of the car, they couldn't have seen more than that it was a dark-haired woman driving.

Telling herself to stay cool and think, Delilah turned off toward the hotels. She drove down the road, looking at the hotels as they rose, bleak and utilitarian above acres of asphalt. No parking garages. That would make it harder to hide the car, but she'd deal.

She pulled into the parking lot of the Super 8 and tucked her car into a line of parked cars. Taking her bag with her, she left the vehicle, throwing the keys into a drainage grate as she walked, hunched with pain, to the motel.

It was warm, but Delilah worried that her wound might start to bleed through. She stopped in the shade of a couple scraggly trees near the lobby entrance and checked her shirt. No blood yet, but the tearing pain stabbing little icicles through her lower back and stomach weren't comforting. She pulled a sweatshirt out of her bag and zipped it partially up. The pill bottles made a sound like a rattle in her sweatshirt pocket, reminding her she had them.

Delilah debated taking a painkiller, but shoved the pills into her bag instead. She needed to stay sharp, awake. Once she was on that tin can of death she could take drugs and hopefully sleep the flight through.

Unless he's there too. Still unable to decide what she'd do about Ted if he were on the same flight, Delilah forced away those thoughts.

"Excuse me, miss?" A man's voice startled her and she almost swung her bag up to hit the elderly guy who stood just off the curb next to a taxi.

Delilah gave herself a mental shake and held her bag close. "Yes?"

"Are you the one waiting for the taxi?"

"Yes," she said with a small smile. "I guess I was."

He held the door open for her and Delilah climbed inside. The driver had his air conditioning running and the chill was a welcome relief to the growing heat outside.

The driver got in and Delilah said, "The airport, please."

"Sure thing, miss."

She leaned back into the tan pleather seat. She had to go. Whatever happened, she would have tried to help them.

She sat silently the short trip to the airport, staring out the window, looking for cops or, if she was honest with herself, some divine miracle that would make this whole mess just go away.

Delilah found neither.

She realized the cabby was talking to her after a moment as they pulled into the departures line.

"What airline, miss?"

"Oh, um." She looked out the windshield at the signs and chose one. "Delta is fine, thank you."

He pulled up beneath the Delta sign and told her the fare was eight dollars.

Delilah handed him a ten, the first bill she peeled off the roll in her pocket, and told him to keep the change.

The airport was a swirl of people even on a weekday morning. She walked to a giant screen that had all the flights listed and searched for something, anything, going to Portland in the next few hours.

There was one from US Airways leaving in just about an hour. Praying there were seats left, Delilah walked slowly to the check-in desk.

She stood patiently behind two girls about her age but with too much metal in their faces as a family of five, two parents and three toddlers, tried to check in a large pile of bags. Time ticked by, minutes that Delilah didn't have to waste. She hoped the security line wouldn't be too long, she'd heard nightmare stories from others about airport security.

She had no knives or knitting needles or bottles of water on her, however, so she hoped she'd be through without an issue. The pills worried her a little, but she could always say they were aspirin or allergy medication if she had to. There wasn't a name on the bottles at least.

Finally a busty middle-aged woman whose hair color definitely came from a bottle arrived behind the counter and called over the girls with faces like sieves. Then it was Delilah's turn.

"Hi," she said. "I need to get to Portland, Oregon. Today."

"We have a flight leaving in about an hour that would get you to Portland about two this afternoon, local time," the woman said, her fingers clacking on the keys. "There are some seats open, but you'll be pushing it to get on, they'll be boarding soon."

Delilah wondered if the woman typed as fast and thoroughly as she talked. When the woman finally took a breath, Delilah said, "Okay, that's fine. How much? And I need only a one-way ticket." She dug her hands into her pockets to stop the tremors of fear that danced through her fingertips.

"One-way? Two-fifty-seven. I have an aisle or a middle seat?"

Shit. "Um, do you have an exit row maybe? I like room."

The woman made a face at her that clearly implied that if Delilah liked room she probably should have booked her flight more than an hour in advance.

"No, though I do have a seat in first class right at the front, plenty of leg room there." Her watery blue eyes glanced over Delilah and her expression made it clear she didn't think much of what she saw.

"How much for that seat?" Delilah ignored the woman, mentally calculating how much money she had.

"Eight-hundred-ninety-six dollars."

"I want that one." Delilah dug into her pocket and counted out the bills. It would take most of her money, but money didn't matter. Delilah could always find a way to get more if she needed it.

"Name and Identification, please?" The woman's eyes widened a little at the wad of cash, but she became all business once again.

Delilah pulled out her fake driver's license. She checked the name and address quickly before handing it over, mentally reminding herself who she was supposed to be.

She gave her name and filled out the little form the woman gave her. Her stomach felt like an anthill, tiny feet burning their way through her insides. A part of her hoped that something would go wrong now, just a little wrong. Just enough to take away this decision. She could run from here, say oh well, she'd tried.

But the US Airways woman handed her back her ID and asked if she wanted to check her bag.

"No, thanks," Delilah said. She took the printout with her gate number on it and the boarding pass.

It was good, she reflected, that she was so fucked up physically. Walking slowly wouldn't attract much attention and her wound kept her from running anywhere. She walked to security and held out her boarding pass and ID again.

The older black man, who looked bored enough to be barely conscious, only glanced at her face before marking her boarding pass and waving her into line.

She watched the other people go through the machines, noting how they removed their shoes and coats and belts. A couple people were taken aside, randomly as far as she could tell, and given a once-over with a wand-like device. A drug-dog, a German Shepherd, spun in little bored circles around his keeper to one side.

Delilah sighed and wondered what had happened to Max. Hopefully he'd made it home or been picked up by someone nice. He'd sort of saved her life, she felt pretty rotten about leaving him out in the rain like that. It'd seemed necessary at the time. She could add it to her list of fuck-ups in the last two days.

Bending over to remove her sandals made her whimper and Delilah bit her lower lip hard enough to taste blood. She removed her sweatshirt as well, glancing down to check for blood. Her tee-shirt remained clean.

She emptied her pockets into her duffle bag and put it all on the belt. She watched her bag start to go through the machine, then turned to the small woman who beckoned her through the metal detector. There was no reason to be nervous, but that didn't stop her. Visions of a tiny cell with no windows and only a single locked door took over her mind.

Delilah forced herself to smile and stepped through the detector. The woman's eyes flicked up to some screen or something, and then she nodded.

"Thank you, go through." The woman pointed her back at the conveyor belt where Delilah's stuff awaited, piling up with the gray bins of others.

Relief shot through her and then was gone again. She pulled on her sandals and her sweatshirt, lifting her bag carefully so as not to aggravate her stitches worse. She pulled out the little bottle of painkillers and tucked it into her sweatshirt pocket.

She'd made it through security. But now she had to go to the gate, and get on the plane.

Flying tin can death-trap. And that was if Ted wasn't waiting at the gate for her. She hadn't seen any other morning flights on the giant screen. So either he was waiting for her or he was long gone. Either way, how would she handle him?

With the ants in her belly swarming over as her stomach turned to ropes, Delilah walked slowly toward her gate, her bag clutched in front of her like a shield.

Thirty

Delilah skirted the gate, watching for Ted. The hum of conversations seemed somehow farther off than they were, an infernal buzzing in her ears, as though everyone were speaking a different language. Walking by a cinnamon roll vender nearly knocked her over, the hot, sweet smells waking her hunger. But she couldn't think about food, or anything else. Not yet.

Not until she confirmed that Ted wasn't at the gate, waiting to get onto the same plane she was. It would be hard enough to walk down the closed corridor to a tin deathtrap. If he'd boarded already, if he were waiting for her.

She shivered and zipped up her sweatshirt. Hovering near a column, she scanned the crowd around the gate. Not too many people, that was good. Tall, handsome Ted should stand out in this group. Most everyone else looked like college kids going home with a family or two calming little children, or a group of business people. She eyed the business people the hardest, shifting to make sure of each face. If Ted were going to hide here, that would be his kind of folk.

Her heart thumped hard in her chest as one man rose to his feet. His back was to her, but he looked broad and well-built enough to possibly be Ted. Delilah struggled to recall how long Ted's hair had been, what the exact shade was. All she could remember clearly was his face, those empty cold eyes and his damp mouth pressing against her.

The businessman turned and even before he'd started walking toward a magazine kiosk she relaxed. He looked good through the shoulders, but in turning he'd revealed a gut barely held in by a belt that cost more than Delilah had on her. She glanced at his face anyway, just to be sure, and confirmed that this wasn't playboy Teddy.

Two men in TSA uniforms walked by and abruptly Delilah knew exactly what she'd do if Ted showed his face here. There were multiple exits, fire doors, other gates. She could maybe even slip away into the growing crowd. After she yelled something like "that guy has a gun" or perhaps a bomb. It was an airport so they'd have to take something like that seriously. Anything to delay him, get him into custody.

Some of her fear faded away as the plan formed and she studied each person approaching the gate, half-hoping now that psycho Teddy would appear.

One of the people in uniform behind the check-in counter called out that they'd be boarding soon, special-needs passengers, people with small children, and first-class first. Delilah sighed. She wouldn't be first on that plane. No need to sit there terrified any longer than necessary.

With a final glance around for anyone resembling the man who'd stabbed her, Delilah turned back the way she had come and walked down the line of food stations. The cinnamon rolls called to her, hot and sticky. But her aching belly told her that she'd just throw up if she ate anything solid, and there was nothing in the world that would get Delilah into a tiny plane bathroom.

Though the flight was over five hours long, she decided she could risk a smoothie. She had to eat or drink something and it would help the pills she planned to take go down a lot better.

She got a strawberry and banana smoothie, paying way too much for it, and leaned on the counter while she waited for the young blonde in a ridiculously colorful uniform to finish making her order. The last day had caught up to her and she blinked rapidly to keep the world in focus.

"Miss, a number four?" The blonde's voice was low and pleasant.

Delilah shoved off the counter and tried to smile. "Thanks," she said.

About half the waiting people had boarded by the time Delilah got back to her gate. She decided not to sit down and wait, fearing she'd never get up. Instead she took small sips of the cold smoothie, sliding ice crystals back and forth through her teeth and trying to pretend she was just another girl going home.

That thought made her laugh and she wiped banana and berry bits off her chin with one sleeve. She *was* going home, in a way. Born and raised in Oregon, though her father hadn't moved them to Portland until she'd been in middle school. She hadn't been back in years, not since the final fight with Jake, the final fight with Colin.

She closed her eyes, forcing the memories away.

Time passed too quickly and soon Delilah was nearly the last person at the gate. She walked forward, pulling out her boarding pass and ID.

The small man ran her ticket through the barcode scanner, glanced at her ID, and then waved her through.

She took a couple shallow breaths and stepped into the tunnel. Though it was probably six feet wide, Delilah felt squeezed in and she had to work to not hyperventilate. *Slow, easy breaths, Dee.* This wouldn't kill her. The plane might, but not this damn tunnel. There was an exit at the end, a door hanging open as a couple guys passed strollers and an oversized bag outside.

She paused by that opening to warm, fresh daylight.

"Miss? We're getting ready to close the doors." A flight attendant stepped away from the entrance of the plane and beckoned to her.

Delilah nodded, not trusting her voice, and forced herself to cross into the plane.

It was worse in here, tight and dark compared to the tunnel. She handed her pass to the attendant and was shown to the first seat. Delilah let the woman put her duffle bag up overhead. The seat was big and cushy, half-swallowing Delilah as she sank into it. She set her smoothie into the cup holder and slowly pulled her seatbelt closed across her hips.

The flight attendants started locking down the plane and Delilah shoved a fist into her mouth to keep from telling them to stop. Thousands of people fly on planes and don't die, she told herself over and over. She would be fine. With the cup holder and seatbelt she could almost trick herself into believing she was in a car. Almost.

At least no one was sitting in the seat next to her. With shaking hands she pulled out the painkillers and fished out three. With a sigh she dumped one back into the bottle. She was running low on pills and anyway, the flight wasn't that long. If the drugs and her own exhaustion knocked her out too hard, she might not wake in time. She hoped two would be enough. Delilah glanced around and then swallowed both pills with a couple sips of her smoothie.

"Blanket, miss?" One of the flight attendants, having sealed the death-trap, offered Delilah a folded square of blue-gray fabric.

"Yes, thanks." Delilah didn't even bother with a smile. She took the blanket and unfolded it over herself.

The plane started to taxi out of the gate, the engine humming and rattling. Delilah swore she heard creaking and even cracking in the wall near her head. She leaned into the window and watched the sunlit asphalt slide past beneath them. Listening to the safety briefing, Delilah made herself finish her smoothie and handed the empty cup to one of the flight attendants as they passed by to take up their seats in the front.

Delilah had just convinced herself this wasn't so terrible, after all, the door was right there near her and the ground really only a few feet away, when the plane started gaining speed. The pavement became a blur and then suddenly she felt almost weightless as the tin can lifted off into the sky. Somewhere behind her, in the economy class seats, a baby started crying.

Delilah closed her eyes, thinking of sunlight and ocean and huge open spaces. She tried to trick herself into believing she was in a car, driving far far away from any troubles, entirely in control. Driving toward dark pine and fir forests, cities with clean streets, and clear, fresh air filled with the scent of rain. Toward a man with warm, dark eyes who loved her, his face full of forgiveness and his arms strong as they folded around her body. Going home.

Mercifully, the pills started doing their magic and the pain faded to a dull ache as her mind floated away from the hum of the plane and off into dreams.

Thirty-one

It was technically his day off, but Sam couldn't help showing up the next morning. He didn't know how fast Mike's lab could run the DNA or if CODIS would even have a hit for them. But it didn't matter. If he were at his desk, he would be ready to do whatever was necessary to help Donna.

Her large, scared eyes had haunted his sleep, the lingering smell of clove cigarettes and rain followed him around his dump of an apartment as he'd manically tried to undo years of neglect in a single night. Sam's car and home were cleaner now, but his head stayed cobwebbed and confused.

He walked through the bull-pen and flicked the light on in his office. It was still early enough that either everyone was out on patrol or sleepily wandering in for the shift change at seven. From the delicious, acidic smell cutting across the usual almost musty smell of the station, Sam knew someone was in the tiny break room brewing fresh coffee. He made a mental note to go get some soon. After he checked his email.

He swiveled his chair around and sighed. Propped in his seat was a large yellow wheel lock with a giant pink bow on it. Rocco and Petty. Great. Sam shook his head and pushed the heavy metal bar onto the floor, nudging it under his desk with his foot. He'd deal with them later.

Sam opened his email and his heart started beating a little faster as he saw a message from Mike's lab address, the time stamp saying it was sent twenty minutes before he'd arrived at the office.

Hey Sam, the email began, *got those samples. I'll start on this right away and see what we can get. I'll call you with results whenever that is. Maybe later today? You owe me, so call your damn sister. TTYL Mike.*

Sam stared at the email for a moment and then sighed. Guiltily, he tried to remember the last time he'd called Nina at all and couldn't. He did not want to talk to his sister, to hear that mix of pity and exasperation in her voice.

He got up out of his chair and headed toward the break room to get a cup of coffee. He'd call Nina soon. Part of getting his life back on some semblance of a track. Sam knew he needed to reconnect with people, people like Nina and Ronnie and all those who had patiently put up with his crap over the years.

Later. After all this was settled, one way or another. Meanwhile, it looked like coffee and a lot of solitaire while he waited. His fingers itched and Sam considered going out for a smoke, but shoved that craving aside. No more smoking. He smelled too much like an ashtray already. Well, an ashtray mixed with cookies. At least cloves had a bit of sweetness in them to cut the acrid tobacco scent. But he'd had enough.

Sam grabbed a cup of coffee and walked quickly back to his desk with his head down. It was too early for the Lieutenant to be in, but he was still nervous and not in the mood for idle chatter this morning. He had no idea how far the story of last night and his car had spread. Knowing Rocco and Petty, probably everywhere. Those two could spread gossip like it was peanut butter on toast.

Sam's stomach growled as he shut his office door. There was jerky and a Snickers in his desk that could keep him going for a while yet. Those and coffee. He set the cup down on a paper napkin already ringed with multiple stains.

Solitaire, or catching up on paperwork. Sam sat heavily in his chair and ran a hand through his thinning hair. Then he dug into his jean's pocket and pulled out a quarter. Heads, solitaire. Tails, work.

The coin flipped into the air, spinning around and around as it fell.

The hours ticked by and the remainders of Sam's coffee grew stale and cold in his cup. Though his quarter had landed in favor of computer games, he ended up doing a bunch of paperwork, filling out some forms, checking over his people's schedules and reports for errors, and other busy work he usually hated and put off. And refreshing his email and checking his phone every few minutes.

There were five ignored messages from Nina on his cell, as well as two from their mother, and one that he thought was a dentist appointment reminder. No call from Mike yet.

Finally, just as he decided to open a new game of solitaire, his cell rang, the number coming up as unlisted.

"Detective Arbichaut here," Sam said, not sure if it was the FBI lab.

"Hey, Sam." The sound of Mike's baritone through the cell got Sam's heart pounding again. Sam was sure that Mike had found something or he wouldn't have called.

"Got something for me?" Sam forced himself to speak calmly.

"Maybe. I'm still sorting some of these results. There was a lot of mixing and contamination. Looks like so far, from the house in Daytona, we've got two females and one male donor. The male matches the home-owner sample Ronnie sent, so we know who he is. I ran a clean sample from one female through CODIS and got a partial match. Ronnie's supposed to send a sample to match up to female Unsub two, but sounds like she has a lot to handle. And as I said, I'm still sorting here and matching each sample to the others I was sent."

A partial match. It was something at least. "What kind of match?"

"Paternal, I think, from the markers they have in common. I'm emailing you the results and the information from the hit. Looks like the father of one Unsub is in prison on the West Coast for armed robbery and attempted murder."

"Jesus. Okay. That was one of the female donors?" Sam clicked on the email, opening the attachment. Bennie Hill, known aliases Al Noone and Junior Lackey, incarcerated in Salem, Oregon, just as Mike had said. The mug shot showed a thin man with muscular, almost Popeye arms, and short salt and pepper hair. His eyes were bright blue and glared out of the picture on Sam's computer, lips curled beneath a few days growth of stubble in a Mona Lisa smile.

He looked nothing like Donna.

"Female donor number one, yeah. Looks like her DNA matches blood found at that hotel site. Ronnie sure did overdo herself with the samples here. She's got a real mess. How come you're involved? And is she calling in the FBI?"

"I think she'll have to, since it looks like she has a serial on her hands. I just figured I'd help her out with my connections, you know—" Sam trailed off. This looked like a huge dead-end. Donna hadn't looked Caucasian, though he supposed she could be half. He sighed and scrolled through the email, looking over what Mike had found so far. Most of the technical jargon was beyond him, the results looking like a lab report with all sorts of weird tables. Something stood out, however, and he leaned in to study the screen.

"Female Unsub one, she's the daughter of this Bennie? What does this 'possible NA descent' result here mean?"

"Native American," Mike said. "There were markers that indicate she might be of Native descent. As I said, we're still sorting stuff, but I threw my best guys on this with me and we're going as fast as we can. It's a slow day right before the weekend, so you got lucky there."

Native American. Donna certainly could be that. Sam opened up the picture that Ronnie had sent him. High cheekbones, dark eyes, that hard-to-place and exotic look. Definitely could be.

"Thanks, Mike. Look, Ronnie is slammed with these cases, so why don't you hold off on getting her all this stuff until it's all sorted, okay?" Sam chewed his lip, hating the idea that was coalescing and forming up in his mind like a cancer.

"You sure?" Sam could almost hear Mike shrug. "Okay. But call your sister. Please."

"Nag, nag, nag." Sam chuckled. "I will. Thanks, man, I do owe you. I'll tell Ronnie to call you when she can. Try her tomorrow if you don't hear before her then, yeah?"

"Sure thing. We'll keep on this. It's a fun puzzle, that's for sure."

Sam snapped his cell phone shut and leaned back in his chair. His thought was madness, but he ached to do something, to be active again. To help Donna.

Bennie Hill. Al Noone. Junior Lackey. Either this guy had a sense of humor about aliases, or whoever made the fake ID seriously did.

Sam pulled up the crime information. Bennie had been arrested during a payroll steal on a private armored car company in Washington. One guard had been shot, though he lived. It was thought that Bennie had at least two accomplices, but he'd insisted that he'd been alone despite witness testimony to the contrary. He took a plea and got thirty years, with possibility of parole in twenty. After two years of good behavior, his transfer request to the Oregon State Penitentiary was approved on "family" grounds.

That was promising. Sam wondered if Donna still had relatives living in Oregon or even a home base there. He still wanted to believe she was just a girl in the wrong place at the wrong time, even if the evidence in his own experience didn't uphold it.

The cancerous and likely horrible idea continued in Sam's mind. He pulled up a flight schedule. Damn. He could fly direct to Portland and then rent a car and make the hour and a half drive out to the OSP, but he wouldn't arrive until pretty late.

Sam clicked back over to the OSP page and picked up the land line.

After asking to be transferred to the warden, and waiting on hold while someone on a saxophone butchered Beethoven, Sam got through.

"I'm Detective Arbichaut with the Jackson CAP unit," Sam said, which was all true, more or less. "We've got a case here which one of your inmates might be able to help out with."

"In Florida?" The man sounded skeptical and Sam couldn't blame him. This would take some quick talk.

"Bennie Hill. His daughter might be a witness in a serial case, and we need to locate her. I'd appreciate if you'd allow us to send someone out to see him tonight; I can have a detective there by nine or so."

"I'd need authorization, and confirmation. I mean, I can see you're calling from Jacksonville, but I'd need some forms filled out."

"Not a problem, we're coordinating with Lieutenant Ronda Brown of the Daytona Homicide Unit, I have her numbers right here." Sam read off Ronnie's office number, the direct line. She'd forgive him. Especially if he called her immediately and begged for leeway on this. "We've got to get a guy on a plane soon, however, if we're going to move on this information. He can fill out the forms there."

"All right." The warden sounded harassed but resigned, which suited Sam just fine. "I'll call the LT. She says go, I'll have the forms ready and a guard standing by."

"Thank you, sir." Sam hung up and then immediately dialed Ronnie's personal cell. After her late night, he doubted she'd be in the office, though the office phone might route to her work cell, but he wasn't sure if she'd answer that.

The personal one, however, she answered.

"Sam, what do you want?"

"Hello to you, too," Sam said. Now the fun part. Hopefully she was still on his side. She'd always looked out for him before. It was time to call on that goodwill and spend it like it was his last day on Earth.

"Seriously, do you have something for me? I'm running on not enough sleep here."

"I might," Sam said, "but don't get too excited. I need to follow it up, just in case. You gotta trust me on this one, Ronnie. If it is something, I'll toss it to you, I promise. I'm not a grandstander, you know me."

"So you do need something. What did you get?" Ronnie's voice was thin, weaker than the night before, like she'd been using it to scream non-stop for hours.

"I have to go to Oregon and talk to an inmate. I need your back-up word on this with the warden up there, he should be calling you soon."

"Good fucking God, Sam," Ronnie said and Sam wondered if she'd just been swearing all night instead of screaming. The thought almost made him laugh.

He missed her, and the crew down in homicide and the late nights and despair and the ugliness and joy and shared pain that came from working long hard hours mopping up after the worst humanity could conceive to do to itself. He missed it so much, so suddenly, that it was a physical jab in the gut and for a moment Sam couldn't say a damn thing.

"Please," he finally mumbled. "Give me this. I need to do something, Ronnie."

"Sure, Sam, sure," she said more softly, as though even a hundred miles away she could pick up on what had just sucker punched him. Then, her tone sharper again, she said, "But you better damn hand off anything you get to me if it pans out. Cause I can't cover your ass for real, not while you're Jacksonville's."

"I know," he said. "Thanks."

"Don't thank me, go do something useful." She hung up and Sam sat, staring at the phone for a moment.

Then he clicked on flight information and booked a seat on the next flight out to Portland. It was his day off. About time he took a little vacation. He sent off a quick email to his Lieutenant. No one would miss him until Saturday. He booked the flight and then signed out of his computer after printing a couple of pictures: Donna Utley and Theodore Whitechapel.

His fingers tingled as he turned off his office light and walked out, closing the door behind him. Home to pack an overnight bag, and then he'd be on his way to do some good, or, as Ronnie said, at least something useful.

Thirty-two

Ted rented a car, a newer Mazda Sport, nothing too fancy since he didn't want to stand out. The car was silver, a nice, neutral color just like hundreds of others. Perfect. It was cooler in Portland, no need for the AC as he drove away from the airport. His first stop was a hardware store marked out on a piece of scrap paper by the helpful rental attendant.

It amused Ted that he'd managed to put together multiple kits and then had to ditch them in the last twenty-four hours. He hoped this would be the final one. In his mind he could see Delilah's tired, thin face reeling in horror as she returned home to his messy surprise. He wished he could have stuck around for that, but this little gambit seemed like a lot more fun.

He laughed aloud as he scanned the radio stations for something worth listening to. Freedom. Complete freedom. No more pretending, no more hiding. Delilah had ruined his façade, but now he could see the mask for the fake little walls, the pretention that it had been. He had money and a plan.

A plan that involved hurting a whole lot of people. Starting with the ones that his sneaky little Delilah cared about most.

An hour later, kit assembled and tucked behind the passenger seat, Ted drove toward downtown Portland. He'd slept on the flight, but was hungry and felt rumpled and grimy from all the travel. With the time difference it was barely noon. Hardly the time of day to go to a bar, though Ted contemplated getting something to eat at Jake's fine establishment.

He finally decided on a getting a hotel room. There were quite a few offerings as he turned off I-84 into the east side of downtown. He settled on a Double-Tree hotel near a mall. Getting a room was simple; it was the middle of the week, after all. The desk girl tried to quibble over it being early, since check-in was not until three, but Ted talked the pretty brunette into letting him have one of the Presidential suites immediately after he gave her the traveling businessman sob story and one of his blinding grins.

The room was well-appointed, with a Jacuzzi bathtub big enough to drown a person in. Ted contemplated trying, thinking about the young desk clerk and how late she might work that night, but reigned in the impulse.

Wouldn't do to throw out *all* propriety and caution to the winds. He'd checked in under his new name, so it was best to keep this location free of scandal until he was sure what the next move was. There would be enough death soon. Desire tingled through his body at the thought, riding in his bones like a deep ache.

Showered, shaved, and with a clean shirt on, he replaced the opal cufflinks in the new shirt. They were quite stylish and Ted liked having something against his skin that Delilah had touched.

He returned to the desk and got directions to No Man's Land from the perky little clerk. The hotel had completely unnecessary air-conditioning, which Ted suddenly appreciated as he watched the clerk write out quick directions for him. The chill air and the breeze that wooshed in every time someone came through the big front doors caused her nipples to push against the thin material of her shirt. Her bra was delicately lacey and showed through just enough where the hard nubs forced their way toward Ted's hungry gaze.

Another time, he whispered silently to those promising breasts, *I'll see you later.*

Thirty-three

No Man's Land was a corner establishment in the south-east part of Portland with big carved wood doors lacquered black and band posters plastered to the front windows. Ted pulled into the tiny parking lot and then drove around the back, parking as far from the front as he could while staying away from obvious tow zones. He climbed out of his car. There was a dumpster in a high fenced surround. A couple of older-model cars were pulled up behind like his was; he assumed they belonged to bar employees.

There was a back door, but it looked like a fire exit and, when Ted carefully checked, was locked tight. He wandered around the front and stepped inside.

A fat bottle-blonde leaned against the L-shaped bar, her black apron denoting her as an employee. She was talking quietly to an unhealthily skinny young man with bright green spiked hair who stood behind the bar like he worked here, though he had no apron or anything resembling a uniform. A group of three college-aged men sat at one of the booths against the wall facing the little parking lot, and a couple talked quietly in one of the few tables in the floor space to the left of the entry.

To his right was a room taken up mostly by a pool table with wrinkled blue felt and stained-glass lamps hanging overhead. There was a cheap dart board with a big piece of plywood behind it on which someone had scrawled names and arrows pointing at various holes in the wood. No one was playing either darts or pool.

At the back of the seating area, next to a hallway, was a little platform that Ted guessed passed for a stage given the live music schedule written out in neon on the whiteboard hanging on the wall behind it. Two middle-aged black men wearing work boots and jeans sat at the bar, nursing pints of something dark and foamy.

"Hey honey," the fat woman said with a wide, wet pink smile. "Seat yourself, I'll be right over, or you can sit at the bar."

The whole place, once Ted stepped more fully inside, stank of beer, fried food, some kind of spicy incense, and peanuts. A shell crunched under his foot as he slid into the furthest booth, taking a seat where he could see the whole place and the front door, as well as the door behind the bar that he guessed led into the kitchen.

There were more shells under the table, carelessly swept there the night before in all likelihood. A black glass bowl full of peanuts still in their shells decorated the scarred table. He

ANNE BAINES

shoved it away, toward the dust-streaked window. It was all very low class, but Ted sighed and resigned himself to slumming. He wanted to see this Jake Leventon, to scout him out. There was no reason to go rushing into anything. *A good hunter studies and knows his prey.*

His prey apparently only served the greasiest sort of bar food dressed up with names that Ted supposed were meant to sound cheeky and fun. When the cow waitress finally stopped her incredibly important conversation with the anorexic bartender and came over, Ted ordered a "Bam! Bam! Burger" with a side of fresh melon and a pint of dunkelweizen. He was in the famed Northwest, so he supposed the least he could do was enjoy a decent beer. He idly wondered if the burger title referred to one of those perky, cliché TV chefs. Emily loved those stupid cooking shows. He smiled. Yet another thing he would no longer have to tolerate.

He waited for his food to arrive and studied the place. Behind him would be the edge of the parking lot outside, which put the back door at the end of the hallway with the bathrooms directly behind his table.

A woman in her thirties, wearing a leather jacket covered in little metal studs, came in just as his food appeared. She sat on one of the chrome and purple faux-leather bar stools. There was muted rock music thrumming over speakers tucked into the cobwebbed corners of the ceiling, so Ted missed whatever she said to the anorexic.

He had just taken the first sip of a not-too-shabby beer when he heard a door opening behind him. A moment later,

Jake, the man of the hour, or at least, Ted's intended hour later, appeared.

Blood rushed into Ted's ears and for a moment all he could hear was his own heart beating a hungry rhythm inside as the tingling grew in his bones. His prey wore a black tee-shirt with a faded gray *No Man's Land* label printed across it and blue jeans that had seen a lot of wear over a pair of hiking boots. Jake's skin looked darker than in the pictures, especially under the soft bar lighting, and his hair was longer, dark curls forming around his ears and falling over his forehead. He looked almost muscular next to the scrawny bartender. Almost. Ted estimated that he had at least two or three inches and a good thirty pounds on the black bastard.

The acid anger rose as Jake scooted onto a seat and started chatting casually with the woman in the leather jacket. This puny, dark-skinned asshole had touched Delilah, put his dick inside her, and spawned a brat with her.

Ted realized he was not only staring, but glaring, and forced himself to look down at his burger just as the bovine waitress came over.

"Need anything else, honey? Water?" She put her hand on the table and leaned over, invading the air around the table with her cheap perfume that stank of some overpaid idiot's conception of vanilla and flowers.

Ted hadn't even noticed that she'd failed to deliver water to the table. In any establishment he dined in regularly, water was offered and provided, usually with or without carbonation, depending on preference.

"Yes, I'd like the bottled water, and a glass of ice." He hoped the water would cool his rising murderous desires.

"We serve tap here. The environment and all. But we got a great filter, so it's pretty much the same." Her wet pink smile was back and she leaned in further.

Ted wondered if her sagging, carbohydrate-inflated breasts would knock over his beer and carefully moved it out of the danger zone.

"Sure," he said with no intention of drinking whatever she brought. Filtered was definitely *not* the same, but he hardly expected this overgrown white trash hag to understand such distinctions. He couldn't see around her and panicked a little until the cow finally took the hint and heaved herself upright, leaving him a line of sight to his prey once again.

Ted forced himself to eat the burger, chewing each bite carefully to buy himself time as he watched Jake chat with the woman. The meat was well-cooked, just enough pink in the middle, and he grudgingly admitted to himself that the spicing on the burger was better than he'd expected. Of course, the menu and ambiance had set his expectations quite low already, so the food being above par was more or less like being taller than Mickey Rooney.

By the time Jake shook the woman's hand, Ted had finished the burger and sipped his beer, leaving the melon after he realized it really didn't go well with either burger or beer. Jake walked right past him, close enough that Ted could have reached out and hooked an arm around the other man's thigh in an instant. Or stabbed him in the femoral artery without even having to do more than shift in his seat.

But Ted sipped at his beer, keeping his head turned a little away, as though looking into the parking lot for someone, his blood rage turning his vision spotted and blank in time to his pulse. Jake passed by him, unmolested.

The cow came back to see if his water needed a refill, but it was untouched. Ted waved her off, asking for the check. He decided he'd nurse his beer, check out the back hallway, and then decide his next move.

Minutes ticked past as he sipped the beer and considered having another. He was tired from his recent travels and more alcohol could let slip the killer before it was prudent. But it did feel good to sit and think about his prey, so near and unsuspecting. He loved this first stage of the hunt. He'd never hunted a man before, but an alpha had to defend what was his, and Jake had defiled his vision of lovely, deceitful Delilah.

Ted sat, lost in a bloody fog of death and desire, letting the anger ants settle in his stomach around the heavy meal he'd consumed. Finally he finished his drink and rose, taking the check with him.

He walked into the back hallway. The bathrooms were on his left, as he'd thought. On his right was a wall covered in hideous gold and black wallpaper that looked like brocade fabric but to his tentative touch proved to be a faux velvet and foil sort of concoction. Ted shuddered. He'd definitely need another shower after this venture.

At the end of the short hallway was the rear door; it had a push bar on it for fire safety and an un-lit exit sign precariously hung above. To his right was another door that had a narrow plaque stuck to it that read "Bossman" in gold foil lettering.

Ted considered trying the door, but he had no plan and none of his tools on him.

He sighed and turned away, walking back out to pay his check. He decided he'd pay, sit in his car and watch the flow around the bar for a little while, and then, if no immediate opportunity presented itself, he would go back to the hotel, take a nap, and return closer to closing time. He wanted the woman and child as well, and to give Delilah a sporting chance to show up in town, if she'd gotten his message. Better to follow his prey, he decided, and watch. For now.

The blonde cow tried to engage him in banter, or at least what her low-class idea of flirting might be, but Ted just stared at her, anatomically cutting her apart and envisioning her body rotting beneath a bed of blooming Plumeria. In death, at least, she'd finally smell like what a truly fragrant flower should, and the blooms were often just the same deep pink blushing shade as her garish, wet mouth. She shut up quickly after eyeing whatever expression these thoughts evoked on his face and gave him his change.

He didn't leave a tip.

Thirty-four

Delilah, groggy from the drugs and her too-short nap, tried not to run off the plane. She clutched her bag and walked through the airport, hungry for fresh air and her first sight of a city she hadn't seen in years.

She'd hoped that sleeping would help the pain in her gut, but unfolding from the seat hurt seemingly worse than it had before. Her bandage had dried out again, tape curling and sticking to her shirt as she slept. Her head felt full of fog and cobwebs.

All she wanted was to lie down and sleep for a week. Maybe a month. The hours on the plane had been a teaser, and her body was trying to make her sorry for it.

A cool breeze and overcast sky greeted her as she left the airport. Daytona Beach, Atlanta, the smoggy, humid southern summer and all the bloodshed and fuck-ups of the last hours faded back a little in her mind as she stood on the curb and breathed in.

She caught a shuttle out to long-term parking. It was broad daylight, but the middle of a weekday, so Delilah hoped that no one would be paying too much attention to her search for a car. The vague thought that this habit of hers should be changed up, that it made her awfully predictable, wandered through her brain, but she wasn't in a mental or physical state to think about a different plan and shoved the idea aside.

After she made sure Jake and the little girl were safe, then she could wallow in self-doubt and examine all the idiot moves that had brought her here. After she found Ted and figured out how to get rid of him.

And to find Ted, she needed wheels. Without a valid credit card to go with her fake ID, and low on cash as she was, there was really no question about a rental. She knew she might have to ditch any car she drove depending on how this situation panned, and leaving a paper trail wasn't on her list.

Well, more of a paper trail. She'd already fucked that up royally in Florida. Paper and blood and fingerprints. Jesus. Might as well yank off her shirt and paint "Arrest Me" across her breasts.

Delilah sighed, aware that she was slowly wandering down an aisle. She started her search for cars that might have hide-a-keys, and older cars that might be easier to break into. She had no tools, but there were ways around it, and she'd learned early in life that most cars carried the tools necessary to steal them already inside.

A tiny ray of luck pierced through her pain and brain fog. A dark green Toyota Corona station wagon. Delilah bit her lip and looked around. No one was nearby, though she'd noticed a security patrol vehicle cruising around as the shuttle was offloading.

Delilah stepped up to one of the passenger doors and pumped the handle quickly a few times. The handle had resistance and she could hear the mechanisms inside the door clicking and grinding in protest. She pumped it again a few times and then pulled hard toward herself.

The door opened, even though the lock was down and supposedly engaged. It was a trick Colin had taught her about these old Toyotas. Oftentimes the locks broke but in a way that owner's rarely noticed since the door would stay locked if someone yanked on it once or twice. But pull a few times in succession and bingo, open door.

She unlocked the other doors and tossed her bag into the passenger seat. The glove box had nothing useful in it. The car's soft beige upholstery smelled like it had been cleaned recently with something lemony, but scattered fast food wrappers and a few empty Tupperware containers littered the floor. A handful of receipts from gas stations were shoved down between the middle divider and the seats.

Even the thought of leaning over the rear seat to check the compartment in the cargo space that usually held the jack and a tire iron made Delilah's guts churn with anticipated agony. She pulled up on the little knobs and laid the rear seat down flat, then crawled into the rear of the car and opened the side compartment.

Just a jack. *Damn.* No tire iron, no screwdriver, nothing. She was going to have to figure out a way to get the steering console open without tools. It was possible, but annoying. Urgency and frustration helped clear the fog in her head, but the pulsing pain radiating out of the wound threatened to take over.

Delilah slammed the panel back into place, jarring her wrist. It wasn't fair. Her life had come down to this moment, kneeling in some sloppy stranger's car while a crazy man could be out there doing horrible, gruesome acts on the one person who'd ever really given a damn about her.

"Shut up, Dee. Do what you have to," she said the words aloud, forcefully. Ted hadn't killed her, he hadn't won yet. As long as she was alive and active, there was a chance she could do something about Jake. And Esther. It wasn't the little girl's fault. She was the victim of all sorts of bad choices her parents had made, and the product of maybe the one good choice Delilah had ever agreed to.

She hadn't wanted the baby. At first she had, a little, since the pregnancy represented a possible way to get Jake back to herself, to bind him to her forever. But months into it she'd seen the truth. Jake loved Nancy and, despite his stupid indiscretions, was committed to making a life with her, a straight-up life.

Maybe if his father hadn't had the stroke. Maybe if Delilah had agreed to go straight.

By the time she saw what a mess she was in with a baby on the way, it was too late to do anything legit about it. But Delilah knew a lot of non-legit people. Instead, she'd let Jake talk her into delivering the baby and giving it to him. Her. Esther.

She saved Esther's life once. On her hands and knees in the station wagon, Delilah gritted her teeth and started to back out. She had to do it again. Go forward, do something right and good again.

Her hand brushed away a Jiffy Lube receipt, uncovering a metal spoon. It was one of the generic cafeteria spoons she remembered from school with a shallow dish and a narrow, squared off handle.

"When you're super fucked," she muttered, quoting Colin again, hearing his slight lisp in her mind. "Improvise, girl."

Crouching as best she could half inside the car, Delilah made short work of the steering column's plastic housing, prying it open with her spoon. The screw holding the ignition barrel gave her some trouble since her injuries prevented her from bending over too far, so she had to use the narrow end of the spoon on the tiny screw pretty much blind. Finally her fingernails scraped under the screw and she pulled it out.

Then it was simple: jam the spoon end into the hole in the barrel, twisting it until the mechanism turned and the check oil and engine lights flicked on. The radio, an old cassette player, flipped on, blaring some man's deep, soothing voice.

She slid awkwardly into the seat and pulled the door shut. This time she remembered to buckle her seatbelt, though pulling it across her body caused another nauseating wave of agony to shoot up from her guts.

She hit the power button on the self-help or hypnotism tape or whatever it was and then turned the spoon one final time after pushing in the clutch. The car choked for a second, then started. She gave it a little gas and then let down the emergency brake.

It was a small accomplishment, but she had wheels under her again. Tiny muscles in her neck and forehead relaxed and she let out a slow, long breath.

It wasn't until she was almost to the pay kiosk that she realized she had no ticket to hand to the attendant.

Thirty-five

Fortunately for Delilah, the attendant bought her story about losing her ticket, charged her for a full week, and was slouched too low in his booth to notice the other side of the steering column where the ignition barrel and spoon key dangled, only sort of hidden with the ill-replaced plastic housing.

She forked over the cash without complaint, giving him a fake smile even though he barely glanced up. She guessed she wasn't the first person to lose a parking stub.

She drove toward No Man's Land, her mind easily finding the path, retracing what had once been familiar highways and roads. The afternoon sun broke through the clouds and highlighted the taller buildings across the river as she drew closer to downtown. In her teen years, these streets had been her playground, the seedier corners of this little city her real school. She passed the turn off that would have taken her toward her old stomping ground, to Kimbo's Auto Shop where she'd spent so many summer days boosting car stereos. Or she could keep going, drive by her old school, though she'd skipped so many classes she could barely remember the layout. She'd mostly shown up to make extra cash selling fake ecstasy and oregano passed off as pot to idiot classmates. Until Colin put the brakes on that.

She licked her lips and headed toward No Man's Land instead, shoving away the memories once again.

The bar was just as she remembered and a phantom pang of longing made her chest hurt as she slowly drove past the black lacquered door. The parking lot was nearly deserted; the bulk of the workday lunch crowd had disappeared by now. She came in around the back and smiled at the sight of her Mustang.

Her smile faded as she drove back around, out of the lot, and parked down a side street. The Mustang meant Jake. Delilah couldn't even begin to pull apart and sort her emotions over their impending face-to-face meeting. She twisted the spoon and shut off the car, leaving the doors unlocked and the spoon on the seat as she climbed out.

She didn't know what to tell him, what she even really wanted. Jake to run away with Esther to somewhere crazy Ted couldn't follow? Jake to let her stick around so she could deal with Ted herself, somehow?

Sick, exhausted, scared, hurting. Delilah could admit to herself that partly she just hoped he'd see her and be at least sympathetic. In a dark, secretly optimistic part of her mind she wanted his strong arms to wrap around her, his soft voice telling her he was here for her and everything would be all right. All she had to do was close her eyes and she could almost feel him beside her again, the years between them shifting to minutes, moments.

For a brief second she paused in the parking lot, leaning on the dumpster surround. The smell of grease and trash dissipated in the face of memory and for that one moment there was only the seaweed and brine, moonlight and the rush of waves, and Jake's hand sliding gently up and down her bare back, his fingers counting her vertebra one by one.

Then reality reasserted itself, the dull, angry ache of her belly and searing nausea dragging her away from fantasy. There was no ocean, just the sound of cars going by. Delilah shivered, thinking that either her wound had gone bad and gotten into her brain somehow, or she needed to lay off those damn pills.

The back door was the same as when they'd been teens together. Maybe Jake's old man had meant to replace it, but she supposed a stroke would sort of kill those ideas. The cover plate over the lock was sheered off, something she and Jake had done back when she was sixteen. Delilah ran her fingers over the scarred metal and smiled again.

They'd gotten so damn drunk off the booze in the bar that they'd never made it out again. Boss Leventon had found them half-naked and passed out, all tangled up together.

"Bad news Squaw," she muttered as she pulled out her driver's license. That's what Jake's father had called her on that morning. First time he'd used that particular nickname for her, but it certainly hadn't been the last.

Her ID slid into the crack of the door and she wiggled it around until the tongue of the lock depressed and the door clicked open to her gentle pressure. She opened it slowly, only enough to squeeze through, and then closed it just as carefully behind her.

The hallway was exactly as she remembered. Peanuts and beer filled her nose, bringing on another wave of nausea. Delilah walked forward a few steps, placing a hand on the velvet wallpaper to steady herself.

She traced one of the fleur-de-lis designs with a fingertip. It looked like Jake had left the place exactly as his father had put it together. She looked out into the main room, moving forward just enough to see the bar.

Her heart punched her breastbone at the sight of Jake's back. She knew it was him, even if his hair was different than she recalled, no tight braids, just loose curls. But she recognized the slight tilt of his head, the way he draped his arm half on the bar. He was talking to a punk-looking woman in a studded leather jacket.

Bridget, the waitress who Delilah was pretty sure had worked at this place as long as it had existed, started toward the back booths and Delilah stepped quickly backward into the rear of the hallway, out of sight.

She turned and tried the door to the office. It was, in true Jake Leventon fashion, unlocked. With a tiny sigh she let herself in.

The office was different. The army-green filing cabinets were the same, but the patterned glass-topped desk, computer monitor, and two cushy chairs were definitely not old man Leventon's choices. There was a tack board full of pictures, some from the bar, most of Jake and his family.

Delilah checked the second door, the one that led directly to the kitchen, and found it unlocked as well. She considered locking it, but she'd had enough of tight, closed off spaces for a while and left it. It was unlikely anyone would bug Jake, and even less likely anyone working here besides maybe Bridget would remember Delilah at all.

She twisted her hands inside her sweatshirt pockets and stared at the pictures on the wall, her mind spinning with what the hell she'd say to him.

After what felt like years, Delilah heard the handle turn. She stepped further into the office and leaned back on the heavy metal and glass desk, facing the hallway entry.

"Hi, Jake," she said softly, her voice thin and weak against the rush of her pulse in her ears. She held out her hands, half in supplication, half in welcome.

He stood in the doorway a moment, then stepped in and shut the door behind himself. He looked good, filled out, older. There were tiny laugh lines around his eyes that hadn't been there before and he had a small pink scar on his chin she didn't remember.

"Fucking-A, Lil." Jake walked around her and sat down with a sigh in one of the chairs.

That popped the last vestiges of the fantasy. *So much for a warm hug and a knight in shining armor getting this kitten out of the tree*, she thought. At least he was still using his pet name for her. No one besides Jake ever called her Lil.

"Now do you believe I'm serious, Jake?" She could cut right to it, if that was how he was going to be after nearly six years. "I got on a fucking plane."

He knew what that meant, was one of the only people who would understand. If he wanted to.

"You hung up on me," he said. He wasn't looking at her, not quite. His eyes kept darting around, to the tack board, the door, the computer monitor which had a spreadsheet displayed on the screen.

"I know," she said, looking down at her hands. Her fingernails were dirty and needed to be trimmed. "I'm sorry, Jake, but this is important."

"This guy, Ted?" At her nod he continued, "You sure about him?"

"That he's fucked in the head and dangerous? Yeah." She glanced back up, but Jake still looked through her.

"I meant about him coming here," he said, shaking his head as though the gesture itself would make her answer no.

Delilah considered. "Sure? I don't know. But he found my home, followed me from one state to another. My gut says yeah, he's coming here."

"Your gut? For fuck's sake. If he's coming here, then give me everything you know so I can get police protection, or," he added as she grimaced and tried to cut in with a protest, "Hire somebody to cover us privately. I'm sure some of the weekend bouncers wouldn't mind helping my family out. But I need more to go on. The description you gave me is like half the people who might visit this place. There've been two or three who might be him eating here today, even."

"Tan? Like California tan?"

"Sure, that describes a guy eating lunch right now." Jake shrugged and then froze, his eyes finally catching Delilah's.

Ice formed in her veins and her hands shook for a moment before she turned and threw open the office door. She staggered down the hallway and scanned the dining room, her dark eyes searching each booth, each of the few faces. She wasn't sure what she'd do if he were there, but visions of grabbing a steak knife and giving the bastard an eye-for-an-eye treatment drowned out rational thought.

Delilah had never killed anyone, but she figured if she were to add murder to her list of offenses, starting with Ted wouldn't be the worst way to do it.

The booths were empty, though she could see the un-cleared remains of a meal in a couple of them. The front door was swinging shut, as though someone had just walked out. Crazily, Delilah envisioned it was Ted, that he was just outside, and the thought froze her solid for a second.

Jake came up beside her and Delilah shook her head.

"Hey, Dee!" Bridget's bubbly voice called out, but Jake raised his hand to get the waitress's attention and shook his head emphatically no. Bridget's pink mouth made a little oh, but she turned back to the bartender, a thin young man Delilah didn't recognize and the two of them exchanged a look.

Not her problem. She doubted Ted would have come in and then left, but what the hell did she know. Delilah shook herself a little, thawing out from her fit of fear as Jake touched her shoulder gently, briefly.

They went back to Jake's office and Delilah leaned against one wall. The chair looked inviting, but she feared to sit. Movement at all seemed to exacerbate her injury and her belly was getting angrier by the minute as the drugs wore off and the throbbing ache won back more ground.

Jake sank back into his chair and ran his hands through his thick curls. Delilah jammed her hands back into her pockets, remembering the slightly coarse feel of his hair, the brush of his full lips over her forehead, the caress of his tongue against her ear lobe.

Then he looked her over, truly looked, for the first time since he'd come into the office and found her there.

"Jesus, Lil. You look like hell," he said, his tone softening. A little worried crease formed between his eyebrows.

She could only imagine. "Hell, huh? I've upgraded from feeling like shit then."

She got a quick twitch of his lips, almost a smile, for that.

"Tell me how this happened."

Delilah looked away from him. She'd come all this way, if he was going to let her help him, save him, she knew she'd have to give him a little more.

"You remember Looney Ray?"

Jake nodded, the line between his eyebrows growing deeper as he tilted his head.

"He kept diamonds in his damn ice tray, did you know that?" Delilah twisted her fingers together inside the fabric of her sweatshirt and went on without waiting for an answer from Jake. "Ever since I found that out, well, I've had this thing about freezers. Like a superstition."

Jake snorted and Delilah looked up. Skepticism, pity, and something she couldn't read shifted across his face. For the first time, Delilah saw a gulf between them, a gap in who they were, in their lives. She'd felt the cracks years ago, but hadn't seen the chasm for what it was. She felt her heartbeat slow and a tiny fire deep inside of her flickered, not quite out, but starved for fuel, guttering.

It was simple. Delilah was a pro, a heister, a career sort. Jake, well, he wasn't. He'd really gone straight. Maybe just been that way the whole time. She pressed down on those thoughts and swallowed hard, continuing her explanation. If Jake noticed her sudden pause, he said nothing.

"Basically, I opened the wrong freezer. Ted's freezer. It had a girl's head in it. This Ted guy showed up and stabbed me. Then he chased me around a couple of states and now he's coming after Esther." *And you*, she thought, but stopped the words.

"Fucking-A." He looked like he didn't want to believe her but he knew her well enough not to ask what she'd been doing in this guy's house in the first place. There was that, at least.

"He's evil, Jake." She bit her lip. "Get protection, that's a good idea. You have a gun?"

"Yeah," he said and swiveled in the chair, opening one of the filing cabinet drawers. Jake pulled out his father's .45 Colt revolver. It looked clean enough, the ivory grip polished, the barrel and cylinder gleaming.

"That thing loaded?" she asked.

Jake flipped open the cylinder. "Looks like it. I clean it every few months."

"Few months? When was the last time it was fired?"

He snapped the cylinder back in place and laid the gun in the drawer. His dark eyes met Delilah's own and the lines around them crinkled as he half smiled. "Remember when we stole that Winnebago and went down to Crater Lake?"

She smiled back, the memory bittersweet. "I shot a deer from the car."

"A four-point buck. Almost broke your nose with the recoil, too."

She chuckled and that little movement of her stomach muscles brought a wave of pain up from her gut. It was definitely getting worse.

Jake half-rose from his chair, his arms coming up, and a strange expression on his face. But whatever he'd been about to do, about to say, died before manifesting and he fell back.

"I've got a gun. I'll call up Moose and see if he's free to tag around with Nancy and Esther. School just started, so she'll be watched during the day by a lot of people." He glanced at the clock on his computer. "Nancy should be out picking her up soon, in fact."

Delilah nodded. It was something. Not enough, not against Ted, but maybe it would be. And this was a hell of a lot better than cops or doing squat. But until he implemented the private security measures, they'd be vulnerable. And Jake wasn't up to real vigilance, it wasn't in his nature.

"You have to fix that back door, Jake," she said. "And if your home security is as crap as this bar's, he could be sitting in your living room right now and you'd never know." Bile burned her throat as an image of Mr. Palmer's mutilated corpse took over her brain.

"We've got an alarm on the house, with a service. I spent enough time with you to know that's a good investment." He didn't smile, letting the words carry their full sting.

She shrugged and let it go. "Do you set it?"

"Yes," he said sharply, then, with a grimace added, "Well, Nancy does."

"When she's in the house?"

Jake's look told her the answer to that, and it wasn't a good one.

"Riiight." Delilah pushed herself away from the wall and crossed the short distance to the desk. She leaned down, getting in closer to Jake even though it hurt in more ways than just physical.

He smelled a little like his bar, and underneath that of Old Spice deodorant and a fresh bread sort of scent that identified him as Jake. As her Jake.

"Let me tail them," she said, pressing her fingers to his lips to stop the automatic protest. "Just until Moose can. You'll be working here until closing, won't you? You're just like the old man, I bet."

Jake wrapped a hand around her wrist, pushing her back. His fingers were warm, strong. "Nancy will throw a shit fit, Lil."

She swallowed a stupid, catty response about how she really didn't care and shook her head. "No, she won't. Because she'll never even see me. I promise. You know how good I am." She smiled with the last part, but doubted it reached her eyes.

He pushed the chair away and stood up. "Yeah. I know." Pacing to the kitchen door and then back to the desk, Jake rubbed his hands over his face. "You just have to be you, don't you?" he muttered. She guessed it was more for his benefit than hers and stayed quiet.

Another round of pacing and he stopped, looking up at her, his lips pressed into a pale line on his dark face. "Nancy sees nothing, you don't talk to her, you don't talk to Esther. Got it? Just follow. And you fucking call 911 if you see this guy and they are in any danger."

She raised her hands in a mocking gesture of surrender, regretting it even as the movement brought on more dizziness. "Okay, okay. Geez."

"I'll give you directions." Jake flopped back into the chair and grabbed a pen. She waited as he wrote them out. "Just for today, you'd better be gone by tomorrow," he said, handing them over. "And seriously, Nancy can't know about this."

If I had a nickel for every time I'd heard those words from him, I could go to the movies. She held her peace, barely.

"She won't know, I swear. I'll keep an eye out, Jake. They'll be safe." She tucked the scrap of paper into a pocket.

"I mean it, Lil." His eyes glinted, hard and flat. "Gone by tomorrow."

"I swear," she repeated. *Like hell. Not until you're safe and this is ended.*

Deep inside, in the soft secret place in her heart, the tiny flame guttered. All the things she'd just promised, well, only about half were lies.

"The road to hell, and all that clichéd jazz," she said softly as she slipped out the back door and headed toward her car.

Thirty-six

Ted sat in his rental car outside the crappy little bar, hands gripping the steering wheel tight enough that his joints started to hurt. He burned to take out a knife from his kit and go back in. He'd stab the fat cow first, just beneath her jiggly chins. The anorexic freak behind the bar wouldn't give him trouble. Ted knew those types, sissy little emo boys barely out of college with liberal, pacifist sissy ideas. The kid would probably faint at the sight of all that beautiful blood spurting from the waitress.

Then he'd go take care of anyone in the kitchens, efficiently and quickly. They were collateral, obstacles in his way.

Jake would be the prize, and Ted very much ached to collect on what he felt the man owed him. He'd cripple him, just enough to make death take a while. And that scrawny, beta-male little asshole would learn exactly why it was happening to him.

Forcing himself to release his grip on the wheel, Ted rubbed his hands over the fake leather and took deep, calming breaths. Jake was just bait, a toy, a means to a glorious pay back. He knew he'd better keep this in mind, or he risked letting Delilah, lovely scared Delilah, slip away for good.

And the bitch couldn't win.

He decided he'd better leave; head back to the hotel and calm himself down, think out the next steps and make sure he was well-rested for the evening. Then he could return to the bar and follow Jake to get to the whole family. He wanted all of them.

They were the bait.

"Eyes on the prize," he said into the stillness of the car.

And then his prize appeared, slipping out of the bar through the back door.

Stillness. Perfect calm took over, Ted's focus coalescing on the hunched figure crossing the back lot and moving toward the street. She glanced around, but her dark eyes, made more vulnerable and hollow-looking by the exhausted puffiness and dark tint beneath them, stared right past him, not even looking into the car.

He knew he could grab her right now. She hardly looked in a state to fight back, though Ted remembered her attempt in his house with a little smile. She'd try, oh yes, his Delilah would certainly try.

But he had nowhere to take her, no plan. He didn't want to just kill her; that would be far too easy. She needed to suffer, to look into his face and give up all control, give up all will to live as she finally saw the reality that Ted held her entire life in his hands. That he had all the power.

She would whimper and beg before he was done and he would erase all thoughts of the black guy she clearly still cared for. Her final thoughts would be only of Ted.

He wondered how she'd gotten into the bar. She must have come in just after he left, and exited out the back for some reason. Ted didn't fancy the thought that she'd been in there the whole time, perhaps tucked away in the kitchen, or in the room with the "Bossman" sign on it. So close, perhaps even in the same room as that asshole, Jake.

Ted growled, surprising himself with the sound. Delilah turned down the sidewalk, moving almost out of sight, and then crossed the street and got into a station wagon.

She wasn't going to escape him this time. As much as he wanted Jake, he could live with mopping up that particular insult later, after he'd enjoyed the main course.

Ted turned on his car, and prepared to follow the prize.

Thirty-seven

The school was a private one apparently, just south of Portland. Given what she knew of Jake's experiences in the public school system, Delilah didn't really blame him for wasting money on a place like this.

By the time she arrived and turned onto the tree-lined road, the big U-shaped pick-up lane in front of the school was half-clogged with parents collecting their offspring. Jake had written *red Civic* on the directions, so Delilah pulled over, parking in a bike lane just outside the turn-around.

She fumbled out her bottle of painkillers. Six left. Damn. Carefully she dumped one into her hand and broke it in half, dry swallowing the chalky pill. If it just took the edge off the gnawing pain, she could deal with the leftovers. She hoped.

For a moment as she scanned the parked and waiting cars with their bright swarm of children and parents, Delilah panicked. She could check the house after this, of course. She knew the address and more or less where it was. But if Ted was already in town, what if he'd grabbed Nancy and Esther already?

Then she caught sight of a red Honda Civic with a brunette leaning against it and relaxed a little. Jake's wife. The thought stung, but less than it might have before the conversation in the bar. After a moment the woman straightened up and a little girl, her dark skin standing out from the other children, walked down the shallow school steps and into Nancy's arms.

Esther.

Delilah sat very still, trying to feel something, anything like what she thought she should. But it wasn't there. There was no instant recognition, no sudden motherly feelings or really anything at all except a little curiosity and slight disappointment.

The little girl wrapped her arms around Nancy's leg in a quick hug and then started pulling off her backpack as Nancy opened the passenger door for her. Esther seemed smaller than a lot of the other children currently flowing in a steady stream from the school. Delilah wondered if that was because of her illness. She'd never asked Jake about the specifics.

Delilah sighed and slowly got out of the car. Jake didn't want Nancy to know anything, but that was stupid of him, selfish. She guessed that Jake's wife would want to know, would probably take this more seriously than he had. Nancy had a typical person's fear about criminals, lumping the world into categories of those who obeyed arbitrary rules, and those who wanted to rape and pillage all they surveyed.

Jake was a terrible liar, but the champion of lies by omission. Delilah hadn't really seen it in action until their affair. She doubted that Nancy would ever have heard about it if Delilah hadn't gotten pregnant, if Jake hadn't felt a duty to raise the baby. She hadn't cared back then what Nancy knew or didn't know. Jake had been halfway hers again, if only for a short time.

But it mattered now. Jake's life was on the line. This mysterious child that had ripped her way out of Delilah's body was in danger. She might not feel motherly, but bile burned her throat at the thought of a man like Ted putting his hands on that cute little girl currently setting a My Little Pony backpack into the car.

And Esther, if Delilah wanted to face the meat of it all, was her last excuse, her last reason to even stay connected to Jake. She was the link, the chain tying them together across the chasm.

Nancy didn't see Delilah until she was right next to the car. Then her hazel eyes widened and her already pale face blanched, her body tensing and flinching away.

"I'm calling the police," Nancy said, pushing Esther, who looked questioningly up at her, into the car. "Buckle your seatbelt, honey." Nancy fumbled in her purse, coming up with keys and then a cell phone.

"Wait, Jesus," Delilah said, halting a few feet away. "Just hear me out, please."

Tiny hairs rose on the back of her neck and movement in her periphery caught Delilah's attention as Nancy hesitated, watching her. Delilah looked to the side. Just another car coming around the turn-about.

Then she looked more closely and her legs went numb. Driving the car, staring right at her, was crazy Teddy.

Thirty-eight

Ted followed Delilah from the bar, keeping a couple car lengths behind her station wagon. She left the city, getting onto a freeway and driving south. He almost lost her at a four-way stop, but caught back up as she pulled over and parked along the side of the road just at the entrance to what looked like a school.

He had no choice but to drive ahead and then turn around. As he drove by a second time, he saw her get out of the car and looked where she was heading.

A brunette in a light blue long-sleeved shirt and white capri pants, helped a young black girl into a red car. The little girl in the pictures, the woman the same as well, though prettier in pictures than in person, at least from a distance. She looked more rumpled, less fresh, and plumper, gone soft around the edges.

"Nancy," Ted said, rolling the name in his mouth. "Esther." He smiled. They were right here, all together, just as he'd envisioned. His threat in Atlanta had done its work, baited the trap nicely for unsuspecting little Delilah.

He burned for a closer look and decided that driving past wouldn't hurt anything. There were enough cars coming and going from the busy pick-up circle that he didn't fear detection too much. And he needed to find a good place to follow them from.

A mother holding a baby on her hip with a little boy wearing a Spider-Man backpack got in his way as he approached Delilah, forcing him to slow more than he liked. He stayed calm, as calm as he could anyway given that the woman who'd escaped him, who probably thought she could still escape him, was mere yards away now.

Then her head turned, as though she were a mouse sensing the shadow of the descending hawk. Her thin face was pale with exhaustion and her eyes were dark hollows of pain. So frail, so vulnerable.

Then a snap of recognition in those agonized eyes and she raised her hands a little as though to physically fend him off as fear drained the rest of the color from her cheeks.

For a moment they just stared at each other, then Ted was past. He slowed and looked behind him. Delilah had grabbed the brunette, shoving her into the car. Then, with surprising energy and agility, his prey slid over the hood of the Civic and yanked open the driver's door.

Face twisting with anger at her audacity in trying to evade him once again, Ted yanked the wheel around and threw the car into reverse, ramming backward as the full force of his barely contained rage thrummed through his blood. The bitch wasn't getting away. Not this time.

Thirty-nine

Delilah peeled out with the Civic, ignoring the intense pain in her belly and Nancy's incoherent shrieking.

"Fuck, shut up," Delilah said through gritted teeth as Esther started crying and saying "Mommy, mommy" over and over.

"Stop the car," Nancy said, reaching for the steering wheel. Then her eyes widened and she let go as Ted's car slammed into reverse and nearly hit them. "What the-?"

"That guy, he wants to kill Esther." Delilah spit the words out, concentrating on not running over parents and small children as she gunned past Teddy and out of the turn-about.

"What do you—" Nancy started, but Delilah cut her off.

"Later, Nance. Gotta lose him." She pulled a hard left, narrowly missing a car coming the other way.

Ted kept up, careening out onto the road behind her and then gaining ground.

Delilah floored the gas and hissed as the slow automatic transmission shifted gears with a whining protest. *Why the fuck did Nancy have to drive this stupid econo-car?* The engine in this thing was about as powerful as a lawnmower and about as responsive. Not Delilah's idea of a get-away car. She needed at least six cylinders for this shit.

But the little car handled well enough. Time to improvise.

Nancy had her cell phone out again and was trying to dial a number while simultaneously calming Esther and putting on her seatbelt. Delilah spared a moment to slap the phone out of the frazzled woman's hand.

"Don't," she said and whatever was on her face or in her tone stopped Nancy from reaching down for the phone.

Delilah knew the area, knew the roads. This was her home, her turf. She had that advantage on crazy Ted. The Civic couldn't beat Ted's vehicle in an all out race, but between her driving skills and knowledge of the roads, Delilah bet she could escape him.

She was willing to bet their lives on it.

A wild, manic glee seared through her as adrenaline wiped away the pain and fatigue. Ted crowded close, perhaps intending to try to nudge her car off the road. His mouth was pressed in a tight smile, his body leaning forward over the wheel, intent.

Delilah laughed, the sound mostly a hiccup and burble in her throat. She pulled a hard right, running a blinking red light and gunned the car forward again, eyes ahead, searching for the next turn she'd want to take.

"Not gonna happen, asshole," she muttered as he made the turn and tried to catch up again.

"Who is that, Dee?" Nancy craned her head, looking behind them.

Delilah risked a moment to adjust the side mirror and slide the seat up a little. Fortunately she and Nancy were about the same height and she only had to tip her head a bit to see out the rear-view mirror.

"A murdering bastard. Jake and I will explain later." Delilah knew she was being obtuse and bitter, but she wanted Nancy to be afraid, and maybe a little mad at Jake.

And right now, she really didn't give a damn about family politics or what the hell Jake would think.

Another turn, but again Ted kept up. Delilah wove around slower cars, trying to put distance and obstacles between herself and Ted. She had to slam on the brakes as she ran a red light to avoid a truck. Damn. Her timing was off a little. Maybe from injury, maybe exhaustion, maybe the painkillers. *Take your pick.*

"He's still behind us, do something." Nancy's shrill voice grated, rising in pitch as she twisted around, watching the silver car with its maniac driver catch back up to them as Delilah was forced by the flow of traffic to take another quick right.

"No shit." Nancy was right. This wasn't going to work. In a better car, in a different area, maybe. If she was healthy and rested, maybe. But ifs and wishes wouldn't sell horseshoes, as Colin had told her often enough.

"Everyone buckled in?" Delilah asked, a dangerous plan forming in her mind. She'd pulled off a move like it before, twice, and tried it another time that hadn't ended well at all.

"Yes, what are you doing?"

Delilah spared a glance at Nancy. Her round face was pale and sweaty, her eyes full of fear and her mouth pressed into a quivering line. She didn't look much like the man-stealing bitch Delilah preferred to consider her. She just looked kind of vulnerable, and scared as shit.

"Hopefully? Saving us." Delilah tried a quick, reassuring smile. Nancy's expression didn't change, so she was pretty sure that had failed.

Ted gained ground and Delilah slowed just a little. There was an intersection ahead and she had to time this just right.

Ignoring the bright stab of pain, she dragged her seatbelt across her body and fumbled the tongue into the catch.

"Hang on," she said, as much to herself as to the now-quiet child and terrified Nancy.

The roads were clear, only one car slowly turning left at the four-way stop ahead. Just before the intersection, as Ted sped toward them, she slammed the brakes while jerking the car hard to the right.

He'd almost reached her bumper at that point and had no choice as his speed carried his vehicle past her.

Whipping the car back to the left, Delilah punched the gas, flooring it again. The nose of the Civic hit Ted's car along the passenger side. They were thrown against their seatbelts and Delilah heard, in an internal, sickening way, something tear in her belly. Liquid heat spilled across her stomach. Metal squealed, a headlight shattered, and the cars crunched together for an interminable moment.

She hit the brake again, letting Ted's car spin away, out of control, across the intersection. There was no time to see if he'd crash or escape the spin. Delilah yanked the Civic left. The car responded with a whine and the smell of burning rubber filtered in through the air vents. She guessed something was scraping against the left front tire, but the car would be okay. For now.

She took a quick right, looping back almost toward the school and headed for the I-5 onramp.

"I don't see him," Nancy said, voice less shrieky now, but still breathless. "Essy, are you okay?"

Esther must have nodded, because Delilah heard no response but Nancy reached a reassuring hand back and relaxed a fraction.

Delilah looked in the rear-view and sagged in relief. The road behind was clear of any sign of Ted.

Forty

Ted's rental car spun fast and he panicked for a moment as his head hit the driver's side window, forgetting to twist the wheel in the direction of the spin. He jammed on the brakes, and the car finally stopped after spinning across the entire intersection and bumping up against the curb.

His head throbbed and a wet trickle of blood started to worm its way through his hair. Frantic, Ted looked around, the rage ants in his blood beating a murderous tattoo in time with the pulsing of his heart.

No Delilah. The little red car was gone, and he had no idea which way she'd taken.

"Fuck," he said, then repeated it several more times as he slammed his hands down on the steering wheel, over and over.

A car pulled over and a young couple climbed out, the woman getting on her cell phone, the man coming toward Ted's side of the car.

His mind a blank, angry slate, Ted pulled out the murder kit and grabbed the hunting knife out of it. He was out of his car and on top of the blonde young man before the kid could do or say more than "Are you okay?"

Another car had pulled up to the intersection, so Ted made it quick. He grabbed the blonde's hair and whipped him around, stepping in close as he stabbed the knife into his throat. The hot mist of blood barely touched Ted as he dropped the gurgling soon-to-be corpse and charged the shocked woman.

She wasn't Delilah. Too tall, too much breast. But she had dark hair. And she was here, not running like a scared little bitch. She'd do, for now.

There was no time to savor anything, to even smell her hair or get a good look at her face, though her eyes were greenish and her wet mouth wide open in a scream his knife cut short.

Someone else was yelling as the woman fell to her knees, her manicured hands coming up to try to stop the blood flowing from her belly. Ted had jammed the knife in quickly, once, twice. This stupid bitch wouldn't survive that. Not like Delilah had.

His world narrowed to the sound of screaming, the smell of blood and car exhaust, the horrible death rattle of the woman's punctured lungs as she threw up blood onto the pavement, narrowly missing his shoes.

But he had to go, get out of here. The last shreds of sense, of poor old Ted faking that he was one of the sheep, cried out to him to get away.

He tossed the knife into the car and pulled away from the curb. He didn't know where he was going, just away, far away, before the police arrived.

Deep breaths brought his heart rate back down. He'd just killed two people. In broad daylight and no one had even tried to stop him. Ted licked his lips, arousal replacing the anger.

He turned onto a random street, then turned again, checking behind him for pursuit. Nothing so far. His right cuff was wet with blood, fingers slippery with it as well, and his head ached from his own injury.

When he was certain he'd driven far enough away, Ted pulled into a little parking lot behind a convenience store. There was a towel in his hunting kit and he used it and some water from a bottle he'd taken out of the hotel mini-fridge to clean himself off.

Then he unzipped his pants and stroked himself. The power of his actions consumed him. He'd lost Delilah, but he could find her again. He'd always find her again. So much death, so much fear.

That woman in the intersection, she'd been asking for it. She'd seen him stab her boyfriend, yet had stood there, a sacrificial lamb, an offering, no, an apology, from the universe for letting Delilah escape him a third time. Her fear was his balm, soothing him.

He sought release, leaning back into the seat as the dead woman's face transformed into the fat waitress with the wet pink mouth in the bar, and then into the face of the hotel clerk with her thick, hard nipples. And finally, at the last moment before all thought dissipated into glorious sensation, there was Delilah with her vulnerable eyes and warm, soapy scent.

Ted cleaned himself up again and got out of the car. His sleeve wasn't too bad, he folded the cuffs in half and the blood hardly showed against the dark material. He needed directions back to downtown and the bar.

Jake would run, especially after this fiasco. He'd take his little family and tuck his tail between his beta-male legs and trust in the police to do something about Ted. That's what insufficient males did, let other people protect them, do their dirty work.

"News for you," Ted muttered to the phantom Jake in his mind as he walked around the building, "The law can't touch me." Almost two decades and the law? They didn't even know Ted existed, though he supposed that as soon as Emily got home later tonight all this would change.

But it would be far too late and they'd be searching for a man who didn't exist anymore.

He'd keep an eye on the bar, and if he couldn't follow Jake away from it, that was not really a problem, just a minor setback. Tonight, after the place closed, he'd break in. There had to be personal papers, something with Jake's information on it. Ted would find him, and he knew now, without any doubt, that, as long as they were under threat, wherever Jake and the little girl went, Delilah would follow.

Plan reconstructed, Ted ran a hand through his hair, checking on the small cut. It had stopped bleeding and his fingers came away dry. He would salvage today, and every transgression Delilah committed would be filed away. Ted knew he'd collect on her debt, very soon.

Forty-one

Delilah drove north, almost on autopilot to the bar. Her vision kept blurring, focusing in and out as though her eyes were a broken camera lens. She ignored Nancy until the other woman leaned down and retrieved the cell phone from the floor mat.

"What are you doing?" Delilah said, surprised at the weakness of her own voice. She reached with one hand to try to slap the cell away again, but Nancy pulled it in against her body.

The car swerved partially into the middle lane and Delilah switched her ragged concentration back to the road.

"Calling Jake," Nancy said, doing something with the phone in Delilah's periphery. "Take us to the bar, now."

"Already going there."

"Good." And then, as the phone apparently connected her call, "Jake?" Nancy swallowed and glanced at Delilah before resuming her one-sided conversation. "We almost, I mean,

259

someone just tried to run us down in his damn car. No, she's okay, we're fine. Why didn't you tell me *she* was in town? No, don't even start, someone just tried to... I don't want, oh. Okay. Yes, she is. Yes. I understand. We're coming right now. Passing Tigard. Yeah. In a few. Love you." She hung up and let the phone drop into her lap.

From the back seat Esther finally found coherent words. "Are we going to see Daddy?"

"Uh-huh, Essy. This lady is going to drive us."

"Why'd we hit that car, mommy? And why are you crying?"

"I'll tell you later, before bed, okay? Why don't we practice your Spanish alphabet?" Nancy glanced again at Delilah and then twisted around and started prompting Esther. The exercise seemed to calm them both and Nancy made no move to call the police or hinder Delilah's driving.

Delilah drove in a haze, trying to ignore the spreading wetness in the bandaging on her stomach. She was pretty sure she'd torn her stitches, but she didn't dare stop the car and ask Nancy to drive. That woman would leave her behind and bleeding in the street in a damn heartbeat.

She risked a longer look in the rear-view mirror, forcing herself to sit upright so she could catch a glimpse of her daughter. Esther looked healthy enough, though thin and a bit frail with her legs tucked up against her chest. The little girl had Jake's eyes, more brandy brown and rich than flat black like her own. But she had Delilah's straight, narrow nose and the same high cheekbones. Drying tears had left pale streaks on Esther's face, like salt sprinkled on fresh churned earth.

She's kind of beautiful. And so damn small.

Delilah shivered and then blinked rapidly to discourage her own tears. Anger and fear washed through her, shoving back the pain. That bastard had tried to kill this tiny, sick girl, this strange hybrid between Delilah and Jake that had become her own miniature being.

She focused on the road, sustained by visions of Jake and her getting more guns and hunting Ted down, plotting his horrible and dire murder. Jake would take her seriously now. Despite his sheep-wife's desires, Jake wasn't totally a straight little plebian man. He'd see the logic in protecting his family the professional way.

Ted was a problem, and together, she and Jake could fix it.

Forty-two

Jake met them at the back door as she pulled the car around to the back of No Man's Land. Delilah barely mustered the strength to push herself out of the car and walk the short distance across to him.

Esther ran right into Jake's arms and he held her tight, glaring at Delilah. He kissed Nancy on the cheek and ushered them all inside.

Delilah read the tension in his body, the knives in his eyes. He seemed mad at her, but that wasn't practical or useful right now. It was Teddy who was the problem. Delilah's quick actions and driving had just saved everyone's lives.

Bridget was in Jake's office and offered them all a nervous smile as she held a hand out to Esther.

"Hey, Essy, want to go see Amos and get a soda?" Bridget said.

Esther looked at her daddy and, as he nodded, grabbed Bridget's fingers and followed the cheery waitress out through the kitchen door.

For a long moment Nancy and Jake just held each other and, if she hadn't been in so much damn pain already and using all her concentration to stay upright, Delilah would've felt even worse. She stood alone, one hand against the back of the second chair, feeling small and unwanted.

"We have to do something about Ted," she said when it seemed like the others weren't going to break apart anytime soon.

"Oh, you're going to," Jake said, glaring at her again over Nancy's head. His eyes narrowed and the venom in them stabbed into Delilah as sharp as any knife.

She peeled her hand away from her sweatshirt and held it up as though to ward him off. It was damp and pink with blood.

"I will." She wanted to tell him her plan, though the details formed on the drive eluded her as she stood before Jake. "We'll talk about this, but maybe Nancy should go join Esther and Bridget. You know, in case. You can explain everything to her later," she said to Jake.

"No, he won't." Nancy pulled away and turned on Delilah. "You're going to explain. You're going to tell them everything, every damn thing. None of your shit this time. You brought this on us."

Them? "Who is them?" she said slowly, biting off each word.

"Nancy!" Jake made a cut-it-out gesture with his hand and Nancy flushed, looking down.

No. Nononono. "You called the cops?" she said it like a question, but Delilah knew the answer even as the words came out.

Jake's expression darkened even further. "Yeah. I did. They'll be here any minute now. And you're going to explain it all to them. All of it. You brought this shit on us."

He'd never yelled at her before, not like this. Not even when they broke up or when she threatened to abort his baby if he didn't leave his then-fiancé.

Walls. Closing in. No way out. "No, Jake, no. I can't go to jail. You know that. You fucking know." She couldn't breathe, couldn't think.

"I. Don't. Care. You're going to tell them every damn thing and protect our daughter. Am I clear?" His tone had quieted, but every word stayed sharp and ugly, his full lips peeled back in a horrible snarl.

The cops. He'd called the fucking cops. He was turning her in. No one did that unless they were serious enemies. It was the lowest of the low sort of play, a fucking bottom-feeding move.

Total betrayal. The guttering flame of whatever they'd shared, those seemingly sunlit and faraway days, flickered and went out.

She turned and reached for the door.

"No you don't, no more running," Jake said, lunging for her.

Her fist met his side and then her knee came up and thrust into his groin. For a moment they were both doubled over in pain, but Delilah recovered quicker and threw the door open.

"Hey!" called a man's voice.

Two uniformed officers were making their way through the bar. Delilah didn't hesitate and threw her weight into the push bar on the back door, fleeing into the parking lot.

She half-staggered, half-ran to the sidewalk, expecting pursuit at any moment. No time. She needed wheels but couldn't remember what she'd done with Nancy's keys.

An older man in a suit jacket walked down his front steps from the house almost directly across the side street, talking on a cell phone. He had keys in his hand and the car parked on the street in front of him beeped, parking lights blinking.

Delilah dashed across the street, desperately sucking in air to keep herself conscious as agony tore through her body and her vision swam with the now familiar red dots. The man was nearly to the driver's door when she caught up to him.

Her palm smashed upward into his nose, knocking him back as the phone went flying out of his hand. She snatched his keys with her other hand and was half-inside the car before he had even regained his feet. Blood ran down over his mouth as he yelled something at her, but she slammed the door shut and started the car.

She peeled away as the two cops ran out into the street behind her. A quick right, then a left, and she was out of there, heading toward the major roads.

For a while, even after she made it onto highway 26 and out near Gresham, she drove with her eye mostly on the rearview mirrors, half-expecting blue and red lights and the terrible scream of the sirens. She drove recklessly, weaving through the double lanes, doing just enough to not crash.

At first her only thought had been to get away. She had nowhere to go, no one to turn to. Jake turned her in. He was probably spilling all her secrets now. Bastard. Traitor.

She wished she'd listened. Wish she'd realized sooner that he wasn't really a part of her world. Delilah had been good to him, helped him with the baby she hadn't even wanted, sent so much money over the years, especially after Esther got sick. And she'd trusted him. Loved him. Believed him when he swore the same.

Fuck. She'd fooled herself, thinking that the daughter she'd given him would still tie them together, that if he loved Esther, it would mean he still loved a part of Delilah, too. Bitterness choked her but she refocused on the road in time to swerve around a minivan. Jake didn't trust or love her, didn't even want to give her a chance to help them, to protect them.

Tears running freely down her face now, Delilah merged into an exit lane before she realized exactly where she was going.

Colin. His was the only place left *to* go. Though it had been over five years since she'd driven down this road, taken the familiar turn at the dead oak tree, Delilah still auto-piloted right onto the gravel driveway.

The trailer, what Colin had always referred to as a "manufactured home", looked exactly the same, it's faded yellow paint almost cheery in the sudden late afternoon sunlight. Colin's rebuilt cherry red Shelby was parked beneath the carport.

Delilah didn't remember even stopping the car, or really getting out of it. She put one foot in front of the other, forcing herself to stay upright, mumbling it was only a few more steps.

Then her fingers found the doorbell and it seemed like Colin appeared instantaneously, his bright blue eyes wide.

"Delilah?" he said in a mix of shock and concern. "Is that blood?"

It was the concern that felled her. She gave in to the agony, to the exhaustion. Her head pounded, an angry buzzing ringing around inside her skull and a terrible sickly sweet smell invaded her nostrils, as though she'd pushed her head down over a bowl of rotting fruit swarming with flies.

"Surprise," she managed to say before she stumbled across the last two steps between them and collapsed.

Forty-three

Delilah's eyes fluttered open and for a moment she couldn't place where or when she was. She lay on a soft bed in a room with rose-colored walls and a window hung with navy blue curtains. "First Blush", she remembered. That was the paint color. She'd picked it out herself and helped Colin put it up. There was still a large stain on the subflooring beneath the royal blue carpet.

Colin. She turned her head and saw him sitting beside her, watching the few beams of sunlight dancing through the curtains. He wore a flannel shirt and had a bit more belly than she'd remembered, but his coppery hair was still thick and in its usual pony tail. Delilah struggled to sit up but her body refused to respond to her commands. Her leaden limbs felt as removed from her control as the pain in her belly.

"Shh, baby girl," Colin said, getting up from the big arm chair. "Lay back."

Baby girl. Her dry lips cracked in a slight smile. He couldn't be that mad at her, not if he'd kept her room exactly the same, not if he still used the little joking name between them.

Baby girl was what her mother had written on the birth certificate, refusing to even give the newborn Delilah a name.

"Jake," she said, her voice sounding thin and far away, as though someone else were speaking. "The cops. That car, it's hot."

He picked up a glass that had a straw sticking in it and gently guided it to her lips. She sipped. It was tea, alfalfa, clover, and mint mixed with milk. Colin had always been a great believer in tea.

"I guessed about the car. It's in the pole barn, under a tarp. What's this about cops?" Colin helped her take another sip.

She tried again, struggling for coherency. "Jake, he called the cops on me. He might tell them about you, about here. Not safe."

Colin laughed, his deep blue eyes disappearing for a moment into the wrinkles and crow's feet around them. "Only way any piggies are getting into my home is by stepping over my corpse." Sobering up, he added, "what the hell happened to you, baby girl?"

She didn't know why she'd come here, but she hadn't expected this. Caring. Concern. Not anger or indifference. No judgments.

"Oh god, Colin," she said, squeezing her eyes shut in a vain attempt to stop the sudden tears. "I'm so sorry." She'd said such horrible things to him before she left, blamed him so much for Bennie's incarceration, blamed him for Jake choosing Nancy even. Called him some pretty awful things, things worse than "fag".

He made a brushing-off motion, whisking imaginary dust from his shoulder. "I know. I'm sorry, too. Shouldn't have taken you five years. But nice of you to come by for tea." He winked at her.

She tried to laugh and it brought on the deep ache again, forcing her to face the reality of why she'd ended up in this bed. "Am I dying? The doctor said I might."

"What asshole doc said that? You pulled out a stitch and might have some infection. I cleaned you up. With some rest and good care, you'll come through."

She nodded. Rest sounded really good. She took another sip of tea.

But Ted was still out there and now she had no way to help Jake. She hoped he'd run away, but wouldn't bet on it. Maybe at least now Jake would hire some big men with guns. But no one knew what Ted looked like. Delilah doubted Nancy had gotten much of a look.

"I fucked it all up, I screwed up so bad," she said, tears irritating her eyes before sliding down and dripping into her ears.

Colin sat on the bed and gripped her cold hands between his big, calloused palms. He smelled of pipe tobacco underlain with the chemicals he used to develop photos.

She told him the story in fits and starts, leaving out almost nothing. He sat quietly and listened, letting her work it out of her system. He shook his head when she finally got to the part about Jake calling the cops on her, clear dislike on his face.

"This guy," she said after she'd finished the horrible saga. "You remember Mirikov?"

"Kimbo's enforcer? Always sat in the back room cleaning guns?"

"Yeah. I thought he was scary, those eyes so cold and flat, looking at everybody like they were piles of meat waiting for slaughter." Delilah swallowed as her body started to shake. "This Ted, he's worse. Worse. I looked into him today, at the school. I saw evil, like demons in hell evil."

"Hey, hey, shhh," Colin said, gripping her hands again as the shudders wracked her body.

"No! You don't understand. I couldn't do anything. I kicked him, hit him, clawed his fucking face but nothing connected, not really." Delilah pushed away the memory. "I didn't even see him grab the knife, never saw it." She pulled her hand free from Colin's and scrubbed at her eyes. "He's going to kill them and I can't do anything."

"But you have," he said, stroking a stray lock of hair off her feverish forehead. "You escaped him, baby girl. You stopped him again at the school today. You're alive and he has no idea where you are. As stupid as Boss's boy can be sometimes, Jake'll take care of his family. You're winning."

She sniffed and took a gulping breath, trying to see it the way Colin described. "What time is it?"

"Does it matter? You ain't going anywhere." Colin picked up a spoon from the nightstand and poured a measure of dark pink liquid from a plastic medicine bottle.

"What's that?" she asked as he helped her tip her head up.

"Liquid codeine. Drink up."

She did, grimacing at the medicinal taste. Even after another couple sips of tea the sharp aftertaste stuck around.

"I'm sorry," she said again.

"It's okay." He smiled at her. "I blamed myself, too. About Bennie I mean. I should have gone back for him once the others split and the job went bad. But we all live with mistakes, baby girl. We do what we have to and we survive."

Her body had stopped shaking, the pain slipping away again and her thoughts eluded her as a gentle fog rolled into her mind.

"I'm sorry," she mumbled. She had no right to expect this warmth, this welcome from him. But it was here, Colin was here, a rock she could cling to as the world fell apart.

"Sleep," he said, pulling the comforter up over her arms.

She let go of her fears, of the pain, and slept.

Forty-four

Sam stopped in Portland only long enough to check into the cheap hotel he'd booked online. Then he turned his rental car toward Salem. He'd checked his messages after the plane landed. The interview with Bennie Hill was approved. Mr. Hill had agreed to see him for preliminary questioning without the presence of an attorney.

There'd been a "What the hell are you up to?" message from Ronnie, but she'd smoothed things with the warden as promised.

The prison loomed in the dark, bright floodlights lending an eerie glow that identified the structure long before Sam pulled up to the main gate. He showed his badge and ID and was escorted into the visitor's center.

They made him leave his wallet, keys, and anything else that wasn't clothing at check-in. He barely got them to let him keep the pictures and a notebook, since he was there to get information, after all. He wasn't allowed to bring a pen in, instead they handed him a short pencil.

"Expecting trouble from Mr. Hill?" he asked the guard escorting him.

"Not really. Bennie's a keep to himself sort. But we have to be careful. Never know what these animals will do."

Bennie was already sitting at a low table in the visitor's room. He didn't get up as Sam entered with the guard, instead leaning back and evaluating the stranger who'd come to see him so late in the day.

"Hi, Mr. Hill," Sam said, sitting down across from him. "I'm Detective Arbichaut." He laid the photographs face down on the table.

"They said you're from Florida or something. I ain't been to Florida in my life, so you're just wasting time." No preamble or pleasantries with this guy. Bennie had a mouse under one eye that twitched involuntarily, making him resemble the spinach-eating cartoon character even more. He looked tired, worn out, not quite as hard as he had in his mug shot.

Fine. He didn't want to chitchat, well, Sam could get to the point, too.

"I'm here about your daughter."

"I don't have a daughter," Bennie said, but his shoulders hunched up and he leaned forward toward Sam, eyes intent.

"Yeah, you do." Sam flipped over the first photo, revealing Donna's face.

Bennie's eyes flicked down and his mouth tightened. "Never seen her before. Hot little thing, though."

"She's in danger. I'm not after her, Mr. Hill. I'm after the man who stabbed her and is trying to finish the job."

The crook's eyes met Sam's and they locked gazes as Bennie seemed to be trying to decide if this was a trick.

"How do I know you aren't lying?" he said finally, licking his lips.

Sam flipped over the second piece of paper, revealing the note and turned it toward Bennie. He waited while Bennie read it.

"I have to find her before this guy does," Sam said, letting some of his frustration and urgency infect his tone. "Help me."

"I don't know where Delilah is," Bennie said, holding up his hands. "I'm sure you've checked visitor's logs. She don't exactly come by to talk to her old man."

Sam hadn't checked the logs, not wanting to try the warden's patience and lack of followed procedure until it was absolutely necessary. But he had a real name now, which was something.

"Give me something, please. This guy has killed people, will kill again."

Bennie sighed, his barrel chest deflating. "Go to No Man's Land up in Portland, talk to the owner, Jake. Maybe he can help you. But my guess is that my girl's in the wind and neither you nor this killer are gonna find her." He rose and motioned to the guard, shaking his head to forestall anything Sam might say. "Good luck, detective," he said, putting a slight sneer on the last word as he held out his hands for the cuffs.

Sam watched him walk out of the room and then stood up, gathering his stuff and making a note with the stubby pencil.

He spent an hour filling out paperwork before he was finally allowed to leave. His phone gave him directions to No Man's Land, a pub with decent reviews. He sat in the rental car and considered options.

It would be after midnight before he made it back to Portland. Sam wasn't sure what time bars closed there, but he was hardly tired. It couldn't hurt to at least swing by and scope out the place. He doubted the owner would be in that late, but he could probably confirm that this Jake guy actually existed before he wasted any more time.

Delilah. Still a D-name. Sam smiled ruefully at himself. He'd been a cop long enough to figure out that trouble almost always came down to money or women. Guessed he wasn't an exception, not even a little bit.

He left the prison behind and drove down the dark highway with the strange notion that he was searching for a lot more than just this one girl.

Forty-five

Ted drove past the bar, but the two police cruisers in the parking lot deterred him from going inside. He was a little surprised over police presence, given his Delilah's criminal ways. If she'd been picked up, taken in for questioning or because the murder in her hotel room in Florida had caught up to her, she'd be out of his reach.

But he shook off that worry quickly as he turned around and set off for the airport. The police weren't competent enough to have sorted out the hotel murder and track her here. He'd heard all about petty squabbles between departments in the same city, much less in different states, from Cora. Her father was always harping on the need for better communication, more cooperation. Many of his cases crumbled due to investigating incompetence.

Which suited Ted just fine. No one had even suspected they had a serial in their midst. The police wouldn't have his Delilah. Not so soon.

And they never would, if he had his way.

He didn't know how good a description of the car the witness at the accident would be able to give, or if either Nancy or Delilah had managed to see his license plate. Ted felt it would be prudent to ditch the Mazda and get something completely different.

He parked the car in the economy lot at the airport and took a shuttle in, walking across the lanes and back to the car rental places. He chose a different company and stood impatiently in line as the sole representative took her merry time, chatting with the woman and two children she was supposedly helping.

Finally it was his turn. When she asked him for any preferences, he smiled.

"A decent-sized trunk," he said.

The car was a dark blue Dodge Infinity. The trunk was plenty big enough to fit Delilah into if it came down to snatching her off the street. Ted tossed in the small duffle bag containing his hunting kit and slammed the door shut.

Secure that he'd done enough to stay under police radar, Ted drove back to the hotel. He would change his shirt, take another shower, watch a movie, and kill time until midnight.

The wait was rough on him, but he wandered around the two-room suite, televisions going in both the sitting area and the bedroom, fantasizing about taking on Delilah. *Patience.* Patience was the virtue of all good hunters. He'd find the family she seemed to care about so much, and, just as she had already, she'd show up, drawn like a moth to his bloody flames.

At eleven thirty he couldn't take it anymore. It was close enough to midnight.

The bar parking lot still had a couple cars in it by the time he arrived and Ted positioned his own car across the street at an angle where he could see the front door as well as the bank of windows in the dining area.

There was a light on, even after two women, one of them the fat waitress, left the building and got into one of the remaining cars. After a few minutes the lights flickered off and a large man walked out the front door. He closed it behind him and then, as far as Ted could tell, jiggled the handle as though making sure it had locked.

Ted watched as the man climbed into the last car and drove away. He made himself count to one hundred before pulling on his gloves and getting his hunting kit.

He crossed the street and tried the front door himself, glancing around for witnesses. A car or two drove past, but going fast enough that Ted doubted they even noticed him.

He walked around to the back. The Mustang he'd seen parked there earlier in the day was still parked in back. Ted hesitated, wondering if the car was just parked here all the time, or if someone was still inside. After a scant moment he shook his head at his silliness. If someone was still here, he'd deal with them appropriately. The calm of the hunt washed over him and his fingers started to tingle.

Ted set his bag down and pulled out a pen light. Examining the back door, he found that the covering plate had been sheered off at some point in the door's past and never replaced. Ted smiled. The universe was still handing him presents, it seemed.

He pulled out a credit card and pressed his ear to the door. He heard no movement or signs of anyone inside. Holding the pen light between his teeth, he worked the card in slowly until he was able to pull it up and depress the latch.

The door eased open. The hallway was dark, as was the bar beyond it, but light spilled in from under the office door. Ted turned off the pen light and put it back in his bag, removing the big knife instead.

He quietly and slowly turned the knob. Then, keeping his grip on the knob with his left hand, he thrust the door open, eyes darting about the room, squinting against the light.

The office was empty.

Ted took a deep breath, almost laughing at his own anticipation. Then he heard movement and looked across the small room. There was another door there, its placement leading Ted to guess it led to the kitchen.

He left the hallway door ajar and crossed the room, scanning the hinges to see which way the door would swing. The handle of the kitchen door turned, and Ted crouched next to where it would open, knife in hand, a wild smile twisting his handsome face.

Forty-six

Jake checked the freezers, making sure there was enough of everything to hold until deliveries on Monday. He felt conflicted about even being at the bar, but things weren't set up to run without him. His father had always liked to be a constant presence, and Jake had never messed with any of the procedures much after he'd taken over.

Besides, Nancy and Esther were safe for the night, he was sure of that at least. Only his father, Delilah, and Jake himself knew about the little cabin in Neskowin. It was off an old logging road, tucked into the hills. It had a generator, because his dad had always wanted a place off-the-grid, as he put it, in case the whites changed their minds about equality. Tomorrow afternoon they could drive back into Portland so Esther could have her treatment, and then they'd see about how to proceed.

The plan hadn't made Nancy happy, but it was the best Jake could do. The bar needed him, too, and cell reception at the cabin was weak at best. He could admit to himself, if not to his wife, that he hoped Delilah might come back that night. Tell him something more, work things out. She'd come once, so she had to care something for their daughter, for him.

Jake sighed. He also wanted to let Nancy cool off. He'd have heard worse already if there hadn't been so many people around that afternoon. Like this was his fault. Once again, Delilah had shown up and fucked him over, putting everyone around her in danger.

Being stuck in a one room cabin with Nancy at the moment didn't sound good. This way, she could sleep off some of her anger, and he hoped by the time he arrived she'd be asleep or too tired to yell.

He would get things fixed up at work so they could do without him for a couple days and then drive to the coast to be with his wife and child. Besides, he had needed to stay in town to hire a couple guys to watch his family and the bar.

His justifications sounded thin in his mind, but Jake shook it off.

Moose had just left. He'd agreed to pick up a friend who worked with him sometimes and meet Jake at the Neskowin cabin. Jake had printed directions for him, so hopefully he'd be able to find the place.

The police said they'd issue a bulletin on the car and check with police departments in Florida to see if this story of Delilah's, what little she'd told Jake anyway, held up at all. He should expect a follow-up call from a detective in the morning. Good thing he'd hired on Moose and his friends, since the police had left without even offering so much as an escort home for Nancy and Esther.

Jake stood in the dimly lit kitchen and folded his arms. Delilah, he was sure, could have helped this. He knew her claustrophobia, her fear of jail. Hell of a profession she'd chosen. But no, she'd done what she always did when things got rough. Run away.

But she'd always gravitated back to him. Jake wasn't sure she would this time. Not after the thing with the cops. He'd been so damn scared and angry, plus there was no way he could have stopped Nancy from calling the police anyway.

"Keep telling yourself you're doing what you have to," he muttered.

He paced around the kitchen for a long moment, making sure the ovens were shut off, the dishes clean and in their racks, and that everything was ready for prep in the morning. Everything was in order. No more reason to be here. Only thing to do was to shut down the computer, turn out the lights, and get on the road. He just had to pray that he could smooth things over with his wife.

Jake walked through the kitchen and opened the door into his office.

Forty-seven

The door swung open and Ted had a split second to recognize the dark figure above him before he struck. The sharp knife caught for a moment on Jake's pants, then cut deep into the back of his ankle as Ted slashed with practiced efficiency.

The thin black man tumbled to his knees with a high-pitched scream. Ted thrust the knife into Jake's side. Jake tried to put his hands up, but Ted rose from the crouch and slashed again and again, slicing deep gashes into his biceps and across his palms.

Jake stopped trying to fight back at all, curling into a ball, bleeding arms up to protect his head.

Ted chuckled at the pathetic shape and kicked the little man until he retreated against one wall. Jake's terrified eyes met Ted's gaze. He was clearly waiting for the end.

Too bad for poor Jake. Ted wasn't even close to finished with the bastard. He stepped back, leaning against the desk, and contemplated his whimpering victim.

Jake edged to one side, toward the filing cabinets.

"Something you want? Or are you just looking for somewhere to hide?" Ted looked around the small office. The computer was on and the fans hummed. There were some papers on the desk and one of the filing cabinet drawers was partly open. Ted leaned over and pulled it open more.

A gun. A six-shot revolver with a nice ivory grip. Ted lifted the gun from the drawer and grinned at Jake, who deflated like a garbage bag when the wind is done toying with it.

"What," Jake said, then licked his lips. His face was a study in suffering and Ted knew the man wasn't going to make it much longer. "What do you want?" Jake tried again, this time getting the words out more or less coherently.

"What do I want?" Ted repeated. "You to suffer and die, but that's easy enough. We're already headed there, aren't we? At least, to the suffering part. But first you are going to tell me where your little brat is." He fingered the gun and twirled it around on the desk, watching Jake with narrowed eyes.

"No." Jake started shivering. Shock was clearly setting in.

"Wrong." Ted left the gun on the desk and bent over his victim. He took the knife and trailed it over Jake's belly.

The black man curled into a tighter ball, but it was clear his arms and legs weren't responding well. Ted easily kicked the man's knees apart and brought the knife down, resting the tip on Jake's crotch.

"You fucked her. Was it good? Is she a tight little bitch? Does she like it rough?"

Jake kept shaking his head and trying to lift his arms. Ted easily batted them back down with one hand. He pressed the tip of the knife in, sliding it through the jeans a bit to the side of the zipper where the material thinned. His eyes on Jake's brown, terrified eyes, Ted saw the exact moment the knife hit flesh and felt a little rush of excitement.

Apparently killing a man could be interesting, after all.

"Tell me where they are."

"Delilah, she's… gone." Jake gurgled, his pitch rising into a scream as Ted pressed the knife in deeper.

"I. Don't. Believe. You." Ted mocked him; imitating Jake's pained, halting speech. "The sick brat. Where's little Esther?"

Jake's eyes flicked beyond Ted, toward the desk, and then back. He shook his head again and squeezed his eyes shut.

Ted stood up, pulling the knife up and then out as he rose and watched Jake curl up again. He turned and looked again at the desk. Did Jake want the gun? Was that it? Or was it something else?

Setting his boot against Jake's now bleeding crotch, Ted leaned his weight forward.

"Give me your full attention, asshole. You're going to die. Slow, fast. Doesn't matter to me." Though it did, but lying to victims to give them some hope never hurt. "But your wife doesn't have to. Pretty woman. I can leave her alone. Maybe even the little girl. I just want Delilah, and she'll come after her kid just like she did today. So you be a good boy and tell me where they are, and I'll see what I can do about letting your family live. I'm going to find them one way or another."

Jake convulsed, his whole body shuddering now, and a growing pool of blood smeared the floor around him. "You'll never... find." But his eyes flicked again to the desk and his eyebrows creased with worry that showed through his agony.

"Is it something on the desk?" Ted looked down at the papers. One was an employment application. Others were delivery orders and random business papers. Not much help there. The computer was on and the monitor displayed a desktop with an oak tree on a hill. "Is it the computer?"

Jake closed his eyes again but the fear that flashed over his dark face gave him away.

Ted moved around the desk and leaned over the computer. There were a few windows minimized in the taskbar. One was Google Maps.

Bingo. Ted clicked it open and found driving directions from Portland out to some place in the coastal range near a town called Neskowin. Probably one of those Indian names, he guessed. The directions didn't seem to go anywhere, ending where Google said there wasn't a road or anything.

"That's where I'd keep someone, too, all nice and tucked away." Ted hit print and the printer on top of the filing cabinet queued up the page, printing slowly.

Ted turned to get the papers, distracted for a moment.

Jake, with more strength than Ted had given him credit for, lunged for the gun. Ted turned, slamming his fist into Jake's face as the man half-rose from the floor. Jake's injured leg, the Achilles tendon severed, wouldn't hold his weight. Ted forced him back down with another blow, coming around the desk. Then he drove the knife point down into the hollow of Jake's collar bone.

Blood spurted and Jake fell away.

"That was stupid. And you got blood all over me. I hope you feel like you accomplished something." Ted kicked him. "You did, in fact. I'm going to kill your wife, but not before I teach her how a real man treats women. She'll understand many things before I finish with her. She's going to beg for the end. And then maybe I'll do your little girl. She's what? Five? Never killed a child before. Esther and I can lose our virginities to each other."

"Fuck... you." Jake pressed his hands to his neck, but the blood sluggishly flowed between his fingers.

"You shouldn't have fought me, and you really shouldn't have fucked my Delilah." Ted hit the power button on the computer and then unplugged the office phone cord. "You'll die soon enough. Keep pressure on that wound and draw it out for me, will you?"

He picked up the gun and walked around Jake to the kitchen. Jake was still shivering and bleeding when he came back a minute later with the worst of the blood wiped off his hands and pants.

"Good night, Jake. You'll see your family very soon."

Smiling, feeling better and better with each passing moment, Ted left the bar through the back door, Jake's final words lost behind him.

Forty-eight

Sam drove through the quiet neighborhood, amazed that this city seemed to shut down so early. Maybe it was different on weekends. He doubted the bar would still be open and as he approached the place looked dark except for the illuminated sign sticking out from the corner in neon purple. There was a small digital sign that read "Closed" in the window and Sam slowed to read it.

Good thing, too. He nearly hit a pedestrian jaywalking right in front of him. The guy wore dark clothes and carried a small duffle bag. He froze for a moment in Sam's headlights as though he'd expected to be seen, or else not even noticed the approaching car.

For a brief moment, Sam saw him clearly and thought he was going insane. The guy looked just like the man in the photo on the seat beside him. Dead ringer. Sam remembered to breathe and then the moment was gone, the man crossing in front of him and walking toward a parked car.

That was Theodore Whitechapel. It had to be. Sam had spent too many hours on the plane staring at his face. He wasn't imagining it. Whitechapel here, at the bar. Had he found Delilah already? Done something to her?

Torn between going and investigating the bar and following the alleged serial killer, Sam turned left and swung around. He pulled up to the stop sign and watched as Whitechapel pulled away from the curb.

Sam mentally flipped a quarter but made up his mind before the figment could land heads or tails.

The bar was closed. This guy was right here, and clearly headed somewhere. Sam had to stay on him, at least until he could notify the police. If Sam was lucky, Whitechapel might lead him right to Delilah.

He turned out and followed the dark blue sedan, keeping back enough on the nearly empty road to be casual. His phone was still in the cup holder on the center console next to him. Sam fumbled with one hand and picked it up. He had an earpiece for it for hands-free use, but hadn't taken it with him.

The screen was dark. Sam glanced down quickly, not wanting to lose sight of the car ahead. Using a phone while driving was dangerous and possibly even illegal in this state, but he figured this was one of those exceptional circumstances.

The phone turned on, then beeped, and turned right back off. No battery.

"Fucking kidding me." He had a car charger thingy. In his now cleaner car, back in Jacksonville. He couldn't even remember the last time he charged his phone up. Monday maybe? He'd been so busy all day with travel and driving that he hadn't even thought about it.

Tossing the useless device into the seat, Sam focused on the sedan ahead of him. He'd just have to follow Whitechapel and then figure out how to notify the authorities from there.

A comforting and indulgent fantasy of taking the bastard out himself danced around Sam's mind. Ronnie had sounded so upset, shaken even, about the crime scene at the Whitechapel house. Whatever this bastard had done to the DA's daughter, it was bad if it could rock a homicide lieutenant with Ronnie's experience.

Of course, Whitechapel might be armed and Sam didn't have so much as a pen knife on him. He sighed. He'd stick with the plan he'd come up with. Tail and then report.

Unless Whitechapel put someone else's life in danger. Sam's mouth set in a grim line. There'd be no more killing, not if he could help it.

Whitechapel's car took a quick right and Sam tapped the breaks, then followed, swinging wide into the intersection.

Forty-nine

Jake lay in his own blood and listened as the back door closed. The pain was too much for his body and his mind shut it away. Blood seeped through his fingers, slower now as his pulse weakened.

Esther. He remembered the first time her tiny hand had grabbed his finger, her bright blue newborn eyes staring at her daddy. They got ice cream every Sunday and then he'd carry her to the top of Mt. Tabor and tell her about volcanoes and dinosaurs or whatever her interest was that week.

Bubblegum ice cream, pink and blue with little flecks of candy in it. She'd open her little mouth and stick a blue tongue out and say, "See-food, daddy."

And he'd always left work and gone to the hospital while she got her transfusions. Read to her. She still requested *Good Night, Moon* most of the time.

He was her daddy. As long as he was still alive, he had to protect her. And he'd failed. That bastard was going to win.

Anger pushed back the pain enough that Jake dared to open his eyes. He wasn't dead yet.

It hurt to breathe, to move. So Jake gave up on breathing, not caring if the movement killed him. His left arm responded to his silently screamed commands and slowly he extracted his cellphone from his jean's pocket.

9…1… Then he stopped. The police. They'd never get to the cabin in time, if they could even find it. Even Moose probably wouldn't be able to get out there.

Besides, Jake didn't want this horrible man scared away. Ted had to die. Moose wouldn't kill for him, not readily enough.

Jake understood now what Delilah had been so afraid of. That man wasn't human. Evil. Just evil. No reasoning or bargaining or driving away evil. Only one thing to do.

Stop it. Kill it. Destroy it.

And there was only one person in the world who would do that, without question, without reservation. The only other person who would kill to save his smiling little girl with a bright blue tongue.

Jake hauled himself across the floor to the desk on his elbows and one good knee. He didn't even try to rise, just pulled open the drawer with his hand and found the black ledger with memory instead of sight.

He didn't know where Delilah was or how far she'd run. But there was one place she might have gone.

Jake flipped open the ledger, smearing blood on the pages. His eyes didn't want to focus and his heart was like a lead weight in his chest. He found the number he wanted and dialed his final hope.

Fifty

"Baby girl." Colin's voice floated in, interrupting a dream Delilah couldn't quite grasp hold of.

She opened her eyes. One lamp was on, the soft yellow glow illuminating her room. The world outside the windows was dark. She braced herself for the return of the pain, but only a dull ache greeted her. She felt fuzzy, but alive.

Colin held a phone out to her. "It's Jake," he said. She couldn't read his expression. Worried, perhaps.

"Jake?" She took the phone, wondering why Colin even had one in the first place. The rule he'd taught her was no personal phones, and definitely no business over the phone, except perhaps pizza.

"Lil. Get him." The words came out in little gasps and Delilah barely understood. Teddy. It had to be something with that psycho.

"Where are you? What's happened?"

"Bar. He cut me. He knows where Essy—" Then a rush of air and the sound of plastic hitting a hard surface.

"Where is he? Jake?"

There was no response, though she could hear harsh breathing.

"Jake, I'm coming to the bar. If you can hear me, just hang on." She waited a moment, but got no response.

Ted had gotten to Jake, somehow. This could be a trap. She was aware but too angry, too scared to care. She'd warned him, she'd fucking told Jake that Ted was dangerous, that he wouldn't be stopped. But Jake hadn't listened. He never listened. Stupid Delilah, just trouble, never right.

"Dee? Are you all right?" Colin put a hand on her shoulder.

She threw off the comforter and swung her legs out of bed, testing her belly as she gripped onto Colin's arm and stood up. Sore, but she'd manage. She felt a hell of a lot better than earlier at least.

Not that it mattered. She'd do what needed to be done.

"I think Teddy got to Jake, at the bar," she said. She stepped away and opened her dresser. Her old shirts and pants where all still there, clean and folded neatly. She wiped at her eyes with one hand. No time to get maudlin.

"It could be a trap, be bait for you." Colin shook his head. "Let me go instead."

She laughed and regretted it as the ache got a little sharper. "Fuck no. This is my mess, my fault. I'll take care of it, the way I should have before." She pulled on a pair of jeans and turned to face him. "I've been an idiot, Colin. Playing around with fire, thinking I was too smart to get burned. And now

302

everything I care about is burning down around me. I've got to deal with this." *No more running*, she told herself silently.

"I'll go get that car out of the pole barn for you. Drink some water and take another spoonful of that codeine. It won't knock you out," he added at her skeptical look. "Just keep the edge off the pain so you can do what you have to."

"Thank you, Colin." She stepped forward and kissed his cheek. "Oh, one other thing." Her dark eyes grew hard and shiny as a beetle's. "I need a gun."

Fifty-one

She'd never driven so fast in her life as she did that night. The rental car's speed topped out around one hundred and it took all Delilah's skill and concentration to get around what little traffic there was.

She got into south-east Portland and ran every light, every stop sign. She didn't care about traffic cameras or getting pulled over. Jake was in trouble. He could be dead by the time she arrived and every second was one for which she'd blame herself forever if she showed up too late.

And there was their daughter to consider. So tiny, so frail, and yet perfect. A little girl that Delilah didn't even know, just a face in pictures until this afternoon. But she was Jake's, a part of him, a part of what he and Delilah had shared. Before life and choices and stupid fights had torn them apart.

She's a part of me, too.

She drove into the parking lot and slammed the brakes, barely taking time to turn off the car. The Glock 9mm Colin had given her rested in her lap, cold and heavy. Loaded. Delilah picked it up, unbuckled her seatbelt, and climbed out of the car.

The night air was cool, a light breeze lifted her hair and teased the back of her neck. The neighborhood looked to be asleep and she didn't see movement in the businesses across the main street or the houses beyond.

There were no lights on in the bar that she could see and the parking lot was empty except for the Mustang. She walked around to the back door and tried it. Locked, of course. It took too many seconds for her to fumble out her ID card and jimmy the catch open.

She flicked the safety off the gun and yanked open the door.

No one in the hallway. The office door was slightly open and the sickly sweet smell of fresh blood swamped her.

Delilah rushed into the office, gun up, eyes darting around. Jake lay on the floor next to the desk in a messy smear of bright, wet blood. Biting back a shocked cry, Delilah moved past him, checking the door to the kitchen. The kitchen was empty, one light still on.

She grabbed a handful of napkins from one of the steel shelves and dashed back to Jake. For a horrible moment she couldn't find a pulse or sign of life, but then he took a shuddering breath and his eyelids fluttered.

His shirt was slashed and the grey material darkened by blood. Shallow cuts lined his arms and hands. The worst wounds were in his neck and his leg. His jeans were soaked with blood, one leg extended, the cuff slashed open and she thought she could see bone inside the gaping wound. She pressed napkins to his neck first since it was still bleeding in slow, pulsing bubbles in time to his heartbeat. Frantic, she looked around for tape or anything to help her apply better pressure.

"Lil," Jake managed, his eyes opening.

"Shh, I'm here. Don't speak." His dark skin was so pale, already looking blue-ish and taught over his bones. Masking tape. She saw a roll in the open desk drawer and leaned over him to grab it.

His fingers closed around her wrist with surprising strength.

"Cabin. At the cabin. Essy. He's gonna—" Jake broke off with a spasm and shivers wracked his body.

Delilah pressed a folded napkin to his neck with one hand and put her thumb on the tape. Quickly she wrapped it tight around his shoulder, trying to build up pressure for the wound. He'd lost so damn much blood already. That bandage seemed to hold and she pressed gently on his head as he tried to raise it.

"Shhh, Jake." There were so many cuts, so much blood. She made another napkin pad and bound the deep, gaping cut in his leg as best she could.

"No," he whispered and one injured hand pressed something into her leg. She took it. The keys to the Mustang. "Go. Kill him."

"They're at your dad's cabin?" She laid her hand against his cheek, tears flowing down her face in cold streaks. She felt more than saw him nod.

His cell phone had fallen beside the desk. Delilah grabbed it but again Jake caught her arm. He still looked like death warmed over, but her triage seemed to have given him some strength. There were still too many cuts and wounds.

"I have to call," she started to say.

He cut her off. "Go."

She pressed the phone into his hand after typing 9-1-1 into it.

"I love you," she whispered, picking up her gun.

"Drive," Jake licked his lips, his head lifting slightly, "like hell."

Vision blurred with tears, Delilah fled the bar. She took only a moment to adjust the seat in the Mustang, not bothering with her mirrors. She knew the way to the cabin. Jake had taken her out there multiple times. It was where they'd first made love, and the secret place they'd met after she'd tried to come back, after he'd met Nancy.

It was where she'd conceived Esther.

She didn't know how much of a head start psycho Teddy had on her. A half an hour, perhaps, given how much Jake had bled. Some of the blood had been sticky, already starting to turn brownish. She didn't know whether there was any way to make it out there in time. But she could try. And she could drive like hell.

The six-cylinder engine roared as the muscle car in its fully restored and upgraded glory shot down the road. Jake had taken care of her baby. The thought brought on another rush of tears and she wiped angrily at her face. There would be time to cry later, to be afraid. Her hands were bloodstained and she scrubbed them into her dirty jeans.

No more crying. No more running. This night wasn't going to turn into one more thing she'd feel sorry about later.

The flicker of resolve she'd felt back in Atlanta, the inner strength that had gotten her onto the plane, came to life again, hardening inside her until she felt invulnerable and utterly focused.

Teddy had stabbed her, hunted her down, attacked her love, and was now trying to destroy the vestiges of family that Delilah had. She'd never killed anyone before, but she doubted she'd lose much sleep. Theodore Whitechapel deserved to die.

"Should have let me go, Teddy," she said to his phantom as she turned onto highway 26 and floored the engine, shifting up. "Should have fucking let me go."

Jake watched Delilah leave and then closed his eyes. He hadn't gotten a chance to warn her about the gun that Ted had taken, but at least Delilah had her own gun. She'd do what she had to, his Lil always did. If he could trust her for anything, it was that she'd survive.

He lifted the phone but the screen had gone dark. It was diffucult to think, though the pain had become familiar and no longer so awful. It lay on him like a blanket. He wished he weren't so damn cold.

9-1-1, that was what he was supposed to call. He shivered, his vision blurring into little red dots. Too cold.

The phone slipped from his fingers. "Good night, moon." His lips moved but no sound came out. The shivering and pain subsided and he fell into a warm, unending dark.

Fifty-two

Ted followed the directions, heading toward the river. He regretted not staying around to watch Jake's final moments, but he had quite the drive ahead of him according to the map. It was satisfying enough to know that the stupid pathetic black man's last thoughts would all be of Ted and what he was going to do. Fear, power. Heady stuff.

Ted was free. Truly free. All those years of careful planning, all the times he's taken extra precautions, extra care to never be detected. God, he'd put up with Cora and her plastic, bitchy ways only so that he could keep track of the DA's office and get wind if anyone realized a serial killer was hunting in Daytona Beach.

Of course, no one ever had. He'd fucked that stupid bitch, bought her stupid gifts, and promised her that he'd think about leaving Emily, all the usual bullshit that so-called normal men put up with from the women who tried to control them.

And it had been for nothing. No point. He could have killed her a year ago and put her beneath his garden for all the good she'd done him. At least then she'd be fertilizing and helping create beauty in the world.

He tuned the radio to the AM dial and searched for a news station. He'd watched all the local news in the hotel that day, but seen nothing at all about a manhunt or any bulletins out of Florida. There'd been a five minute segment about the intersection stabbing in Tualitin, but they'd gotten what little facts they had pretty much wrong. The focus had mostly been on his car, which he didn't have to worry about. As far as he could tell, no one had any idea what he'd been up to or who he really was.

It was so… easy. Pathetic. All that care, all the lies and the carefully manicured and developed façade had been for nothing. He could have been having so much more fun.

But he was free now. And once he'd settled into whatever place lay at the end of his map with dead Jake's plump wife and sickly daughter, he'd do what he could to make up for lost time, at least until Delilah showed up. Perhaps he should have left her another clue. But he had a feeling she'd guess where Jake would squirrel away his family. If she wasn't there with them already. She'd been with them in the car that day, it seemed likely she'd have stuck around to help protect her kid.

He laughed aloud at that idea. She'd gotten away from him again, so she probably felt safe, cocky even. Stupid little bitch. He'd teach her, show her how to beg for him, how to beg for death. She'd crumpled readily enough in his arms once.

There wasn't much traffic, though a few cars were on the road, especially as he neared the bridge. One car seemed to stay behind him, even when Ted experimented and slowed down, giving the guy room enough to get into the other lane and pass.

He wasn't sure if he was being paranoid, but decided to take a quick detour and drive around the next block, just in case. He signaled and turned right. The car did the same.

Ted signaled again and turned right again. Again the car followed.

Not paranoia. The other car's headlights were too bright, blocking any view of the driver. Ted wondered if it were Delilah. How long ago had this car been following him? Since the bar? He hadn't gone far, yet.

He thought about stopping and just shooting the driver. But it might be the cops, though he doubted it. The make of the car looked all wrong for police. Ted took a hard right and the car struggled to keep up, swinging wide into the intersection.

Definitely following. He thought he could make out only one person in the car and the silhouette looked too tall and bulky to be his tiny, deceitful Delilah.

"Time to play, asshole." Ted muttered. He didn't want to start shooting here, the prudent side of him whispered. Gunshots would bring out police and there might be witnesses. He had a full tank of gas; he could lose a few minutes running this jerk around in circles.

He'd let the other guy make the first move. If the guy just wanted to follow him, oh well. He'd have a nice little drive around town. If the other car proved too persistent, Ted figured he could find a quieter, lonelier place on his little drive and take care of the idiot.

He glanced in the rearview mirror again. The car was still on his tail, hanging back. He wondered if the man inside knew he'd been made. Ted had no idea who it could be.

Jake was dead. His silly, wounded Delilah was probably hiding in a cabin, thinking she'd won, thinking she was safe. It seemed unlikely anyone had followed him from the bar. He'd seen no one there.

Ultimately, it didn't matter. He could afford to play around with this unknown factor for a little while. No hasty decisions yet. He was still a hunter and this new prey would learn soon enough it had chosen the wrong target.

Fifty-three

The first hard right worried Sam. Then the dark blue car turned right again, basically going around the block, and Sam knew he'd been made.

He cursed softly and decided to ditch all pretense of hanging back or being uninterested in the car in front of him. He got close enough to read the license plate, guessing it was a rental.

Whitechapel knew he had a tail, but he couldn't know who Sam was or why he was following. And on the plus side, Sam doubted Whitechapel would go start killing people while someone was watching. He figured a guy who liked to hurt women would be a giant coward.

He expected Whitechapel would try to lose him, but the man just reversed their course, driving away from the river, staying the speed limit and moseying along as though driving to a friend's house or home from a movie. Sam grit his teeth, tension making his arms ache as he clutched the wheel. He expected the calm to break any moment, for Whitechapel to pull a u-turn or something crazy, maybe even try to assault Sam's vehicle.

He wished he had his gun. He'd never really considered how wrong and weak it felt to be without it. A good detective shouldn't need a gun, he told himself. Whitechapel would have to do something eventually. Sam just had to stick on him, keep watch.

Minutes and miles slipped past and the relative silence inside the car grew oppressive. Sick of the sound of his own heavy breathing, Sam turned the radio on low, leaving it on the first station. It was NPR with the BBC morning news. There had to be some sort of cosmic lesson in that, but damned if he knew what it was.

The clouds broke up, revealing dim stars and a heavy, almost full moon just about at zenith. The moon bathed the buildings in eerie blue light and cast weird shadows that shifted and merged in the headlights.

After a few more seemingly random turns, Whitechapel appeared to be leading him out of the city. The businesses turned to neighborhoods and the lots grew larger, the homes more spread out. It was dead quiet out here, barely even any counter traffic, just the two of them on the road, driving to nowhere.

Sam hunched his shoulders, trying to relieve the tension building in them. He sensed that this was a terrible idea. Driving out to less populated areas meant fewer witnesses, less trouble. If Whitechapel had a weapon, well, he'd be far ahead of Sam in that respect. That the man had made zero attempts to lose him worried him even more.

Sam leaned forward, judging the distance between them, and then looked around at the road. He could try a PIT maneuver, but if Whitechapel had a gun that would probably end poorly. And Sam admitted to himself he wasn't even sure how to do one, having never done it himself. The PIT maneuver had gone out of the books years ago after the top brass kept complaining about replacing so many patrol vehicles.

An orange glow on his dash caught his eye. The low-fuel light. *Shit.*

Sam ran his hand through his hair and looked back up at the blue car. He had to do something, now. Running out of gas wouldn't help him. PIT and confront, or let Whitechapel go.

The hero in him yelled for action. Sam pounded a fist into the steering wheel and shook his head. If he got killed here, that wouldn't help Delilah. It wouldn't help anybody.

"Fuck," he said and turned his car away, circling back toward the last gas station he'd seen.

At the pump, still amazed that people here weren't allowed to pump their own gas, as the grizzly attendant had informed him, Sam leaned against his car and stared up at the moon.

He was a detective, he could still work the crime. Whitechapel had come out of the bar Bennie Hill had told him to visit for information on his daughter. Whatever the killer had been doing or looking for there, it would provide a new starting place for Sam's informal search.

"When you're looking for a killer," Ronnie had always told him. "Always ask yourself, what was the bad guy up to?"

"What were you doing there, Whitechapel?" Sam muttered.

"Sir?" The attendant removed the nozzle as the machine clicked to a stop.

"Sorry, thinking to myself." He collected his receipt and then asked for directions back to south-east and the bar. Apparently Whitechapel had led them in a couple giant circles, because he wasn't as far out from it as he'd thought.

New plan. Go to the bar and see what he could figure out from there. Then maybe he'd call the police and see if he could pull a few strings to find out about the license plate. He considered calling them now, but he didn't really have much other than suspicions. Guilt poked him as he thought of Ronnie. She'd want to know her killer was here, on the opposite coast.

But the moment he told her that, if she even believed an identification made in a split second on a dark road, she'd be out here with the FBI in tow and that would be the end of Sam's involvement. He'd get a pat on the head and a door hitting him in the ass on his way out.

Sam turned onto the road and wished he had a cigarette. At least he was trying to help. It felt good to be doing something, to feel useful at all. Somewhere out there, beneath this eerie moon, was an injured woman running scared. Sam had to keep going.

Fifty-four

Halfway up the winding dirt and gravel road to the cabin, Delilah flicked off her headlights. The cold moon and her parking lights illuminated the landscape enough that she could see the darker edges of the road where the thick salal, ferns, and evergreen trees started.

It was slow going. No car parked anywhere along the edge of the road. Good sign. She figured Ted wouldn't drive right up to the cabin but probably approach carefully much the same way she herself was. Paranoid thinking, maybe. But he'd underestimated her, no way was she going to make the same sort of mistake.

She inched her way around the final turn and the road dipped downward. The cabin stood a few hundred feet ahead, tucked into a clearing among the hills and rolling green second-growth forest.

Nancy's Honda Civic sat out in front on the large square of gravel that served as a parking lot. The porch lights were on and the front and back of the cabin were bright and welcoming. A light was on inside as well, though no shadows moved against it behind the drawn curtains. The side of the wrap-around porch was dimly lit by the windows and empty.

Delilah let out a breath she'd been keeping in for miles. She'd beat him here. Somehow.

She drove the Mustang up and parked beside Nancy's car. She was only half out of the vehicle when Nancy burst from the front of the house and jerked to a stop as she saw Delilah and not Jake get out.

Her eyes widened in the yellow porch light as she saw the gun.

Shit, not the best way to begin.

"Nancy," Delilah said, stepping forward as the other woman backed up onto the porch. She kept the gun against her leg. "Jake sent me. You have to go, right now."

"Get away from me. Get away from my family." Nancy's voice was shrill, the whites of her eyes showing as she held up her hands as though to ward Delilah away.

"Fuck, woman. Ted's coming here. Here. Do you get that? You have to go." Delilah advanced on her, following her into the cabin. Her left hand came up and slammed into the door as Nancy tried to use it to push her out again.

"Where's Jake? What do you mean that man is coming here? Jake said we'd be safe here." Nancy lowered her voice after the first question and glanced behind to where Esther lay curled under a bright orange and brown wool blanket on the futon in the back of the cabin.

Dark circles of exhaustion marred the little girl's face, but she looked tiny and peaceful as she slept, her cupid's-bow lips parted and a light flush to her cinnamon cheeks. Delilah's heart twisted and deep inside something snapped and popped, like a joint suddenly dropping into place.

"Nancy," she said, keeping her voice low and soft. Delilah stepped forward and gripped Nancy's arm, pulling on her red sweater to get her attention. She hoped that Nancy wouldn't notice the flecks of dried blood on her fingers. "Take the Mustang. Take my, your daughter. You've got to get out of here. Please."

Maybe it was the please, maybe the look in her eyes. But the tension shifted in Nancy's body and she slowly nodded.

"Where," she said. The she licked her lips and tried again. "Where do I go?"

"Drive back toward the city. Check into a motel. Not," she said, holding up a hand to forestall whatever Nancy was about to ask, "not under your name. If they quibble about that tell them you're running from an abusive husband or something. Most people are sympathetic to that kind of thing. Don't call anyone until tomorrow."

"No, I'm calling Jake as soon as we get into cell reception," she said.

It must have showed in Delilah's face first because Nancy was already withdrawing and shaking her head even before she spoke. "I don't think Jake's going to answer," she said.

"Nononono." Nancy backed away, tears running her mascara as they welled quick and heavy. "Is that his blood?" She waved her hand at Delilah's stained jeans.

Delilah glanced down. The streaks had turned brown and blackish on the drive. Fuck.

"Nancy. Focus. Focus on Esther. You have to go. She's right here. She needs you, Nancy." Delilah repeated her name, using the cheap psychological trick to pull the woman back into the present situation.

"Okay," she said and wiped a hand over her face which just smeared her makeup worse. "This is your fault."

"I know," Delilah said to her back as Nancy turned away and started gathering up things from the small table. "I'm going to take care of it."

"You can't—"

"I fucking know. Get Esther. Now."

They moved around in silence, Nancy not meeting her eyes. Delilah carried their bag out to the Mustang and held the door open while Nancy gently settled the sleepy Esther into the back seat and tucked the blanket back in around her thin body.

"I need the Honda's keys." Delilah held out the keys to the Mustang.

Nancy nodded and pulled them out of her purse, still not looking up. She looked like she wanted to throw the keys onto the ground, but after a tense second she merely handed them off, taking the Mustang keys instead.

"He's never let me drive it," Nancy said and finally glanced at Delilah.

A pang of guilt followed the momentary elation that statement evoked in her. The Mustang was her car, after all. A gift to him. That Jake had kept it safe and cared for and only his meant something.

Not anymore. Jake was probably gone. Esther was what mattered now.

"Go, Nancy. Don't stop for any reason. If you think someone is following you, find a police station. There should be plenty of gas left."

Nancy nodded and walked around the side of the Mustang. Her sweater looked like old blood in the moonlight. Delilah pushed away her morbid thoughts and watched as the car started up and drove away. She stood on the porch, staring into the darkness until the car's lights no longer winked among the trees.

Ted wasn't here, yet. But he would be. He'd come soon and skulk about in the darkness like a puma.

That thought reminded Delilah of something, something possibly important. She smiled. It didn't touch her eyes.

Fifty-five

Boss Leventon, Jake's father, had bought the cabin from an old black woman who'd led a major strike and advocated heavily for millworkers back long before Boss himself had been born. Fighting Jenny, she'd been called. Crazy Jenny in her later years. She'd built the cabin after her husband died and spent the rest of her years there until one of her grandsons finally dragged her to a nursing home and sold the place to Boss.

Fighting Jenny had been super paranoid that the white man would come and take her away. She'd had an assortment of rifles, some going back to WWI era. And she'd had a bunch of bear traps, the old steel and iron kind with the huge jaws and heavy springs.

Delilah looked around the cabin. So many memories hid here, lurking in the cedar and wood-smoke scent, in the lumpy futon, whispering down the little chimney like ghosts. If she closed her eyes she could almost hear Jake's voice telling her about the place, about his plans for it. There was some decent land belonging to the property, flatter than a lot of the acres around here.

Thinking about Jake, about his long, gentle fingers sliding over her skin, brought on a rush of tears and weakness. She shook it off. What she wanted now wasn't inside the cabin anyway, if they were even still here.

She grabbed a flashlight out of one of the kitchen drawers and walked out onto the back deck. Underneath the rear stairs she found what she wanted. Jake had even preserved the bear traps, folding the half dozen that hadn't rusted out into a tarp.

Her ears and eyes alert for any sign of movement around the cabin, Delilah dragged the tarp out. Her belly protested, nausea returning for a horrible moment. She breathed through it.

The traps were brown with rust but in fairly good condition. They were the old kind, with a big pressure plate and rounded iron teeth designed to keep an animal in place. The springs were strong enough to snap bone.

Delilah walked around the cabin, eyes searching out the darkness. She evaluated the best approaches to the place. If it were her, she'd park down the road and walk up along the grassy edge, staying out of sight of the cabin and off the gravel to prevent undo noise alerting the occupants. With the moon dipping toward the ocean, there was still too much light to put the traps in the road anyway.

She decided on the grass in the dark beside the road, and a couple around in back, where the leafy salal had started to take over the minimal yard and would conceal the metal. She wouldn't put it past Ted to circle around, thinking to get in through the back door.

Starting at every rustle or imagined sound, Delilah managed to set five of the traps. It was harder than she remembered but the late summer grass grew deep along the edge of the road. Jake had taught her how to arm the traps and they'd taken turns finding large sticks to break in the trap.

The chill, moonlit night was a million years away from those summer evenings. Delilah pushed away the ghosts of memory and walked back to the cabin. She was losing energy, the codeine long since wearing off. Her precautions would have to be good enough.

She made herself drink a glass of water from the cistern, swishing the slightly earthy, cold liquid around in her mouth. Then she shut off the lights and powered down the little generator. The resulting stillness was oppressive.

Walking out into the night helped. She took a deep breath and checked the Glock. All was ready. Delilah retreated into the shadow of the porch and leaned against the wall. Blue-silver light bathed the landscape and woke strange shadows that danced in the wind sauntering down the hills toward the sea.

"Come on, Teddy," she whispered. "I'm ready. Let's end this."

Fifty-six

After his mysterious follower cut away suddenly and disappeared from sight, Ted continued driving around. He wanted to be sure the stranger was gone before he headed out to find the little girl and his deceitful Delilah.

He drove for another ten minutes, looping around a few blocks in a big figure eight. His tail didn't reappear. Satisfied that the man must have gotten bored or called away for some reason, Ted picked up the map and got back on track, headed again for the river.

It was like a treasure hunt. X marks the spot. He wasn't sure what was at the end. A house, probably. With luck, Nancy and Esther and his sick little Delilah were all alone out there. But if they weren't, well, that's what the gun was for. He didn't want to shoot any of the women. Bullets made such a mess and often killed a person entirely too quickly.

There'd be no quick end for Delilah. She'd have to beg for it if she wanted the bliss of death, she'd have to acknowledge that Ted was the only one who could give her that release. And he would.

When he was done with her, of course.

The drive was too long. He had trouble staying near the speed limit as he headed toward the ocean, but the last thing he needed was to trip the radar of some bored State Trooper with a small penis complex.

Finally he reached 101 and turned north, toward Neskowin. The town was one of those blink-and-you'll-miss-it stops along the highway. Ted did miss his turn-off and had to backtrack a couple miles, driving slowly. He leaned over his steering wheel and finally saw the askew, faded road sign that marked the beginning of Cold Creek Lane.

There were a couple houses tucked back off the road in the trees, but no lights on. A dog barked somewhere in the distance, barely audible over the sound of his engine. The old logging road was unmarked, a dark gravel drive that turned and disappeared into the trees.

Ted drove up it slowly, unsure where exactly his destination lay. The directions said one-point-two miles. He kept a close eye on the trip mileage counter and at point-six miles turned off his headlights, using the bright moon and his parking lights to guide himself along the road.

At one-point-oh-nine miles, he pulled the car over to the edge, the tires crunching in the brush. Ted turned off the engine and got out. He stood for a long moment, listening. The night air danced through the trees, bringing on an earthy scent and a hint of rain, though the sky was clear. It smelled like autumn and Ted was chilly in just his shirt.

He removed his hunting kit from the car, carrying it in his left hand. In his right he held the revolver he'd taken from the bar. Not knowing what was ahead, he decided it was better to be prepared for the worst.

The road rose in a little bump and then dipped away, revealing a clearing ahead in the pocket valley below. The moon illuminated a cabin and shown on a car that looked almost black in the blue-silver light. He recognized it as a Honda Civic and smiled.

Nancy and Esther were there, at least. He saw no other cars. The small house was dark, the wrap-around covered porch hidden in shadow and nothing moved in or around the cabin. *Good.* They were likely asleep.

The wind was noisy enough that he didn't worry about his careful steps in the underbrush being heard by anyone inside the home. His rustling movements blended into the background as he picked his way down the hill, staying out of the open area and just inside the overhanging trees.

Ted's foot hit something hard and he instinctively stepped back. He bent, feeling in the dark. Metal. Metal teeth, it felt like, though they were dull. He felt around the object and then shook his head.

A bear trap. The kind he'd seen in old Western movies, with a plate and heavy springs. He'd have to tread carefully here.

Then the full realization hit him and Ted's smile widened. Delilah. His deceitful, sneaky little Delilah was behind this.

She had to be. It was possible that this trap had been set months ago and forgotten, but Ted doubted it. A trap, here, right where a good sneak or stalker would approach the cabin? Her work, definitely.

She was here, then. Here and still trying to fight him. His blood sang with lust, the angry ants in his belly starting their war dance. His groin tightened. She was close. So close. Soon he'd smell her soft, dark hair. Her real hair. No more disguises, no more lies between them. He'd teach her the truth of her sad life; carve it into her golden skin.

Delilah. He almost said her name aloud. Instead he straightened up, carefully stepping around the trap. He'd head around the back and then they'd see how ready she was to receive him.

Ted took another step, watching the cabin. The bullet cut through his bicep before he even heard the report of the gun.

Fifty-seven

Delilah had grown stiff and cold waiting in the dark. The slightest rustle of wind or shifting shadows no longer made her jump. Her eyes half-closed and her belly began its dull, protesting ache, reminding her that she wasn't nearly healed just yet.

Light winked in the trees, there for only a moment and then gone. She watched the hill, head cocked, listening intently. Just the wind.

Delilah was still on full alert, but starting to think she'd imagined the light when a glint in the trees beside the yard caught her eye. She turned her head slowly, watching the treeline.

Again. She raised the Glock, taking aim at where the glint had been. It might be nothing.

But she wasn't willing to bet her life on it.

Colin had taught her how to shoot a gun when she was thirteen, declaring that she'd better know or else she'd just get taken advantage of someday. But she didn't use them that often, though she tried to keep in practice.

The recoil surprised her, as it always seemed to. She was ready for the noise, though it, too, sounded painfully loud in the darkness. Was that a muffled cry? Her ears, ringing from the gunshot, strained.

Instinctively, she shifted to one side, knowing she shouldn't stay in place after a shot.

The return shot chewed into the cabin wall a foot from her head. Delilah dropped down to the porch, ignoring the intense pain as her remaining stitches pulled tight.

She saw movement, someone coming toward the porch quickly. She fired the gun even as she rolled for the porch edge. Her body hit the grass and she forced herself up to kneeling, gun ready.

Movement off to her left, so she took another shot. *Go, go, go*, her brain screamed at her. Stationary target here in the moonlight was bad. For a long half second fear mixed with adrenaline, freezing her as time slowed.

Then she was up, dashing around the side of the cabin, seeking the deeper shadows in the back, away from the light of the setting moon.

Two more shots rang out but as far as she could tell, Ted missed by a mile. There were three traps in the back yard, hidden beneath the grass. She wanted to draw him around, give him a chance to step in one.

But to lure him, she'd have to show herself, give away her position.

Delilah took a couple gulping, quick breaths, her back pressed against the cedar shingles. The back door was just to her left and she hadn't locked up when she'd set up her watch outside.

"Delilah?" Ted's voice called from somewhere in the trees behind the cabin. She searched for the sound, but the wind whipped it around, making it impossible to pinpoint him. "Let's talk; I don't want to shoot you."

Then stop shooting at me, she said silently. A crazy, desperate ploy formed in her mind. She willed him to keep talking, to stay there in the darkness behind the cabin a few moments longer.

"Delilah," he said in a sing-song voice that raised the hairs on her arms.

She inched her way to the left and reached slowly for the door handle. Her fingers depressed the latch of the old-fashioned jug handle and she eased the door open. Then she slammed it shut, and dropped prone. She prayed the deep shadows on the porch were enough to conceal her movement and her body.

She heard what sounded like a muttered curse and then he fell for her ploy.

Ted emerged from the trees, moving in a quick, zig-zag pattern over the open ground. Delilah lay still, aiming down the sight of the Glock.

She stilled her heartbeat and held her breath. Closer, closer. He was nearly to the back steps and she started to squeeze the trigger.

There was a sickening crunch as Ted screamed and dropped.

Delilah took her finger off the trigger and shifted to kneeling, moving like a crab to one side, never taking her eyes off Ted.

He continued to writhe in the grass, cursing and making horrible agonized noises. Delilah's smile surprised her. He'd stepped right into one of her traps.

Carefully, because she couldn't be sure if he'd dropped his gun or not, Delilah rose.

"Teddy," she called and stepped quickly to one side, just in case.

His arms came up, one hand shading his eyes as though he could block out the moonlight behind her and see clearly. His hands looked empty and blood darkened one sleeve.

"Delilah," he said, his voice thick with pain. "Fuck you. I'm going to fucking kill you, bitch."

"Shut up, Teddy." She licked her lips and walked forward. He was barely a car's length away now. "I should thank you, you know."

His face in the cold light blanched but his eyes were dark, angry pits.

"For what?"

"For showing me that I do have some motherly instinct after all."

He growled at her and tried to lunge forward as she raised the gun. His effort aborted as the teeth of the trap yanked his broken leg. Whatever he might have said turned into another scream.

Delilah stepped onto the top step and took aim at his head. His eyes widened and he raised his hands as though he could ward off the bullet. A glint caught her eye. His cuff-links. They looked a lot like the opal ones she'd stolen from that house in Daytona Beach a lifetime ago. She realized that it might have been those, catching the moonlight, which first caught her eye from the porch.

"I guess you weren't born in October, Teddy," she said, and pulled the trigger.

Fifty-eight

Delilah turned and walked into the cabin and dropped the gun on the table. She collapsed onto the futon, pulling over herself the knit throw folded on the back. Her shivers subsided as her heart returned to a normal rate.

It was over. No more being hunted down. No more fear.

No more Jake. She smelled him, fresh and warm, spice and peanuts. He was there with her, in the cedar bones of this cabin, whistling a lullaby down the chimney with the ocean winds.

Surrounded by the ghosts of her memories, by the phantoms of better days, Delilah fell into a deep sleep.

It was full daylight when she awoke. She didn't have a watch and the sky was overcast, hiding the sun, but she guessed it was mid-morning from the brightness of the day.

Ted's corpse was still in the back yard. Delilah didn't look too closely at it. She gathered up the tarp the traps had been in and used it to drag the dead body into the woods. She took his car keys, wrinkling her nose at the smell of his vacated bowels. Corpses were definitely not fun, but it gave her a sense of closure to confirm his death in broad daylight.

She dumped him down a ravine a short trek from the cabin. It was all the grave she was willing to give him. It would probably be a long time before anyone came back to this place anyway.

She used a couple big sticks to disarm the rest of the traps and put them back under the deck. Delilah found Ted's gun in the grass and recognized Jake's revolver. She tossed it into the Civic along with her own gun.

Ted's car was just over the top of the hill, pulled over along the side. Delilah used the tool kit from the cabin to remove the license plates before she drove the car up into the trees as far as she could get it before the brush got too thick, but at least it wasn't visible from the road anymore.

She worked mechanically, pushing away thoughts of Jake bleeding out on the office floor. The stains on her jeans popped into her vision at awkward times, threatening another round of tears and tearing grief.

Delilah locked up the cabin and climbed into Nancy's car. The peanut and Cheerio smell made her smile. It was a sign of the lives she'd saved. She'd protected her daughter, that miracle, binding her by blood forever to the man she'd loved and left.

Left to die.

Delilah drove down to the coast, stopping at an overlook. She perched on the metal barrier overlooking the ocean and watched the waves for a long time as she dismantled the Glock. The pieces went over the cliff and disappeared into the rocks and surging water below. She knew she should ditch the Colt as well, but couldn't quite bring herself to toss it over.

The smart thing, the safe thing, would be to get in the Civic and just keep driving. North to Washington, maybe, or south to California. Ditch the car along the way and just keep going. She could drum up work later, after she'd had some rest and time to heal her belly, and her heart.

That would be the safe thing.

Delilah sighed and climbed back into her car. She got back on the road and headed down 101. When she came to the turn-off that would take her back to Portland, she took it.

Fifty-nine

Sam walked into the waiting room outside the intensive care unit. He looked around at the handful of people waiting and found the most likely one. He approached the exhausted-looking woman, a pretty brunette in her thirties.

"Nancy Leventon?" he asked.

"Yes?" She looked up, eyebrows creasing.

"I'm Detective, I mean, I'm Sam. They said you wouldn't mind if I came by this afternoon."

Her face smoothed and she smiled, wan but genuine. "Sam. Thank you." She rose and pressed her hands into his. Her fingers were cold and trembled slightly.

"How is he?" Sam had gone back to the hotel for a quick nap after the police had finally located Jake's wife and child in a hotel just south of Portland. At that point, Jake had still been in surgery.

"Stable," she said, her eyes bleak. "He lost so much blood. He hasn't woken up yet. They say he'd be dead if you hadn't found him when you did, put those bandages on him."

Sam stiffened. He'd told the lie to the paramedics because he hadn't been sure who or why the napkin and masking tape triage had been performed. He doubted that Whitechapel had done it and Jake definitely hadn't had the strength.

"I can't take all that credit," he said softly. "I don't know who bound up the worst of it."

Nancy looked down and dropped her hands from his. "I do," she whispered. "Delilah. She saved us."

"You saw her? You didn't mention that to the police." Sam tried not to sound too eager.

She shook her head and sat back down heavily. "No, I couldn't. She said she'd wait for him, that man after us. She told us to go."

"Where was this?" he asked but Nancy was already shaking her head. He wanted to grab her and jolt the truth out. Visions of the vulnerable, dark-eyed girl who'd stolen his keys with a pretty smile in the bar rose up in his mind. Visions of her cut to pieces and bleeding out, just like the poor bastard Sam had helped scrape up off the floor late last night.

"She made this problem," Nancy said, though it was as much to herself as to Sam. She wasn't even looking at him and instead stared out the window into a sunlit nothing. "She'll be okay. Delilah knows how to look after herself."

Sam sighed. "How's your daughter?"

"Sleeping in pediatrics. She had to get her transfusion today anyway, so they're letting her rest up there." Nancy looked at him and her smile returned briefly.

He wanted to know more, there were so many questions dodging around in his head, but Sam felt impotent to get anything out of this tired woman. He couldn't just stand there until she decided to talk.

"You look exhausted," he said. "I'm dying for some coffee and a sandwich. Want something?"

Again the brief smile, tinged with a hint of relief. "Yeah, if you don't mind. Skim latte with a shot of vanilla."

"I'll try to remember that." Sam returned her smile.

"Plain coffee with skim milk is fine if you forget."

He walked out of the hospital and across the emergency entrance. He'd reached his car and was going for his keys when he saw movement in the corner of his eye. Turning, there was Delilah, standing in the sunlight like a figment, solid and ephemeral all at once.

"Sam," she said.

He walked over, stepping up onto the curb beside her. "Hi, Delilah, or Lia, or is it Donna?"

She laughed, the sound thin but pure. "Delilah will do. You came all the way here? For me?"

"You asked for my help, remember?" He studied her. Her face was thin and drawn, her dark hair mussed as though she'd just gotten out of bed. But she had a secret strength about her and there was no fear in her eyes at all.

"So I did. Bridget told me some Florida detective saved Jake. Somehow I just knew it was you."

"Bridget?" He raised an eyebrow and resisted brushing a lock of hair off her forehead. Part of him was afraid that if he touched her she'd dissipate like a dream.

"Waitress at Jake's bar." She chewed her lip and looked away. "Is he, I mean, he's here, right? Inside?"

Sam answered the question that she didn't ask. "He's alive. Stable. Lost of a lot of blood though. They don't know for sure yet if he'll ever wake up."

She took a deep breath that seemed to shake her whole body but when she turned her dark eyes back to his face they were clear and empty of tears.

"Whitechapel?" Sam asked.

"Not going to be a problem anymore," she said.

"Good."

"What about my daughter?"

That surprised Sam, though suddenly a couple missing pieces fell into place. Like why Whitechapel had gone after Jake and his family in the first place.

"Yours and Jake's?"

She nodded.

"She's sleeping. Nancy said she was tired, but fine."

They stood for a moment, close together but not quite touching. Delilah finally broke the tension by reaching into her pocket and digging out a set of keys.

"Can you do me a couple favors, Sam?"

"Hell, why not?" He chuckled, releasing the tension of the moment. "I can't arrest you, after all. Even if I had jurisdiction, I'm not sure I'd want to. So fuck it, I might as well just continue aiding and abetting, right?"

She blushed and pursed her lips. "You're a good man, Sam."

"Yeah, we'll see. What do you want?"

"Return these to Nancy? I don't think she wants to see me right now." She held out the car keys.

Sam took them. Before he could ask what the second thing was, she leaned in, closing the distance between them. Her arms came around him in a quick embrace. He had long enough to feel her hair, smelling of cedar and wool, brush against his cheek. Then she was away, down from the curb and moving toward the cars.

"Hey," he called out. "You said a couple favors. What's the other one?"

The lights flashed on his rental car as she reached it and opened the driver's door.

"Don't report this for a couple hours," she called back to him. Then, with an impish smile, she ducked into the car and started the engine even as the door closed.

Sam stepped off the curb, feeling for his keys but then stopped. He hadn't even felt her take them from his pocket. He backed up and stood on the sidewalk, shaking his head.

Delilah backed his car out and drove off, one hand sticking out of the window as she waved farewell.

Sam had no idea where she was headed, or what she'd do. Or, for that matter, how the hell he was going to explain this whole trip and its strange results to Ronnie or his own Lieutenant.

But he knew, without a doubt in his bones, that Delilah would land on her feet.

Epilogue

The parking lot behind Poppy's pawn shop was mostly empty of cars. A new Cadillac, done up in deep purple with shining chrome rims, was the only one parked close to the building. Dry leaves blew in lazy circles around the lot and the heavy gray sky promised an autumn storm.

Delilah parked behind the Caddy, blocking it in. There was no sign of Poppy's truck, but him changing up cars wasn't all that unusual. She sat for a moment and let the song on the radio finish, collecting her thoughts. Then, with a deep breath, she got out.

She was ready.

A couple quick taps on Poppy's steel back door were all it took. The view slit slid open and the older black man's yellowed eyes peered out at her. She heard his small exclamation of shock and just smiled, tipping her head to one side.

He probably hadn't expected her to ever show her face in Atlanta again, but hell, she hardly blamed him. She hadn't expected to come back either. But she'd done a lot of thinking while lying in bed shaking with fever and pain as her belly wound slowly healed.

She had unfinished business, and she wasn't going to run away from that shit anymore.

Poppy opened the door, a puzzled smile on his face.

"Delilah," he said, motioning her inside. "Hadn't expected you back. I haven't gotten word that mess is cleared up. You might still be a bad person to know, if you know what I mean." His attempt at polite concern fell flat.

Delilah pulled the revolver out of her sweatshirt and pointed it at his gut.

"I'm pretty sure I'm a terrible person for you to know right now, Pops. After you screwed me out of my ten percent and all." She motioned with her other hand for him to back up, stepping forward as he did. "Let's go into your office."

"Hey, there's no reason to—"

"Shup up and sit down, Pops." Delilah cut him off with a tiny smile and a slight adjustment of her aim downward. "Hands behind your head, please."

He sat in the garish orange leather chair and laced his fingers behind his head. She could smell the fear coming off him like sweaty steam rising in the dim office.

Delilah hitched her hip up onto the desk. Her gun never wavered.

"Now, Poppy," she said, her dark eyes like obsidian stones, her smile small and cold. "Let's talk about the money you owe me."

The end

About the Author

Anne Baines holds a BA in English and a BA in Medieval Studies and thus can speak a smattering of useful languages such as Anglo-Saxon and Medieval Welsh.

She spends her non-writing time jumping horses over large stationary objects, traveling, and (legally) kidnapping and transporting rebellious teenagers for money. She lives in the Pacific Northwest with her husband and a very demanding bengal cat.